Einstein had it all wrong.

Had he participated in speed dating, his theories would never have seen the light of day.

Acclaim for
Four Uncles and a Wedding
TARA First Impressions Award finalist

"Quirky, but lovable, characters placed in out-of-the-ordinary circumstances are a winning formula for an unbridled romp that will keep you in stitches and eager for more. A great, fun read!." — Amazon reviewer

"What a riot!" — Amazon reviewer

"This book is laugh out loud funny with plenty of smiles and smirks along the way." —Amazon reviewer

"I was hooked from the start." — Amazon reviewer

"Really enjoyable with plenty of humour throughout." — Amazon reviewer

Books by Lois Winston

Anastasia Pollack Crafting Mystery series
Assault with a Deadly Glue Gun
Death by Killer Mop Doll
Revenge of the Crafty Corpse
Decoupage Can Be Deadly
A Stitch to Die For
Scrapbook of Murder
Drop Dead Ornaments
Handmade Ho-Ho Homicide
A Sew Deadly Cruise

Anastasia Pollack Crafting Mini-Mysteries
Crewel Intentions
Mosaic Mayhem
Patchwork Peril
Crafty Crimes (all 3 novellas in one volume)

Empty Nest Mystery Series
Definitely Dead
Literally Dead

Romantic Suspense
Love, Lies and a Double Shot of Deception
Lost in Manhattan (writing as Emma Carlyle)
Someone to Watch Over Me (writing as Emma Carlyle)

Romance and Chick Lit
Talk Gertie to Me
Four Uncles and a Wedding (writing as Emma Carlyle)

Four Uncles
And a Wedding

LOIS WINSTON
Writing as Emma Carlyle

Cover design by L. Winston

ISBN-13: 978-1-940795-18-8

"Having a weird mom builds character." – Unknown

DEDICATION

To all the weirdly interesting, sometimes annoying, sometimes laugh-inducing, people who have crossed my path in life and in ways both big and small inspired me as I created some of the characters in this book.

IN THE BEGINNING
Emancipation Proclamation

"This isn't working anymore." I spoke to the ceiling, my voice controlled and emotionless.

Significant Other groaned but didn't turn over. He spoke to the closet. "Women don't always come. You know that. Go to sleep."

Easy for him to say. Some men hold records for the two-minute mile. Significant Other beats them by a full minute and does it lying down. Slam. Bam. He didn't even bother with the thank-you, ma'am, anymore. I felt more like a sperm repository than a girlfriend. I flung back the quilt and switched on the overhead fixture. The room filled with bright light, too glaring for the late hour.

"Hey, come on, Polly! I've got a big meeting tomorrow. I need to get some sleep."

"Fine." Leaving the light on, I stalked into the kitchen and rummaged through the cabinets until I found a box of heavy-duty trash bags. When I returned to the bedroom, he had turned the light off. I flipped it back on.

"What the hell are you doing?"

"You're leaving." I yanked open a dresser drawer and dumped the contents into one of the plastic bags. "Go sleep at the Waldorf."

"Are you crazy?" He jumped out of bed and grabbed the half-filled bag from my hand. "It's nearly midnight."

"Then you'd better hurry if you want your beauty sleep." I grabbed an armload of pinstripes, blue blazers, and khakis from his half of the closet and stuffed them, hangers and all, into another bag. The plastic split down the seam along one side. I didn't care. I tossed the bag at him. "I want you and your selfish ego out of my apartment. Now."

He stared at me, his eyes wide, his jaw hanging down like a broken hinge. "You're kicking me out in the middle of the night because you didn't have an orgasm? That's crazy!"

"No." I fought to keep my voice from rising along with my growing anger. I didn't want to sound hysterical. "Crazy is molding my life around your needs and completely denying my own. No orgasm sex is merely the tip of the iceberg. This is the first sane thing I've done in six months."

He pulled a hanger from the bag, ripping the plastic further. "I was going to ask you to marry me." His speech took on that pathetic, passive-aggressive little-boy sound he slipped into when things weren't going his way.

"I don't want to marry you. I don't love you." Actually, I suddenly realized I didn't even like Significant Other, but I didn't tell him that. I'm not a cruel person.

"Of course you do, Polly. You're just angry right now. Let's go back to bed, and we'll talk this over tomorrow after work."

I raised my arm and pointed to the door. "Out!"

~*~

"We never liked him," said my mother and father in unison.

"I knew you'd come to your senses," said Uncle Aaron.

"Just needed to get it out of your system," said Uncle Francis.

"Atta girl!" said Uncle Emerson.

"About time," said Uncle Cal.

~*~

And that's when the real trouble began. Don't get me wrong. I love my parents and my great-uncles, but in their own way they can be as manipulative as Significant Other had been—only far less subtle. The weekend after my self-proclaimed Emancipation Proclamation the six of them embarked on an all-out campaign to cheat time and beat my biological clock. And like any loving relatives on a mission, they fought dirty.

Top 10 Reasons to Call it Quits After the First Date

10. He's thirty-five and still living with his mother.

9. He shows up for a formal gala at the Met wearing black jeans and a tuxedo print T-shirt.

8. He shows up for a picnic in Central Park wearing a three-piece Brooks Brothers suit, white shirt with French cuffs, and a conservative blue and red striped tie.

7. He kisses with his eyes open and puckers his lips like a fish sucking up plankton.

6. He has a list of his former girlfriends tattooed on his left bicep.

5. He spends the entire date talking about his ex-girlfriend.

4. He spends the entire date psychoanalyzing you.

3. He brings his own silverware to the restaurant and disinfects all surfaces with antibacterial wipes before touching anything.

2. He conveniently forgets to mention he's married.

And the number one reason to call it quits after the first date—

1. Your parents or one of your great-uncles fixes you up with him (which means he most likely falls into one of the above categories.)

ONE
Tall, Dark, Handsome, and Boring

Christmas is a lousy time of year for the recently singled. Actually, it's pretty much the pits for the perpetually single as well. Everyone else on the planet is busy pouring over glossy mail-order catalogs, surfing the Net, or strolling through holiday displays at Saks and Bergdorf's in search of that perfect gift for that special someone.

Unless you have no special someone in your life. In which case, all your friends and relatives are on a frantic search to find you a special someone before the one day of the year when no one wants to admit to being a card-carrying member of Losers Anonymous—New Year's Eve.

There is no escaping New Year's Eve. It's the one holiday celebrated by everyone on the planet, and when you live in New York City, practically everyone on the planet manages to squeeze into Times Square every December 31. Everyone except New Yorkers. We have more sense and too many party invitations.

What we don't necessarily have is a date for any of those parties, and to my butinsky family, that's a dire situation in need of immediate remedy.

"You can't keep moping around about Significant Other," said my mother as we squeezed down a crowded aisle in the men's department at Macy's. It was Black Friday, the day after Thanksgiving and the official kickoff to the Christmas shopping season. A consummate bargain hunter, Mom liked to jump into the fray early. Her fellow crazies packed every floor, swarming up one aisle and down the next like killer bees descending on a jam-packed football stadium.

"I'm not moping." Her assertion miffed me. I'm not a moper. "*I* kicked *him* out, remember?"

"But you're not dating, dear. It's been over two months now. A girl with your looks should have a queue of men to choose from."

Mom always likes to use words like *queue* instead of *line*. Don't ask me why. Probably just to sound unique. As far as I can tell, no one outside of England says *queue* other than literary novelists or people with Netflix subscriptions.

Mom bounced across the aisle. She never walks, strolls, saunters, or ambles. And she's incapable of doing only one thing at a time. Whoever coined the phrase *stop and smell the roses* never met my mother. Instead of taking time to sniff the petals, she rushes headlong into the garden and mows down the bushes. By the time she gets to the exit, she's made two dozen centerpieces, a kilo of potpourri, and a vat of perfume. Her body is always in constant motion, her arms and hands animating every nonstop word.

"Take Millie Sewell's daughter," she continued, "Brittany."

She quickly scanned a table of ties, lifted one for closer inspection, then tossed it back on the pile before turning to me. "You remember Millie, don't you, dear?"

I nodded, biting back the exasperated sigh that filled my lungs. I really didn't remember Millie, not to mention Brittany, but I had learned long ago that a well-placed nod and a smile of acknowledgement fast-forwarded Mom's incessant parables about strangers. And I had no doubt her tale was meant as parable. Mom had a message to impart. For all I knew, Millie and Brittany existed only in her imagination. It was the moral of the story that mattered.

"Well, you'll certainly agree Brittany's no beauty," she continued. "Not like you. She's at least a size twelve to your size two—"

"I wear a size four, Mom."

"Two. Four. There's hardly a difference." She brushed away my comment with a wave of her hand. "Anyway, as I was saying, Brittany's a frump." Mom had a low opinion of women who didn't take care of their bodies. She herself still maintained a size six figure. Dad said it was due to centrifugal force. She whirled around with such speed that the calories never got a foothold. Instead, they spun right off her.

"Your point?"

"Brittany married an orthodontist. They have a lovely home in Chatham and two adorable children, a boy and a girl. Millie is always bragging about them and shoving pictures under my nose." She wagged an index finger in my face. "And you're not even dating!"

"Maybe I don't want to date."

She tossed me one of her silent when-you-fall-off-the-horse-get-right-back-on lectures. It was hard to believe Mom considered herself a feminist. I suppose back in the day, she wasn't thinking ahead to when she'd want grandchildren.

"Look," I continued. "I don't need a man in my life to feel complete. I'm quite happy right now." Actually, I wasn't. I was lonely as hell, but I kept that bombshell to myself. I didn't need my mother taking out personal ads in *New York* magazine for me or signing me up for Match.com.

"Really?" She grabbed my wrist and steamrolled us through a knot of shoppers crowded around another table. Reaching across several women, she lifted a lemon yellow golf sweater from a pile and held it up. Although she pretended to study the knit, I had the uncomfortable feeling she was actually sizing me up and making it clear with a one-word question that I had fallen far short of expectation. "How about matching sweaters for the uncles?"

"You bought them matching golf sweaters for Christmas last year," I reminded her. "And the year before. And the year before that."

The uncles, all from different sides of the family, had few things in common other than their similar professions, their weekly foursome, and me, their only niece. Under normal circumstances, the first might have kept them apart. However, golf and I, not necessarily in that order, bound them together like blood brothers. Besides, our family circumstances were far from normal.

She held the sweater up to the overhead lights and scrutinized it some more. "But not in yellow."

"Yellow makes Uncle Cal look like death warmed over."

"You'd think with all that fire and brimstone he spews that he'd have a bit of color, wouldn't you?" She dropped the sweater

8

back onto the pile and made a face. At first I thought her pout was a silent commentary on Uncle Cal, but then she turned the frown in my direction and shook her head. Her wild mane of chestnut curls, as uncontrollable as her incorrigible personality, bounced around her face. People often mistake Mom for Bernadette Peters—minus the red hair and voice. Mom carried a tune about as well as she kept her opinions to herself.

Unfortunately, that never kept her from either singing or stating what was on her mind. "What am I going to do with you, Polly?"

"Me?" I picked up the sweater and refolded it. "Mom, I'm thirty-two years old. I have a wonderful career, money in the bank, and own a lovely apartment in Gramercy Park. You don't have to do anything with me."

"I'm talking about your love life—or lack of it. And *my* lack of grandchildren." She added that last part under her breath but loud enough for me to hear.

"How about seafoam green?" I held up another sweater, making it clear that I had no intention of discussing either my love life or lack of offspring with my mother in Macy's men's department.

"You're impossible." She ignored my attempt to change the subject and uttered the one sentence I had heard far too many times over the last few years. "By the time I was your age, you were a pre-teen."

Ah, my mother, the queen of revisionist history. It wasn't like I was planned, and we both knew it—no matter how much she tried to pretend otherwise. "Only because your birth control failed."

She pursed her lips into a thin, tight line before emoting a

9

theatrical sigh. "I suppose one of your uncles let you in on that secret? I can just guess which one."

Actually, she'd told me herself, during one of those obligatory mother-daughter talks during my teen years, but to this day she denies having divulged the secret of my birth to me.

She grabbed the sweater out of my hand and read the label. "See if this comes in an extra-large. I noticed Uncle Aaron's been putting on weight lately."

We continued our shopping expedition, making our way uptown. From Macy's we headed to Lord & Taylor, then Saks, our strides choreographed to the tune of the jingling change weighing down my mother's coat pockets. At each bell-ringing Salvation Army post Mom withdrew a handful of silver coins and tossed them into the red kettle. I added a dollar bill. I refuse to walk down Fifth Avenue sounding like a refrain from *Jingle Bells*.

After a quick lunch at Trump Tower we finished up at Bergdorf's. Mom didn't bring up my lack of mate again the rest of the day, but I knew her well enough to know she hadn't dropped the subject for long. She was merely regrouping after a minor skirmish to prepare for a major assault. The battle began in earnest two days later.

~*~

My family gives new meaning to the word *unorthodox*. Mom and Dad met in Haight-Ashbury in the late sixties during a tune-in-turn-on-drop-out weekend escapade. Both she and Dad are products of nonconformist parents. On my mother's side, my grandparents came from the Lower East Side, only my grandmother was a Russian Jew and my grandfather an Italian Catholic. You can imagine the Romeo-Juliet scenario their romance caused back in the late nineteen-forties.

On my father's side, the situation was no better. His mother was a Boston blue blood who traced her Episcopalian heritage back to the Founding Fathers. So did my grandfather, but he was a Unitarian—in other words, a heretic as far as my grandmother's family was concerned.

Both sets of grandparents are long gone. Mom and Dad were only children, much to the relief of my great-grandparents, I'm told. My great-uncles are the only remaining family—Uncle Aaron Goldfarb, the rabbi; Uncle Francis Xavier Spinelli, the Catholic priest; Uncle Calvin Trusdale, the Episcopalian priest; and Uncle Ralph Waldo Emerson Harmony, the gay Unitarian minister.

Like I said, I come from a very unorthodox lineage, which explains the name my parents saddled me with—Polly Faith Harmony. I suspect they were stoned when they named me. I once asked, but they refused to answer the question, merely raising their eyebrows at the absurd idea that I thought they once smoked pot. I took that as a yes.

~*~

For as long as I can remember, Sunday has been *Gathering Day*. While I attended college, the tradition carried on without me. Once I graduated and returned to the area, moving a short train commute away from my parents, I returned to *The Gathering*. It was expected.

I also resumed *The Rotation*. The first Sunday of each month finds me at Uncle Emerson's Unitarian-Universalist Society in Greenwich Village. The following Saturday I attend Uncle Aaron's synagogue on the Upper West Side. On the third Sunday of the month I show up for—but don't partake in—mass at Uncle Francis's church in downtown Newark, and the fourth Sunday means a visit to Uncle Cal's church in Caldwell, New Jersey. On months with five Sundays, I give myself a day of rest. I was brought up to believe in everything. Consequently, I think I believe in nothing, but I keep this to myself because I like leaving my options open. I also don't want to hurt my uncles' feelings.

On my Catholic and Episcopal Sundays, I take the train to church, then drive to my parents' house in Summit, New Jersey with whichever uncle I've visited that day. On other Sundays Uncle Aaron, Uncle Emerson, and I meet up at Penn Station and take the train.

I should have guessed something was up when Uncle Emerson called Saturday evening to say he and Uncle Aaron had some ecumenical business to attend to and would meet me at my parents' home. Instead, unsuspecting me wound up walking into a minefield.

I arrived at the station in Summit a little before four in the afternoon. Although daylight was already waning, and the sun had dipped below the tree line, I decided to walk the quarter mile rather than calling my father for a lift. Taking my time, I strolled the sidewalks, enjoying the holiday lights and decorations on first the shops I passed in the center of town, then the houses along the residential streets.

Inhaling, I filled my lungs with the crisp evening air, breathing in a mixture of evergreen boughs and the fireplace smoke that traveled up the chimneys of many of the houses. Manhattan never smells as good as the suburbs—especially in the weeks before Christmas—except for the roasting chestnuts from the street corner vendors, and they always smell far better than they taste.

The sprawling split-level of my childhood sits atop a hill at the end of a cul-de-sac. Mom and Dad purchased the house shortly after my second birthday. Before that, we lived in a small cape cod in Clark, but I don't remember it. Mom says that's understandable because both the house and the town were quite forgettable.

After my birth, my parents decided they needed to become responsible adults. Or so the revisionist version goes. According to the uncles, the transformation from hippies to yuppies had more to do with my grandparents reading my parents the riot act. Whatever. The outcome was the same. Mom and Dad put their science and marketing degrees to use and got in on the ground floor of the natural cosmetics and hair care craze. They made a fortune. Theirs was the first company to refuse to test its products on animals. The Harmony line is still the premiere line in its field, sold only in the finest department stores and catalogs.

Several years ago my parents went public with the company and made a gazillion dollars on the IPO. They now spend a good deal of their time working for charitable causes. Each year they donate large sums of money to each of the uncle's houses of worship. My parents are good people.

With everything they do, you'd think my family wouldn't have time to orchestrate my social life. Unfortunately, I'm their favorite charity. I eyed the house with mounting suspicion. From the looks of things they had planned a charity event for this evening.

Cars, jammed nose-to-tail, packed the long, winding driveway leading up to the house. Additional cars lined the street in front of the house. I recognized Uncle Francis's ten-year-old black Lincoln with the dented rear bumper and Uncle Cal's slightly newer Ford Escort with the creased front fender. The uncles had had a little mishap in the parking lot one day after their weekly round of golf several years ago. Both refused to talk about it, but neither has ever gotten his vehicles repaired. "Isn't worth the deductible," they each stated in voices gruffer than normal whenever asked. Then they change the subject.

I trudged up the path. My mother swung the front door open before I reached for the handle. "Sweetheart! We were getting worried." She threw her arms around me and at the same time dragged me across the threshold.

"Having a party, Mom?" I slipped off my coat. Standing in the foyer, I scanned the living room. Something seemed odd. There were few women scattered about the large room. A half dozen at most, all my mother's age or older. The men, on the other hand, except for the older counterparts of the women, all appeared close to my age. I saw two possibilities. Either my mother had decided to throw a party for The Gay Men's Choir or she had deliberately only invited those friends with eligible sons.

"Oh, I told you, dear." She grabbed my coat out of my hands. "When we had lunch on Friday. A little holiday kickoff, remember?" She headed for the coat closet, shooing me into the living room. "Go mingle, Polly."

I decided not to challenge her although I knew she hadn't mentioned a party last Friday or at any other time. This was obviously some devious scheme she had conjured up on her way home after our shopping junket. She gave up too easily that day. Instead of mingling, I headed straight for the bar and poured myself a vodka and grapefruit juice—heavy on the vodka, light on the juice.

"Drinking never solved anything."

I spun around. The voice belonged to a nice enough looking man who could have qualified as a poster boy for the proverbial tall-dark-and-handsome category or a male model on the cover of a romance novel. Either way, he was definitely eye candy. Six-two, if an inch. Thick dark brown hair with a wavy lock falling rakishly over his forehead. Large dark eyes hidden behind wire-rimmed glasses. A short, neatly trimmed beard with an early hint of gray peaking out here and there that made him look distinguished rather than old. I figured he was pushing forty if a day.

"Is it that bad?" he asked.

I might have forgiven my mother except that tall-dark-and-handsome was sounding suspiciously like a shrink. I dated one of those once. Jerome Lerner. He spent the entire evening psychoanalyzing me. Then he had the balls to tell me if we hadn't been on a date, he would have charged me three hundred dollars for a double session!

I told him his unwanted and unsolicited advice wasn't worth three dollars, let alone three hundred, and his parents ought to demand a refund on his tuition. Then I slammed the door in his face. He was the son of a friend of my father's accountant and Number Four on The Top Ten Reasons to Call it Quits After the First Date.

"You have no idea," I muttered in reply to Tall, Dark, and Handsome. Then I took a long swig. "Who are you?"

"Sorry." He extended his hand. "Jeff Jacoby. You must be Polly."

I plastered a smile on my face and switched my glass from my right to left hand to shake his. "And you've heard so much about me, right? Which one of my mother's friends do you belong to?"

His brows knit together as if he were trying to figure out the extent of my lunacy. Only mildly crazy or full-blown nut case?

"None that I know of."

"So my mother picked you up off the streets of Summit and

dragged you to this shindig?" Okay, I admit I was acting a little over-sarcastic, but I resented being ambushed in my own home. After spending all day Thursday cooking and serving Thanksgiving dinners to hundreds of poor and homeless New Yorkers (another family tradition,) then getting bruised and battered at the Black Friday Shopping Roller Derby, I was looking forward to a quiet evening with my parents and uncles. The last thing I expected was being cast as the sacrificial lamb in Mother Maria Ruth—Mimi to her friends—Harmony's very own version of *The Dating Game.*

"Actually, your uncle invited me. We're colleagues."

Ah, a clergy shrink. I doubted any of my uncles was in need of counseling, so I figured they must be working on a case together— maybe some suicidal choir director or Sunday school teacher with a secret addiction. "Which one?"

"Which colleague?" His expression told me he had made up his mind. I was definitely a full-blown nut case.

I wondered if tall-dark-and-handsome was always this obtuse or if his denseness was in my honor. "Which uncle?"

"Oh." I could see I had inched back towards mildly crazy. "Rabbi Goldfarb. I'm his new cantor."

Cantor! He turned slightly and motioned to Uncle Aaron. It was then that I noticed the minuscule *yarmulke* perched atop his head. That made me angry. It was bad enough my mother had donned her Yenta the Matchmaker shawl, but now it appeared she had dragged in at least one of my uncles as an accomplice. "So he's in on this, too," I muttered. Jeff the Cantor was apparently the *ecumenical business* that had kept Uncle Aaron and Uncle Emerson from meeting me at Penn Station.

"Pardon?"

"Trust me." I took another swig. "It's far safer not to know."

"Right," he said, and I could see I had crossed back over into the full-blown nut case department.

"Right."

A moment of awkward silence, lasting the length of an eight-day week, followed. Poor Jeff Jacoby. I could tell he was trying to find some gracious way to extricate himself—from me and possibly from the party. He looked very uncomfortable. I felt sorry for him. He was as much a pawn in my family's matchmaking melodrama as I. "Well, nice meeting you, Jeff." I offered him my best daughter-of-the-hostess smile. Then with a breezy wave, I spun on my heels.

"Wait, please." He reached for my elbow.

"Yes?"

"I was wondering if there's a story behind that." He nodded in the direction of the twin evergreens that stood sentry on either side of the fireplace.

I chuckled. "You mean why Rabbi Aaron Goldfarb's niece has a *dreidel*-decorated Christmas tree in her living room?"

"For starters. There's also a traditional Christmas tree, a Menorah on the windowsill, and a nativity scene on the mantle."

I was tempted to mention the Buddhist shrine in the den, but decided not to. Cantor Jeff didn't strike me as someone with a great sense of humor. Anyway, it wasn't really a Buddhist shrine, just one of those New Age rock and water fountains. As far as I know, we have no Buddhists in the family—at least not yet. "Equal opportunity religion," I explained. "You know, like network television giving equal airtime to political candidates?"

His eyes widened. He released my elbow and took a step backwards as if whatever I had was catchy. "And your uncle agrees with this?"

Definitely no sense of humor. "Relax, Jeff. My uncle is full-grown, one hundred percent, card-carrying devout Jew."

"But not you?"

"That would be a little hard, considering I'm only one-fourth Jewish."

"And the rest?"

"Equal parts Catholic, Episcopalian, and Unitarian. Still want to ask me out?" He blushed so fast and so deep that if I hadn't known better, I would have thought he was having apoplexy. I'm usually not so cruel, but I couldn't help myself. This guy was asking for it. Then the devil hopped off my shoulder, and I felt sorry for him again. "Relax." I patted his arm. "I was only kidding."

The purple receded from his face and neck. He stared at me for a full minute before he spoke. "Yes."

"Yes, what?"

"Yes, I'd like to ask you out."

Now it was my turn to go wide-eyed with surprise. "I...I didn't mean to put you on the spot."

He smiled. "Will you have dinner with me next Saturday night, Polly?"

I glanced over Jeff's shoulder. Across the room, Uncle Aaron nodded his billiard ball head in our direction. What little steel gray hair he had left was clipped so close that I doubted he ever used any of the free Harmony hair care samples my parents supplied him with on a monthly basis. "You don't have to do this," I told Jeff. "It's not part of your job description. Besides, I'm quite capable of getting my own dates when and if I want them."

"I don't doubt that. All the same, I'd very much like to have dinner with you."

I studied Jeff and weighed my options. He *was* a hunk. Not much of a conversationalist, but maybe he felt intimidated after being duped into attending a party thrown by Matchmakers, Incorporated. I could join him for dinner next Saturday night and get my mother off my back for a while, or I could dine alone with a carton of Chinese takeout and the latest Susan Elizabeth Phillips novel. "All right." After all, what did I have to lose?

~*~

My life, for one thing. If it's possible to die of boredom, the following Saturday evening left me feeling like I had escaped with one foot in the grave.

"That bad?" asked Joni when I knocked on her door after the date from hell. Joni Hughes and her twin brother Mitch—their mother got knocked up one night backstage after a Joni Mitchell concert—live in one of the two apartments upstairs from me. Joni, the quintessential party girl, was nursing a mild case of flu that had kept her from her usual Saturday night ritual of club hopping. Mitch was between relationships. The two of them were spending a quiet Saturday night at home with a stack of DVDs.

Initially, Joni and Mitch shared the two-bedroom apartment above me while completing their masters. Both are now well-established professionals in their fields—Joni, a segments producer at ABC and Mitch, a financial analyst for *The Wall Street Journal*—but they continue to live together. Mitch calls it an extension of the womb. I think it's his way of keeping tabs on his impetuous, free-spirited sister.

Joni doesn't seem to mind, though. Mitch is her best friend, and somehow they've worked out the situation as far as dating and sex is concerned. As Joni says, "Anyone who thinks it's weird or kinky isn't my kind of guy, anyway." She and Mitch use their dates' reactions to their unorthodox living arrangement as a litmus test.

Joni, Mitch, and I have been the best of friends since the three of us moved in on the same day ten years ago. Three peas in a pod, only two of the peas are tall blondes. Mitch and Joni suspect their unknown father came from Scandinavian stock because they certainly don't look anything like their short, redheaded, freckled, Irish roots mother. I'm the petite, olive-skinned brunette pea, thanks to my Italian bloodline. Mitch calls us a reverse Oreo. He's known for his warped sense of humor.

"Think of the worst date you ever had, then multiply it by a factor of twelve," I said.

Joni wrinkled her nose. "Ouch!"

"You know that list of Top Ten Reasons to Call it Quits After the First Date?"

"Know them? I co-authored them, remember?"

"Well, I think it's time to add an eleventh reason." I nodded to Mitch who was fixing Irish coffees for us at the bar that separated the kitchen from the living room. "Drum roll, please." He rapped out a kitchen counter crescendo.

"Number Eleven." Thanks to a head full of congestion, Joni's normally sexy voice sounded as husky as Kathleen Turner. "You know it's time to call it quits after the first date when..." she pointed to me. "Take it away, Polly."

"...when he can't carry on a conversation past the third sentence."

Joni's eyes widened in disbelief. I think maybe she was expecting me to tell them Jeff had spent the entire evening talking about himself. Or his mother. Or his dog. Now that I think of it, any one of those subjects would have been more tolerable than his talking about nothing at all for three hours.

"You mean like you said something. Then he said something. Then you said something..."

I finished her thought for her. "And then he said *nothing*. All night. Same pattern. I felt like a dentist pulling teeth. By the time we finished our appetizers, I was racking my brain trying to find something—anything—to talk about that would keep the conversation going for more than thirty seconds. I tried to move the evening along by passing on dessert and coffee, but he ordered some for himself. So then I sat there watching him eat while I carried on a one-sided conversation. I felt like an idiot."

"You said he's a cantor, didn't you?" asked Mitch. He placed the three coffees and the open bottle of whiskey on a tray and carried them across the room to the couch.

"So?" I lifted two of the glass mugs off the tray, handing one to Joni.

Mitch placed the tray on the coffee table, took the remaining coffee, and settled into a chair opposite us. "So maybe he's more comfortable singing his thoughts."

"Great. Just what Polly needs, living her life as an opera."

"Hey, she's halfway there now," said Mitch. He took a sip of his coffee and grinned at me over the rim of his mug. "You're always saying your life's a soap opera, right?"

I thought about throwing a pillow at him, but I didn't want to risk hitting anything—especially the open bottle of whiskey. "Actually, I believe I've said my life would make for a perfect situation comedy—*Religions Are Us*."

"So you put up with a loser for a few hours," said Mitch. He reached for the whiskey and topped off each of our mugs. "Could be worse."

"It is." I sighed. "He's a drop-dead gorgeous loser."

"Typical." Joni flopped back against the couch. "The good-looking ones usually are."

"Or married," I said.

"Or gay," she added. Joni had an unrequited crush on a well-known broadcaster at her network. He hadn't officially come out of the closet, but everyone who worked with him knew he didn't date women.

"Cheer up, Polly." Mitch rose from his chair and plopped down on the couch next to me. He wrapped his arm around my shoulders and kissed the top of my head in that big brother way of his that I found both annoying and comforting—depending on my mood. "You'll always have me."

"Right," said Joni. "Besides, lovers come and go. Friends are forever."

"True, but contrary to the Gen Y *Friends with Benefits* movement, it's not a good idea to have sex with your friends," I reminded her. "That's how we stay friends. I'm not ready for a life of celibacy, but I may have no alternative. Pickings sure are getting slim out there, especially when you're approaching thirty-two and competing against toddlers."

After we hit the big three-uh-oh, Joni and I began to refer to anyone under thirty as a toddler. I worried that nine years from now we'd be calling the thirty-somethings toddlers and the twenty-somethings infants.

"Then we need to find you a boy-toy," she suggested.

I couldn't believe my ears. Surely, she was joking. I stared at her, but her expression remained a study in innocence. You never knew with Joni. She looked at sex as a recreational sport.

I, on the other hand, needed a committed, meaningful relationship before I hopped in bed with a guy. Unfortunately, my track record in that area left much to be desired. I had come to the conclusion that my idea of meaningful and committed wasn't necessarily the male definition. So I hopped in and quickly hopped out—like with Former Significant Other. And his many predecessors. Maybe it was all that Jewish-Catholic-Episcopal guilt running through my veins. Those didactic corpuscles had a tendency to crowd out the more open-minded Unitarian ones.

Joni leaned over and whispered in my ear so Mitch couldn't hear her. "Remember, Polly, when all else fails, there's always the handy-dandy vibrator."

~*~

I looked forward to the following Saturday morning with as much anticipation as a convicted murderer awaiting sentencing in a capital punishment state. The last time I had attended a service at Uncle Aaron's synagogue, old Cantor Herskowitz was still alive and kicking. Now the dearly departed cantor was singing in a heavenly chorus, and after our disastrous dinner date, Jeff Jacoby was the last person I wanted to see. Unfortunately, I had no choice. It was the second week of the month, and Uncle Aaron expected me.

Services at Uncle Aaron's synagogue last two hours, followed by an *Oneg Shabbat*, the Jewish equivalent of a church coffee-hour. The *Oneg Shabbat* is held in a large multi-purpose room devoid of furnishings. The room regularly transforms from reception center to lecture hall to indoor playroom for the nursery school, depending on the day of the week. During the *Oneg Shabbat*, people stand around gossiping until the rabbi approaches. Then the conversation quickly shifts to the sermon of the day with everyone congratulating the clergyman for such an inspiring spiritual presentation.

I don't know the literal translation of *Oneg Shabbat*, but as far as I'm concerned, it should stand for "awkward situation."

Beth Shalom is a revolving door synagogue. One third of Uncle Aaron's flock finds it impossible to sit for two hours without a cigarette break. Another third undergoes cell phone withdrawal after forty-five minutes. The remaining third either suffers from Attention Deficit Disorder or bladder problems. Consequently, very few congregants ever hear the entire sermon. This has a tendency to produce lots of averted gazes and shoe shuffling whenever Uncle Aaron mingles with his congregants.

Since I am neither addicted to nicotine nor cell phones, have a strong bladder, and have never been diagnosed with ADD, I am one of a select few who winds up sitting through the entire sermon.

"So what did you think?" asked Uncle Aaron, coming up to me after the service. He wrapped a beefy arm around me and kissed my cheek.

I am also one of the few members of his congregation unafraid to voice my opinion. After all, he's family. "I thought the choice of subject matter a bit odd, considering you were doing a Bar Mitzvah this morning."

He gave me a puzzled look.

"The story of Noah and the ark? Noah finally lands the boat, and the first thing he does is go off and get drunk? Terrific message for thirteen-year-olds, Uncle Aaron. Besides, isn't tomorrow night the first night of Hanukkah? I expected to hear all about Judah Maccabee and the oil miracle."

"We're doing a special Hanukkah service for the children tomorrow during Sunday school," he said. "Today's sermon was intended as a message about responsibility."

I motioned over to the refreshments table. "Maybe you were too subtle. I don't think they got it."

The other difference between an *Oneg Shabbat* and a church coffee hour is the choice of beverage served—sweet, syrupy purple wine replacing watered-down decaf. Rows of three-ounce plastic cups, half-filled with the stuff, lined the table. The Bar Mitzvah boy and his friends, ignoring the children's table containing grape juice and cookies, packed around the wine like Secret Service operatives guarding the President. Whenever they felt the coast was clear, they reached out and grabbed a cup, quickly downing the contents.

Uncle Aaron glanced around at his congregation. No one was paying any attention to the underage drinkers. He groaned.

"Maybe you need to sit in on one of Uncle Cal's fire-and-brimstone sermons," I said. "He does a great one on demon rum."

"Cal's a hypocrite. You should see the way he drinks us all under the table at the Nineteenth Hole." He winked at me, his face taking on a mischievous, elfin quality. "By the way, Polly, did you hear the one about the rabbi, the priest and the minister who walked into a bar together?"

Only about a million times. The uncles were such regulars at The Nineteen Hole after their weekly golf match that the manager had framed the classic joke and hung it over the bar. I finished the punch line for him. "The bartender looks up at them and says, 'What is this, a joke?'" We both laughed.

My uncles were the most unlikely group of friends ever to walk the earth. They met in the strangest of circumstances. Mom and Dad had shacked up together in a one-room basement apartment in the East Village. From what I've been told, their furnishings consisted of a mattress on the floor, several dozen milk crates, and a bookcase made of cinderblocks and one-by-eights. Strips of batik fabric covered the windows, and a curtain of beads separated the bathroom from the rest of the apartment. They were blissfully happy.

Horrified, each of my grandparents enlisted the help of his or her clerical brother. The four clergymen wound up converging on Mom and Dad at the same time.

As Mom tells it, they all started out screaming at each other and hurling threats, but within minutes the six of them were sharing a bottle of Chianti, exchanging priest/rabbi/minister jokes, and planning the wedding. Dad says it took a bit longer and more than one bottle of wine before a compromise was reached, but in the end they appeased the family by agreeing to make the union legal. Good thing, too, because I was already on the way.

Four ceremonies were held, one after the other, with each of the uncles presiding and the order decided by a roll of the dice. Afterwards, Mom and Dad took off for a honeymoon at an ashram in Idaho, and the uncles headed for the golf course. They've been a weekly foursome ever since.

Uncle Aaron brought the conversation around to the topic I wanted to avoid. "Actually, I was more interested in your date with my new cantor. Didn't you and Jeff have dinner together last week?"

Now it was my turn to groan. I also rolled my eyes.

"What?"

"How could you do that to me?"

"I don't understand. Jeff's a great guy. He's good-looking, funny, smart—"

"Whoa!" I held up my hand. "Back up. I'll grant you the good-looking. But funny? Smart? Are we talking about the same Jeff

Jacoby? How can you tell? The man talks less than a monk who's taken a vow of silence."

Uncle Aaron looked across the room. I followed his gaze. The new cantor was surrounded by a group of congregants, all hanging on his every word. And he was obviously uttering quite a few of them—probably more than he had spoken to me during the span of our date.

"He told me he had a lovely time with you. Said he planned to ask you out again."

"I don't think so."

"You should give him another chance, Polly. He's really an interesting guy when you get to know him."

I had no plans to get to know Jeff Jacoby. I already knew more than I cared to about the man.

I guess Uncle Aaron saw the stubborn set of my jaw because he pulled out his trump card. "Make an old man happy, sweetheart."

Uncle Aaron wasn't all that old. None of the uncles had yet hit seventy. All were the youngest of their respective families and actually only about ten to fifteen years older than my parents. But what could I say?

Jeff wandered over several minutes later. "Hello, Polly."

"Jeff."

Uncle Aaron excused himself, leaving me alone with Jeff. "I didn't expect to see you here," he said.

"Second weekend of the month," I explained. "I divide the care of my soul between my uncles."

"Oh. Right."

I waited for him to say something else. And waited. And waited. And waited. Finally, I decided to put us both out of our misery. "You have a wonderful singing voice. The congregation seemed captivated."

"Thank you."

More awkward silence. I couldn't stand it. "Do I make you uncomfortable, Jeff?" Okay, I'll admit it was blunt, but this was getting ridiculous.

He blushed.

I pressed. "I do, don't I?"

He took a deep breath. "In a way. I've never dated anyone outside my faith before. I guess I'm afraid I'll say something that might offend you."

Wow! Three sentences in a row. Impressive. "I doubt there's much I haven't heard. It's not like I grew up in a convent."

"In a way, I did." He blushed again. "Well, not a convent, exactly."

I assured him I understood.

"Rabbi Goldfarb didn't quite prepare me for your family."

I laughed. "I doubt anyone is ever prepared for my family."

"No, I suppose not." He paused and offered me a shy smile. "Think we could maybe start over, Polly? Give this dating thing one more try?"

I had a sneaking suspicion I was going to regret this, but in the name of making a not-so-old man happy, I agreed to meet Jeff the following day for a late brunch after his Sunday school duties.

~*~

Jeff's choice of restaurants didn't bode well for convincing me to continue our relationship. The Klezmer Kafé was a smoky hole-in-the-wall down in the Lower East Side. New York had banned smoking in restaurants years ago, but no one at the Klezmer seemed to be aware of this. Nearly everyone crowding around the small tables puffed away on cigarettes. Much to the dismay of my stomach, some even chomped on cigars.

The restaurant served traditional Jewish fare from before anyone had heard of cholesterol, clogged arteries, or bypass surgery. Each item on the menu contained more grams of fat than my entire weekly intake.

"I know it's not good for you," said Jeff, apparently sensing my horror as I scanned the menu, "but you have to admit, it tastes great."

The heavy smells of fried you-name-it, mixed with the tobacco, filled air. "Eat enough of this, and you won't be around very long to enjoy anything else."

He shrugged. "I jog five miles a day. Besides, this food is part of our heritage."

"Yours," I reminded him, "not mine."

"Not according to Jewish law."

I raised an eyebrow. "Oh?"

"Since your mother's mother was Jewish, your mother is Jewish. And therefore, so are you."

"Are you trying to convert me, Jeff?"

"I don't need to. You're already Jewish."

I could see the logic behind his explanation—at least from his point of view. It was Jeff's way of coming to terms with dating a *shiksa*—or at least a three-quarters *shiksa*. I wanted to assure him that there was no need to form some convoluted rationale to ease his conscience. I was quickly regretting accepting this second date and had already decided there wouldn't be a third.

His attitude rubbed me the wrong way. I was brought up to believe that you should accept people for who they are. I don't require my dates to fill out a census form stating race, religion, and country of birth before going out with them, and I expect the same consideration from them.

I decided against launching into a lecture on tolerance. What was the point? As far as I was concerned, Jeff Jacoby was history before the first bite of cherry blintz made it to my mouth.

~*~

"And if that wasn't enough to seal his fate," I later told Joni when I ran into her outside our apartment building, "the after-brunch entertainment would have done it."

"Entertainment?"

"A Klezmer band. Think of polka music on Jewish steroids. Then throw in a guy with two left feet—both of which kept landing on mine."

"So much for tall-dark-and-handsome," said Joni. "That'll teach you to break our rules. No second chances. We came up with them for a reason, remember?"

"What can I say? I'm a sucker when it comes to my uncles. Now if you'll excuse me, I think I'll soak my poor feet for an hour before catching the train to Summit."

~*~

Much to my artery-overloaded chagrin, I arrived to find Mom had planned a traditional Jewish menu in honor of Hanukkah. Only my parents would celebrate Hanukkah with a rabbi, two priests and a minister present, but no one sitting around the table seemed to think this was odd. We had been doing it for as long as I could remember. Later on in the month, the rabbi would celebrate Christmas with us—an even odder occurrence and one I doubted the local branch of the Rabbinical Council would approve of, had they known.

The first course consisted of borscht soup with a dollop of sour cream. For the entrée we ate brisket with onions and carrots and latkes with a choice of more sour cream or applesauce. Mom, of course, wasn't Kosher, and Uncle Aaron was a Reform rabbi, so she didn't need to worry about mixing meat and dairy. Dessert was Jewish apple cake. I politely passed on the gold, foil-wrapped chocolate coins that were a traditional treat of the holiday. After my brunch with Jeff, I was certain I'd now need to call Roto-Rooter to tunnel a passageway through the plaque in my arteries.

Afterwards we all gathered in the living room to exchange gifts. Since the holiday came early this year, Mom had done her Hanukkah shopping back in August and September during all the Back-to-School and Labor Day sales. Each of the uncles received golf club covers—but not just any golf club covers.

Mom had done her shopping at The Disney Store, choosing a separate character for each uncle. I could picture the foursome come tomorrow morning as they rolled across the greens in their golf cart, four bags sticking up out of the back, each with multiple stuffed heads of Mickey Mouse, Goofy, Donald Duck, and Pluto bobbing along.

"How did you decide who received which cartoon character?" I asked.

"Random selection," said Mom. "I didn't label the packages."

I did notice, however, that each had come wrapped in a different paper. And Mom looked a bit too innocent. Still, I wondered at the reasoning behind pairing Uncle Aaron with Mickey, Uncle Emerson with Goofy, Uncle Francis with Pluto, and Uncle Cal with Donald. And then it hit me. Uncle Aaron possessed the outgoing friendliness of Mickey Mouse. Given half a chance, Uncle Emerson, with his crazy sense of humor, could out-Goofy Goofy. Uncle Francis bounced around from one task to the next with the energy and determination of Pluto, and Uncle

Cal's feigned curmudgeon exterior mirrored Donald Duck's personality to a "T."

I watched as Uncle Francis placed two of his Pluto covers over his hands like puppets and wondered what the Archbishop of Newark might say about this odd gathering of ours.

"Too bad we have no children around for you to entertain," my mother said to Uncle Francis. Subtle is not a word in Mimi Harmony's vocabulary.

This was all Uncle Aaron needed to jump in and bring up the subject I was dreading. "I understand you had another date with Jeff."

"We met for brunch earlier today."

"And?"

Six bodies inched forward to the edge of their seats, their movements choreographed to the popping of arthritic joints. Six pairs of eyes focused on me through bifocals and trifocals. Six pairs of lungs held their collective breaths. I eyed each one of them before I spoke. "And I'd really appreciate it if the six of you would please stop trying to marry me off."

"Now, Polly, he's such a fine young man. I don't think you're giving him a chance."

"Look, Uncle Aaron, I suffered through one of the most boring evenings of my life last week, but I gave him a second chance. For you. He's not getting a third. We're incompatible. Plain and simple. No chemistry." I threw my hands up in the air. "If you like him that much, why don't you date him?"

Uncle Aaron has lived alone since Aunt Harriet's death from cancer nearly seven years ago. To my knowledge he has never dated in all that time. For all I know, he's adopted Uncle Francis' vows of celibacy. If only my parents and the other uncles would concentrate their efforts on finding a nice companion for Uncle Aaron, maybe they wouldn't have any time to stick their well-intentioned noses in my social life.

What am I thinking? With my luck they'd find a nice widow with a single son and strike up a two-for-one deal!

My father cleared his throat. "I believe you're confusing your uncles, Polly." He nodded in Uncle Emerson's direction. Everyone laughed, Uncle Emerson the hardest.

Leave it to Dad to jump in and relieve a tense situation with a bit of Harmony humor. I love my father. He has a sort of "aw shucks" Jimmy Stewart quality to him in both appearance and demeanor. He's tall and lanky—thanks to the genes he inherited from Uncle Emerson—with a head of thinning gray hair that often flops across his forehead and over one eye. Laid back and easygoing, Howard Harmony is the Yin to Mimi Harmony's hyperactive Yang—a perfect example of how opposites attract.

Sometimes I think Dad's the only one on my side. Unfortunately, Mom outnumbers us both. Don't ask me to explain the math. In my family it's more a matter of voice and perpetual kinetic motion than numbers.

After the laughter died down, we returned to opening our gifts. I doubted I had made my point. When it came to Mom and her incessant meddling in my life, my protests fell on deaf ears. Short of a miracle on the order of changing water to wine or getting a day's worth of oil to last for eight days, her matchmaking attempts would continue to drive me crazy. And she'd employ any tactic to achieve her goal, including recruiting my uncles to join her cause. I knew my mother too well. She was on a crusade of Biblical proportions. Who better to aid her than four men of the cloth?

TWO
Lecherous Jerks and Boy Toys

For eons single, working women the world over have searched out the answer to the age-old question of how to survive the holiday office party. In a word? Forget it. Okay, that's actually two words. No matter how well-intentioned you are, no matter how many vows of temperance you swear to beforehand, no matter how hard you bite down on your own tongue, no matter how many prayers you recite or how many hours you meditate, no one gets through the holidays without saying or doing something really stupid at the annual party from hell.

And there's no getting out of it. Barring divine intervention or a blizzard that shuts down the city, attendance is mandatory—at least if you want to remain on the shortlist for promotion. Also, fail to make an appearance—and I don't mean a popping-the-head-in token appearance—and you might as well kiss that much anticipated year-end bonus goodbye. Instead of a check in your office stocking, you'll find a lump of brown rubber ca-ca from a Times Square novelty store. Our CEO has a Beavis and Butthead sense of humor—juvenile at its best, scatological at its worst.

He also has wandering hands that fail to respond to the threat of a sexual harassment suit, mainly because he knows none of his female employees would ever carry out the threat. Gloria Steinem aside, we're all too smart to commit professional suicide. As anyone who has ever filed one of those suits will attest, it's not worth winning the battle to lose the war. So although we hate to admit it to each other and never concede it to the public, most of us put up with Anita Hill-style sexual crap around the office on a daily basis.

To make matters worse, newly hired male coworkers often see our response—or lack of it—to the CEO's behavior as permission to behave the same way. We quickly set them straight. If a few well-chosen words fail to work, the threat of a knee to the groin usually gets the desired results. However, there are a few dense Neanderthals who consider such warnings a form of foreplay. On more than one occasion, I've been sorely tempted to carry out the threat.

The office is a battle zone. Always emotional. Sometimes physical. There's no getting around that. Multiply an average day's worth of combat by a thousand, and you come close to conditions at our annual holiday bash. The real trick is surviving without either putting your foot in your mouth after too many egg nogs or dumping the aforementioned egg nog—the entire punch bowl's worth—over the head of some lecherous jerk, whether he's the boss or an overly intoxicated drone.

I suppose I could always quit and get another job. I have a standing invitation to join the family hair care and cosmetics empire any time I want. Problem is, I don't want. I love my parents but in small measured doses. After living on my own for so long, going to work for them would be like moving back into my old bedroom.

As far as I can tell, the work world isn't much better anywhere else, so I stay put. If the city is a jungle, the office is the belly of the beast. When you're stuck in the belly, one beast is as bad as another. At least I like what I do—even if I'm not too happy about my present accounts. Most of my coworkers are tolerable, and ever since his most recent marriage a few months ago, the Head Lecherous Jerk is a bit tamer and not nearly as obnoxious. I think his latest trophy wife—number four by last count—is keeping him on a short leash. She used to be his secretary, so I guess she's wise to all his tricks.

Still, I was looking forward to the yearly event with as much relish as doing my taxes. Never having developed the fine art of small talk, I'm not fond of parties to begin with, and I resent forced socialization with people I wouldn't normally choose as friends. Having to work with them five days a week is one thing. We focus on business and get the job done. Our personal lives rarely enter into conversations, and that's the way I like it. My off-hours should be my own. Since it's obvious that the rest of the office staff feels likewise, everyone deals with the yearly command performance by multiple dips into the big bowl of liquid holiday cheer. That's usually where the trouble begins.

~*~

I work for Management Consultants, Incorporated, an organization that organizes organizations. We specialize in small to midsize nonprofit professional groups in the arts, providing executive directors and ancillary staff for organizations not large enough to afford their own on a full-time basis. My responsibilities require me to have public relations, advertising, journalistic, legal, secretarial, and even psychological skills. I coordinate their yearly conferences, publish their newsletters, write press releases, oversee their board meetings, take care of all business-related issues, and do a lot of hand holding. Sometimes the hand-holding takes up a good deal of my day. Believe me, the myth about artists being extremely temperamental is no myth.

The big joke, though, is that with all this organizational skill, you'd think I could better organize my own social life. Not a chance. Which is why I always seem to be available whenever one of my well-intentioned relatives sics another blind date on me. Of course, I haven't done so well on my own, either, so I try to forget my failures at love and concentrate on my successes at work.

At present I'm assigned to three associations—The National Society of Professional Ventriloquists, The American Cloggers Association, and The Medical Illustrators Guild. I'm thinking of getting them all together to write a book—*The Clogging Dummy's Guide to Surgery*. Considering some of the other books the big publishing houses are churning out lately, it should be a tremendous financial success. My cloggers, ventriloquists, and illustrators will make enough money to hire full-time directors, and I'll get promoted to some of the A-list accounts. Okay, so it's a pipe dream, but a girl can dream, can't she?

~*~

My office, along with most of the others, is actually an eight-by-eight-foot cubicle made up of four-foot-high blue-gray fabric-covered panels that branch off on either side of a long corridor opposite the elevator. The configuration leaves little room for privacy.

An L-shaped desk takes up two walls of my office. A computer monitor, keyboard, and two printers cover most of the surface area. Across from my desk, a set of double bookcases hold everything related to my three accounts. I have no window. A framed motivational poster, compliments of Head Lecherous Jerk, hangs on one blue-gray panel. Everyone in the office has one of these posters, each with a different message about teamwork superimposed over a sunrise that peaks out behind a mountain, glimmers over an ocean, or rises above a rolling wheat field. I got the glimmering ocean. Other than that, I have no artwork on my walls, only a generic calendar, compliments of one of our vendors. Head Lecherous Jerk frowns upon individuality in the workplace.

I was sitting at my computer proofreading the latest issue of *Two Clogged Feet*, the monthly newsletter of The American Cloggers Association, when Head Lecherous Jerk placed his age spot riddled sixty-year-old hands on my shoulders and leaned over to scan the text on my computer screen.

"Nice work." If his face were any closer, his lips would have kissed my cheek as he spoke.

I swallowed down the urge to slam my chair back into his balls, pasted a smile on my face, and still staring at the computer screen, asked, "Is there something I can help you with, sir?" Had I turned to face him, we would have locked lips, a thought that sent my lunch backing up into my esophagus.

Head Lecherous Jerk straightened. "Yes, Miss Harmony. I need a favor, and I think you're the perfect person for the job."

I didn't like the sound of this. I pushed my chair back from my desk and stood to face him. I didn't care that he had the advantage of looking down at me as he spoke. From his vantage point I wasn't certain of the view. I also wasn't about to give him any more of a psychological advantage than he already held in the employer/employee dynamic. Head Lecherous Jerk was a short guy, five-five at most. In heels we stood nearly eye-to-eye, and that's the way I wanted it when he asked his favor. "What type of job?"

"One I think you'll thoroughly enjoy."

I raised an eyebrow.

He ignored the silent sarcasm. "The International Society of Choral Directors is looking to replace their existing management firm. Their president is going to be in the city tomorrow and has requested a meeting with me late in the afternoon."

"Our office holiday party is tomorrow afternoon," I reminded him.

"Precisely. I can't very well rush through the meeting and send him on his way because we're having a party. It's too big an account. Under the circumstances, I have to invite him to join us."

Not a good idea, I thought, especially if we have a repeat of last year's fiasco. Prospective clients should not see the people they're entrusting their business to making complete asses of themselves, but I kept my opinion to myself. After all, Head Lecherous Jerk was the biggest ass of all and proved it every year at our annual shindig. "So where do I come in?"

"I would like you to act as his escort for the evening. Stick beside him during the party and get him out as soon as you can."

Escort? I didn't like the sound of that word at all, but I didn't think even Head Lecherous Jerk was stupid enough to suggest I behave as anything less than a consummate professional. I decided not to challenge him. After all, if we landed the account, he might give it to me for helping him out, and The International Society of Choral Directors sounded like a definite promotion over wooden shoes and talking dummies. "You mean before things start to degenerate?"

He wrapped his arm around my shoulders. "Now we're on the same wavelength."

~*~

The next day the office was scheduled to close at four-thirty. The caterers had arrived a little before four and were busy setting up buffet and drink stations in the conference room and throughout the hallways. Jay Steiner, head of accounting and a Grade-A lecherous jerk in his own right, had already purloined a bottle of whiskey and was busy darting from cubicle to cubicle filling coffee mugs. Someone plugged The Barking Dogs rendition of *Jingle Bells* into the sound system and turned the volume up to a deafening level. The party was out of control before it even started. Three howling bars into *Jingle Bells* my phone buzzed. "Ms. Harmony," I answered, straining to hear over the musical mutts.

Head Lecherous Jerk spoke from the other end of the line. "Would you mind stepping into my office, please?"

Show time, I thought, flipping off my computer. I strode down the hall to the big corner office with its panoramic view of Manhattan.

Arlene Flynn, Head Lecherous Jerk's secretary, greeted me in the reception area outside his office. "Go right in, Polly." Rumor had it, the slightly overweight, middle-aged newest addition to our staff was handpicked by her predecessor. Trophy Wife Number Four wasn't taking any chances.

Head Lecherous Jerk was sitting behind his pink Italian marble-topped desk, chosen by Trophy Wife Number Three when he was still paying more attention to her than the secretary that eventually replaced her. Opposite him, in one of the matching white leather club chairs that faced the desk, sat Prospective Client.

Head Lecherous Jerk rose and walked around his desk. "Come in Ms. Harmony." Prospective Client rose and turned to face me. "This is the young woman who will be handling your account." Head Lecherous Jerk motioned to me. "If you decide to sign with our firm."

Faster than the speed of light, I soared from an extreme high to a pit-of-the-stomach low. With Head Lecherous Jerk's first words I thought he had signed the deal and was turning the Choral Directors over to me. By the time he finished his sentence, I realized that the entire account rode on the remainder of the evening. I glanced over at Head Lecherous Jerk. His eyes said, "Don't blow it." All I could think was *shit!*

As he made introductions, I mechanically participated in the formalities, but my mind was on the flowing whiskey and barking dogs at the other end of the floor. Luckily, someone had thought to disconnect Head Lecherous Jerk's office from the sound system before connecting the howling mutts.

Too bad I couldn't disconnect the rest of them from the office. By now I figured Nan Osner, our resident coke head was shaking her bootie on the conference table. Hopefully, she still had most of her clothes on and hadn't yet fallen face-first into the pâté like last year.

Prospective Client, otherwise known as Professor Mason Hightower, Ph.D., of Lincoln, Nebraska, didn't strike me as the type to appreciate the fun and games gearing up down the hall. I studied the austere cut of his conservative black suit, white over-starched shirt, and university tie, and pegged him for a teetotaler. From the pinched expression on his weathered face, I suspected he stored his conductor's baton up a certain part of his anatomy where the sun never shines.

Apparently, Head Lecherous Jerk was thinking along the same lines. "I've had my secretary make a dinner reservation for the two of you at Alberto's. You can give Professor Hightower an overview of how you'd handle his organization." Then he turned to the professor. "You'll like Alberto's. It's a nice, quiet Italian restaurant. Good food. Pleasant atmosphere."

The professor nodded.

I excused myself to get my coat and purse. While at my desk, I stuffed a few newsletters and PR samples into my briefcase. Mason Hightower looked all business, which was fine with me. Small talk on a blind date was bad enough. During a one-on-one business dinner, it could prove deadly. Thankfully, he also looked like he turned in by nine every night, so I anticipated a blessedly short evening.

Okay, I knew I was stereotyping, but the guy looked like a younger, better-dressed version of the farmer with the pitchfork in *American Gothic*. If he smiled, he'd crack the paint. And he *was* from Nebraska. He probably couldn't wait to leave wicked Manhattan and hightail it back to the safety of the cornfields.

Now I was no longer sure I even wanted the account. With a name like The *International* Society of Choral Directors, I had envisioned planning conferences in the great music capitals of the world—Paris, Vienna, Salzburg, Milan. I had a hunch that if Mason Hightower picked the various locales, I'd be traveling to such exotic venues as Milwaukee and Indianapolis.

I'd seen enough of the Midwest with the cloggers and ventriloquists. At least the medical illustrators chose cities like New Orleans and Miami for their yearly conferences. Granted, they were always in the heat of the summer when the rates were lowest, but Miami in August—even in the heart of hurricane season, in my opinion—beat Milwaukee any time of year.

By the time I returned to fetch my charge for the evening, Arlene had ushered the rest of the staff into the conference room and closed the door. Bing Crosby was now crooning *White Christmas* over the sound system, and no time bombs lurked in the corridor between the executive suite and the elevators.

I made a mental note to buy Arlene a Christmas present—a really nice one—if we landed the account.

~*~

As we descended to the lobby, I turned to Professor Mason Hightower and asked, "Are you all right with Italian food? We don't have to go to Alberto's if you'd prefer something different." I figured him for a steak—extremely well done—and baked potato sort of guy and wondered if I shouldn't whip out my cell phone and see if Morton's, Gallagher's, or The Palm had a table available.

"Northern or Southern?" he asked.

I was surprised he even knew the difference. "Northern. The chef is from Turin. The menu contains a heavy French influence. It's definitely not your standard spaghetti and meatballs."

"Perfect. What passes for Southern Italian cooking at most American restaurants bears little resemblance to what you'll find in Rome or Naples. It's like the travesty we call Chinese food here." He shook his head and scowled. "Chow Mein? Chop Suey? You won't find anything coming close to those gluttonous horrors in Beijing."

Perhaps I needed a lesson in how looks can be deceiving. I gave myself a well-deserved kick in my jump-to-conclusions rear end and vowed to become more open-minded toward corn-bred

Midwesterners. "No you won't," I agreed.

Maybe I wouldn't get stuck organizing a conference in Milwaukee after all.

~*~

The professor, who preferred to be called Mace, continued to surprise me over dinner. With his first very dry martini—with an onion, not an olive—he loosened up. By his second martini, he opened up. The farmer with the pitchfork turned out to be a truly cosmopolitan man, having traveled extensively throughout Europe and Asia. He possessed a brilliant wit and a cerebral sense of humor. His stories held my attention. His anecdotes made me laugh.

When he smiled—which he did often—his rugged face didn't crack. Instead, his bright sea-green eyes sparkled, and dimples appeared at the corners of his mouth. His straight, sandy colored hair gave him a rakish air that reminded me of Harrison Ford back in his Indiana Jones days. To my pleasant surprise and contrary to my initial assessment, Professor Mason "Mace" Hightower was actually a good-looking man. A *very* good-looking man.

The evening didn't break up by nine as I had originally expected, and I was glad. We didn't leave the restaurant until after ten-thirty.

"We should take separate cabs," I suggested. "Your hotel is uptown, and my apartment is downtown."

He wouldn't hear of it. "Sorry, but you're going to have to put up with some old-fashioned Midwestern manners. I wouldn't think of sending you off alone in a cab at this hour of the night."

I would have told him that I take cabs alone at night all the time, but the truth was that I really didn't want the evening to end yet. I was enjoying Mace's company too much. When the taxi pulled up in front of my apartment building, I invited him in for a cup of coffee.

"Fake or high-test?" I asked as we entered my two-room apartment and I led the way to the kitchen area, an L-shaped corner sectioned off from the living room by a bar and a row of overhead cabinets.

"Excuse me?"

I turned to look at him. A puzzled expression covered his face. I opened a cabinet, pulled two canisters off a shelf, and held them up. "Decaf or regular?"

"Oh! Regular if you don't mind."

"Not at all." I measured out some beans into the grinder and filled the carafe with water. "I don't see why people bother to drink decaf, actually, but I keep some around for friends who do."

"Might as well drink hot water," said Mace. As I ground the beans and prepared the coffeemaker, he wandered around my living room, originally the master bedroom of the converted brownstone. At the far end of the room he stopped in front of one of two built-in wall units framing the triple bay window that looked out over Gramercy Park. "Meissen, isn't it?" he asked, lifting a porcelain harlequin figurine from one of the shelves.

The man continued to decimate each of my pre-conceived notions. "Yes, I found it at a street fair in Brooklyn. Paid all of five dollars for it."

He flipped over the porcelain and studied the markings. "I'd say it's mid-seventeen hundreds. Fairly rare. You got a steal."

I was flabbergasted. "Seventeen-forty. I've done a bit of research on it."

"Yes, *Commedia dell'Arte*, if I'm not mistaken."

"How do you know that? Most men wouldn't know a Meissen

figurine from a Ming vase."

He placed the figurine back on the shelf and shrugged. "I took a course in the history of European porcelains while I was working on my doctorate in Berlin."

I wondered if there was anything he didn't know. The man was a fount of knowledge. "Make yourself comfortable," I waved to the couch. "I'm going to take my contacts out while the coffee's dripping."

He nodded. "Take your time."

~*~

As I popped my lenses and ran a brush through my hair, I considered the ethics of dating a client. Although I knew we wouldn't see each other often—most business being conducted via phone, fax, and e-mail—I could feel a certain chemistry percolating between us, one I thought I'd like to pursue. I didn't remember seeing any company policy forbidding fraternization between employees and clients, but I had never really spent any time reading over that part of the employee handbook. None of the cloggers, ventriloquists, or medical illustrators had ever fascinated me the way Professor Mason Hightower did.

I took one final stroke to my hair, set the brush back down on the shelf above the toilet, and grabbed a bottle of Blue Rhapsody, Harmony's signature scent. Mom had named it after Gershwin's *Rhapsody in Blue*, in her opinion the sexiest piece of music ever written.

I had spent the evening watching Mace speak, enraptured by his words but also captivated by his very sexy-looking mouth. Anyone with lips like that, I decided, had to score a ten on the Kiss-o-meter. Perhaps with a little olfactory stimulation I'd know for sure before the evening ended. I gave a spritz to each wrist, perched my glasses on my nose, and headed back into the living room.

~*~

"Sorry to keep you—" The rest of my sentence died, trapped in my throat. I stared at Mace. My jaw hung open. I'm not usually at a loss for words, but the sight that confronted me struck with such unexpected force that it literally shut down my brain.

"I took the liberty of adding a splash of brandy to the coffee." He motioned to the bottle sitting on the coffee table next to a steaming mug. He sipped from the other mug, then set it down beside the bottle.

I finally found my voice. "You apparently took more than a little liberty." He lounged sprawled across my couch wearing nothing but a sensuous smile, a pair of socks, and the most enormous hard-on I'd ever seen. I felt the heat rise to my cheeks and wasn't sure whether it was from anger over his brazenness or the size of his penis. I took a step backwards and diverted my gaze, concentrating on the red G-clefs that embellished his black socks. "Is this another form of Midwestern manners I'm not familiar with, or have I missed something?"

He rose from the couch and strolled leisurely across the room towards me.

"Keep your distance." I backed up another step.

Mace stopped. A scowl replaced his smile. Deep grooves ate into his forehead. "You did invite me up to your apartment."

"For a cup of coffee, not a screw!"

"Hell, Polly, you've been sending me signals all night. Then you head off to the bathroom to get more comfortable. To a man that means one thing and one thing only."

Now I *was* pissed. "I said I was going to take out my contacts.

Since when is that a euphemism for slipping into a lace teddy? Jeez! We've just met, Mace. Yes, I was enjoying myself this evening. You're an interesting guy, and I'll admit I was beginning to wonder if maybe we might develop a relationship. But hell! We've never even held hands, much less kissed. What kind of a girl do you think I am?"

I grabbed his pants from off the chair where he had carefully folded his clothes and hurled them at him. "I can't believe you thought you were going to get laid!" I reached for his shirt and sent that flying in his direction. "This wasn't even a date," I screamed, roughly balling his T-shirt up in my fists. "It was a *business* dinner—one that *my* company paid for!" I pitched the undershirt. It hit him square between the eyes.

I scooped up another garment. When I saw what it was, I dropped it like a hot coal. Touching his cotton boxers repulsed me. I kicked the shorts in his direction and spun on my heels.

"You've got two minutes to get dressed and leave."

With that I headed for my bedroom, slammed the door, grabbed the phone, and called Joni. Mitch answered. "I need you down here right now." I tried to keep my voice from quivering. It was bad enough my hands were shaking so hard I could barely hold the receiver.

"On my way," he said.

~*~

When I returned to the living room, Mace was dressed except for his tie, which he had looped around his neck and his jacket, which was draped over his arm. We stared at each other for a moment. An apology would have been nice, but the look in his eyes made it abundantly clear that he thought *I* owed *him* one, not the other way around. Without saying a word, he strode across the room and yanked the door open as Mitch arrived, out-of-breath, shoeless, and half-dressed.

Mace glared at Mitch.

Mitch glared at Mace. "You all right, Pol?" he asked, turning his attention to me.

"I'm fine, thank you. The gentleman," —and I used the term derisively— "was just leaving."

Mitch stepped aside, and Professor Mason Hightower strode out of my apartment, my career, and my life. A moment later we heard the sound of the front door slamming behind him. I'd have a lot of explaining to do come Monday morning.

I collapsed against the doorjamb, closed my eyes, and sighed.

A singsong voice called from the floor above. "Mitch? Will you be up soon?"

My eyes flew open. I hadn't realized I had torn Mitch away from a date. He offered me a sheepish grin. Stepping to the railing, he ran his fingers through his tousled hair and called up the stairwell. "In a minute." Then he turned back to me. "You sure you're okay?"

"Yeah, terrific." When he gave me one of his trademark I-wasn't-born-yesterday smirks, I forced a smile and waved him off. "Really. Go back up to your friend, Mitch. I'm sorry I disturbed you."

"No problem." He bent down and kissed my cheek. "Tell me all about it tomorrow, okay?"

His date called again, this time in a louder singsong voice, "Mitchie?"

"Shh! You'll wake the neighbors."

We both knew that wasn't true, but who was I to correct him? We lived in a converted brownstone, two apartments per floor, on the upper levels. Mrs. Graham, the owner of the building, occupied the first floor, but she was on a cruise through the Panama Canal.

Mr. and Mrs. Dumont, my octogenarian floor-mates, were both nearly deaf. They spent their days shouting at one another or sitting in front of a blaring television. Either way, they'd never hear Mitch's date or anything else spoken out in the hallway, no matter how loud.

Mitch and Joni shared the third floor with Mr. Bentencourt, a businessman in his late fifties who spent much of the year in Europe but also kept an apartment in New York. He had departed for the continent earlier in the week and wasn't due back for several months.

I stepped into my apartment. "Thanks. I'll see you tomorrow."

~*~

An hour later I was nursing a glass of wine when Joni pounded on my apartment door.

"Early night?" I waved her in. Joni, the original New York party girl rarely came home from a Friday or Saturday night date before dawn.

She shuddered. "One kiss was one kiss too many. I owned a St. Bernard that slobbered less." She wiped her mouth with her sleeve. "Yuck!" Joni plopped onto the sofa and waved a piece of paper in the air. "What's this all about? Mitch left me a note that you had a problem tonight."

I poured her a glass of wine, then poured out the story of my strange evening with Professor Mason Hightower. "The worst part is," I said, polishing off my second glass of Cabernet, "I was really beginning to like the guy. I mean *really* like him. It shocked the hell out of me at first because I initially pegged him for a total loser and wasn't sure how I'd ever survive the evening.

"I mean, me, the girl who thinks anything west of the Hudson is the sticks, and some professor from Nebraska! Can you believe it? So instead of a budding relationship and a new account, I wind up with Reason Number Twelve—the bozo doesn't know the difference between an invitation for coffee and a night of hot sex!"

Joni hardly gave a second's thought to the incompatibility between a died-in-the-wool New Yorker and a Nebraska cornpone. Her thoughts were focused on something else. "Let me get this straight." Her brows knit together in deep thought. "You had the hots for him. He had the hots for you—along with some eye-popping goods—and you kicked him out?"

She threw her arms up in the air and sighed. "Polly, honey, we've got to do something about these seriously outdated virtues of yours. Why the hell didn't you at least sample the offered merchandise first?"

I hit her in the face with one of Mom's needlepoint pillows—the one that spelled out LOVE in red letters on a green and blue background like the Robert Indiana painting. "You want him? Be my guest. He's staying at the Carlyle. Enjoy yourself." I thought about telling her I preferred knowing a guy more than two hours before I spread my legs, but that sounded too much like an insult. I might not agree with Joni's morals, but she was my friend, and I wasn't about to pass judgment on her—even if she felt no qualms about passing judgment on me.

"Hey, I was only thinking of your needs. You know what they say, 'Use it or lose it.'"

"I think I lost it a long time ago." I had also lost any chance of dumping the cloggers and ventriloquists for a more interesting account. No way would the International Society of Choral

Directors sign with us now, and I'd get the blame.

~*~

Joni decided I needed immediate help. Afraid I'd join a convent, she signed onto the family crusade. Only, whereas my mother and uncles were interested in marrying me off, Joni's sole desire was to find someone who would make me scream my head off and keep me begging for more. "Good sex is the ultimate high," she repeatedly told me, "and you, Polly, my tight-assed, repressed friend, need to get high."

So the next night I found myself getting dragged—kicking and screaming—to Hudson Tube, the newest "in" spot in Chelsea. The club scene was never my scene. I hated it when I was younger, and I hate it even more now. The music is too loud and the clientele too young—especially now that I'm over thirty.

None of that seemed to bother Joni. She shoved a path through the mass of sweaty bodies gyrating on the packed dance floor and pulled me along behind her. I couldn't help but notice that many of the couples looked more like they were having sex than dancing. The men and women, groping handfuls of backsides, pressed firmly against each other as they performed tonsillectomies with their tongues. Joni didn't seem to notice. She made her way to a ringside table, complete with baby stud muffins and pushed me into a seat between the two guys, neither of whom looked old enough to drink.

"This is Polly." Joni shouted above the din as she motioned to me. Apparently, she and the boys were already acquainted. I wasn't surprised. Joni believed any guy over twenty-five was past his prime and not worth the effort. These two hardly looked past puberty, though.

She introduced her friends as Juan and Carlos. "Actually, their names are Jason and Craig," she yelled into my ear, "but anything Latino is in right now."

"In for what?" I shouted back, eyeing the two. If either of them had an ounce of Latino blood flowing through his youthful veins, it was generations removed and thoroughly diluted. Both were shaggy-haired blondes, similar in build, with matching pouty lips and insolent gazes. Jason-Juan bore a striking resemblance to the kid who had played in the *Home Alone* movies. Craig-Carlos struck me as a rougher, streetwise version of Leonardo DiCaprio.

"Acting and modeling jobs. Carlos just did an ad for Tommy Hilfiger, and Juan's up for a soap spot. Aren't they both simply delicious?" She leaned over and locked lips with Jason-Juan.

I gave her a weak smile that she was too busy to notice. I wasn't sure whether she meant a soap opera or detergent commercial, but I decided it wasn't worth straining my vocal cords to find out. Besides, at the moment Joni had forgotten all about me.

I smiled lamely at the other stud muffin. He offered to buy me a drink. I declined. I wasn't crazy enough to risk getting slipped a tab of Ecstasy or worse. Joni came up for air and told Juan to bring us a round of Cosmopolitans. "Loosen up," she yelled in my ear. "Enjoy yourself. I'll be right back."

As soon as Joni walked off, Carlos reached across the back of my chair, wrapped his arm around my shoulders, and drew me against his chest. I tried to shrug him off, but before I knew what hit me, he had his other hand up my skirt and his tongue down my throat.

I tried pushing away, but there was no place to move. The more I struggled, the tighter he held me. His one hand cupped the back of my neck and held my mouth firmly against his. The decibel level in the room increased. The bass reverberated from the walls, the floor, the ceiling, and throughout my entire body.

Carlos worked his tongue and fingers like a pro. To my horror, as much as I didn't want to feel anything, my body had other ideas, quickly turning traitor. I relaxed into him and started opening up, allowing him to probe deeper with both his tongue and his fingers. A moan built up in my throat and escaped into his mouth. I moved against his hand, the need building inside me until I thought I'd explode.

Carlos laughed into my mouth. "Not here, hot little mama." He lifted me from my chair. Holding me close against his body, his mouth never leaving mine, he danced me around a maze of tables and people, through a door, and down a dark corridor past moaning shadows. Like a willing slave, I followed.

At the end of the corridor he pressed me up against the wall and raised my skirt. I wrapped my arms around his neck. With one hand he tore a hole through my pantyhose and slipped under my panties, entering me with his entire hand. I gasped and panted. My body arched into his. My thighs spread wide to welcome him and offer as much as he wanted of me.

His other hand tunneled under my sweater and claimed a breast. He plundered my mouth with his teeth and tongue, nipping, biting, probing every recess. At the same time, he rolled my nipple, squeezing it until the throbbing pleasure-pain of the sensations shot straight to my womb.

All the while, he never let up with his other hand. His fingers thrust in and out, in and out between my legs. He grabbed hold of my nub and began working it as fast and hard and ruthlessly as he attacked my nipple. I writhed against him, delirious with uncontrollable need. He consumed me with his mouth and hands, and I was helpless to resist him. My body needed him, and he knew it. He increased his rhythm. Faster. Harder. The world disappeared.

"You want it." He repeated the words over and over again into my mouth. "Tell me you want it." He withdrew his fingers. His hand stilled on my breast.

"Yes." I moaned and reached for his hand. I felt empty without him inside me, working me. "Don't stop," I begged. "I want it. Please. Please." I moaned some more. He slipped one finger back inside me and teased my nub. I squeezed my thighs together. My need increased until I thought I'd die if he didn't continue.

Carlos laughed again. "I'm going to give it to you, baby. Now, baby. Now, baby. Now, baby." He thrust the rest of his fingers deeper inside me, harder and faster, keeping time to the words he sang over and over in my mouth. I strained for even more. He laughed over and over, working me harder until I finally shattered with screams that ripped my throat raw and died in his mouth.

I slipped to the floor, my legs too rubbery to hold me, my body shuddering, and gulped huge lungfuls of sweat-filled air. In the darkness Carlos hovered over me, laughing a deep guttural laugh.

"My turn." The unmistakable sound of a zipper sliding down hit me like a bucket of ice and dragged me from my sex-induced stupor back to my senses. I staggered to my feet, pushed him backwards into the opposite wall, and began to run, knocking into bodies as I fought my way back down the corridor. Once inside the main room, I kept going, plowing my way towards the exit.

I felt dirty. I felt stupid. And I felt angry. With Joni for setting me up and with myself for succumbing to Carlos like some sex-crazed teeny-bopper.

But worst of all was the sickening realization that I'd just experienced the best orgasm of my entire life.

~*~

The next morning I stood at the back of St. Benedict's and actually considered walking into the confessional. Only the thought that Uncle Francis might be the priest sitting on the other side of the booth held me back—that and the fact that technically, I wasn't a Catholic and therefore had no right to enter the confessional and beg for absolution. I was juggling enough guilt over last night. I didn't want to add to the load by giving my uncle a heart attack.

Besides, I couldn't really see myself trying to explain to a celibate priest how I had allowed a total stranger to masturbate me to Nirvana. *Forgive me, Father, for I have sinned, but damn, it felt good!* So much for the repentant sinner.

St. Benedict's was an old stone church with enormous stained glass windows built to mimic the towering Gothic cathedrals of Europe. It served a large, predominantly Hispanic and Slavic congregation in the heart of downtown Newark and was filled to capacity most Sunday mornings. I slipped into a pew towards the back, nodding a greeting to several of the parishioners I recognized.

Of all of my uncles, I enjoy listening to Uncle Francis conduct a service the most and was glad to see him stride to the pulpit several minutes later. Uncle Cal is a dear in family settings, but his sermons are either dry as croutons or filled with hell, fire, and brimstone. Uncle Emerson and Uncle Aaron both lean towards using the pulpit for political as well as religious purposes, Uncle Aaron stressing Zionism and Uncle Emerson bouncing back and forth between gay rights and environmental issues. Both Uncle Emerson and Uncle Aaron often sound more like *New York Times* op-ed columnists than servants of God.

Uncle Francis, on the other hand, speaks with a passion and

reverence that could convert a diehard atheist. I hang on his every word, spellbound by the magic he creates inside those cold stone walls. Maybe it's the pomp and pageantry of the Catholic service. Maybe it's the scent of incense wafting across the pews. Or maybe it's the devotion of a man who believes so deeply and fully that he has given up a lifetime of sex to honor his Lord.

This Sunday, however, I allowed the sound of his voice to soothe my soul without listening to his words. I was too busy castigating myself over last night's fiasco. All I kept thinking was, thank God I hadn't had anything to drink or I might have succumbed to far worse. At least I didn't have to worry about STD's.

~*~

 One of the most interesting things about my uncles is that they all suffer from split personalities. Get them out from behind the pulpit, and they become totally different men. Father Francis morphed into Uncle Francis on our ride up to Summit after church.

"You look like the morning after the night before." He studied me while we were stopped at a traffic light on McCarter Highway.

"Gee thanks." I thought I'd applied ample cover-up to disguise the dark circles under my eyes. Guess not. You'd think at forty dollars a tube the damn stuff would work well enough to keep a celibate near-septuagenarian from noticing the aftermath of a sleepless night. Guess I wasn't a very good walking testament for Harmony cosmetics.

"Rough night?"

"You could say that."

"Want to talk about it?"

I shook my head. "Trust me, Uncle Francis, it's best if you

don't know." He frowned, his shaggy black eyebrows growing together into one bushy line below his furrowed forehead. Uncle Francis' jet-black hair had turned white early. I couldn't remember him any other way, but his eyebrows had refused to age with the rest of him. The combination created a comical appearance when he laughed but intensified his features when he grew serious or stern. Right now he looked both serious *and* stern.

"Let's just say I've learned my lesson, and it won't happen again." No matter how good it felt.

"Well, that's nice to know." He stepped on the gas as the light changed. "Whatever *it* is." His frown deepened. His dark brown eyes narrowed.

Then it occurred to me that if I didn't explain further, last night would become the central topic of discussion over the dinner table later. The last thing I wanted was a three-hour interrogation by my parents and uncles. "If you must know, I let my friend Joni drag me club crawling last night. Big mistake." Then I yawned for effect. "I'm too old to stay up all night."

He patted my knee and made a sympathetic clucking sound like a mother hen. The rigid lines around his mouth and eyes softened. "Maybe you should slip upstairs and take a nap when we get to Summit."

"Sounds like a plan."

~*~

As it turned out, though, I didn't get my nap. I also didn't have to worry about an interrogation concerning the bags under my eyes or my wild night out. I walked in the front door of my parents' house and found I had a bigger problem. Apparently, Uncle Aaron hadn't given up on playing Cupid between me and the boring cantor.

THREE
Tall, Dark, Handsome, Boring...and Then Some

My weekend had turned into a nightmarish *Gilligan's Island* rerun. There I was stranded in my own little island hell with the professor, Carlos, and the cantor. Since I couldn't come right out and scream at Uncle Aaron, I opted for sarcasm. I sidled up next to him, kissed his cheek, and whispered in his ear, "I see you decided to take my advice. The two of you make a lovely couple."

His jaw dropped.

I pressed further. "I thought I made myself perfectly clear last Sunday that I am *not*—repeat *not*—interested in pursuing a relationship with Jeff Jacoby."

Uncle Aaron offered me an apologetic smile. "Your mother was being hospitable. He's new in town and doesn't know anyone yet." He shrugged his shoulders as if he had nothing to do with Jeff being invited for dinner—again. Not in a New York minute did I believe that truckload of feigned innocence. It reeked of bullshit.

I stared into his baby blue eyes, telling him just that without saying a word. He quickly averted his gaze. Men of God make lousy liars.

I wasn't going to let him off the hook that easily. "I find it hard to believe that none of your congregants has invited him to dinner. All those Jewish grandmothers with eligible granddaughters? You mean to tell me none of them have extended the new cantor an invitation? Not Mrs. Finklebaum? Or Mrs. Shapiro? Or even God's own social secretary, Mrs. Goldstein?" Estelle Goldstein was known to everyone at Beth Shalom as the unofficial synagogue hostess. Whenever a stranger crossed the temple threshold, she swooped down and extended an invitation, refusing to take *no* for an answer.

"Now, Polly...."

"Don't 'now, Polly' me!'" I was getting really worked up. Lack of sleep, not to mention a massive dose of shame and guilt over last night's escapade, had taken its toll. Then Uncle Aaron's face filled with hurt, and I backed down. I knew he was manipulating me, but I really wasn't up for a battle—especially since the object of my ire stood nearby.

Besides, for all I knew, Jeff possessed twenty-twenty hearing or whatever the auditory counterpart of perfect eyesight is. I watched him out of the corner of my eye as I lifted myself up on my toes and pecked Uncle Aaron's cheek. "I'm sorry. I've had a rough weekend. I didn't mean to sound like a bitch."

Uncle Aaron's face brightened.

A moment later Jeff approached. "Looks like Uncle Aaron has adopted you." I wanted to be the first to speak in order to direct the conversation. "When I was a little girl I used to wish for an older brother. I suppose an older cousin will have to do."

Before he could say a word, I smiled sweetly, excused myself, and went in search of my mother. Maria Ruth Mimi-to-her-friends-and-family Goldfarb Spinelli Harmony had some explaining to do.

I found her in the kitchen, placing little white paper doodads on the standing rib roast. Mom was definitely spending too much of her semi-retirement watching HGTV and The Food Network. She'd developed a passion for sculpting vegetables and folding napkins into intricate shapes. Every meal now included linen origami animals and massive centerpieces constructed of floral radishes, carrots, cucumbers, and celery. Dad suspected it had something to do with menopause, but he was wise enough to keep that opinion between the two of us.

"She's not the flower child I married." He shook his head in dismay as Mom fussed over a stubborn doodad whose frills refused to poof to her satisfaction.

I raised an eyebrow at the CEO of one of the largest cosmetics conglomerates in the world. "Neither are you, Dad." I then turned to my mother. "You and I need to talk."

"So talk," she said, paying more attention to her doodads than her daughter, but she did pause long enough to lean over and kiss my cheek. "How are you, sweetie?"

I scowled at her. "It's about Jeff Jacoby."

"Oh, yes, dear. Uncle Aaron called and asked if it was all right to bring him along. Said he hadn't made any friends his age yet, other than you."

So that's how it was going to be. Pass the buck. I turned to my father. "I could really use an ally here."

"Feeling outnumbered?"

"Definitely."

He knit his brows together in puzzlement and frowned at the

frou-frou garbed roast. "Join the club."

I was on my own.

"Polly, dear," said my mother, totally ignoring my father's comment, "dinner's ready. Would you have everyone move to the dining room while your father and I bring the food to the table?"

"Sure." I threw my hands up in defeat. Score Round One to Mom. I walked back out to the living room and found Uncle Cal regaling the others with the newest addition to his collection of clerical jokes.

"A priest and a rabbi are sitting next to each other on a plane," he said. "The priest turns to the rabbi and asks, 'Is pork still taboo for you?'

"The rabbi nods.

"'Ever cheat?' asks the priest.

"'Once,' admits the rabbi.

"After a while the rabbi turns to the priest and asks, 'Sex still off limits to you guys?'

"'Yes,' says the priest. 'We still take a vow of celibacy.'

"'Ever break that vow?' asks the rabbi.

"'Once,' admits the priest.

"The rabbi nods in understanding. The two sit in silence for awhile. Then the rabbi turns to the priest and says, 'A lot better than pork, isn't it?'"

The three other uncles burst out laughing with Uncle Francis and Uncle Aaron, slapping each other on the back as if they were sharing a joke within a joke. Only Jeff, slightly off to the side of the group, remained silent. And obviously uncomfortable.

I sidled up next to him. "You find the humor inappropriate?"

"Don't you?"

I scowled at him. "Are you aware of how many wars have been

fought over religion? How many people have died?"

"Of course, but what has that got to do with questionable religious humor?"

He just didn't get it. "The world could learn a valuable lesson from my uncles." I paused and speared him with an icy glare. "And maybe so could you. Dinner's ready." I started to walk away, but Jeff grabbed my arm.

"Maybe you could teach me."

I looked up at that to-die-for face of his and decided that life was definitely not fair. How could someone so handsome be so dense and boring? Then I remembered how I had observed him within a circle of admirers at the *Oneg Shabbat* and wondered if maybe it was me. Whatever the problem, Jeff and I had no chemistry, and there was no point in getting his hopes up or prolonging my agony. What I couldn't understand was why he kept pressing the issue. "Why me?"

Jeff's lips turned up into a very sexy grin. His eyes twinkled. "Maybe I like a challenge."

I took that as an insult, but instead of saying anything, I held my tongue. Then inspiration struck. I returned his smile with what I hoped was an equally sexy one. "Dinner at my place next Saturday night?" Although somewhat startled by my abrupt about-face, Jeff quickly accepted the invitation.

Jeff liked a challenge? Fine. I'd serve him a heaping dose of the ultimate challenge. As I ushered everyone into the dining room, I decided I was either incredibly clever, extremely wicked, or both. Either way, as I planned it, Saturday night should prove interesting. Especially for someone who enjoyed a challenge. Besides, turnabout was fair play.

~*~

I have to give Joni credit. She had accomplished exactly what she set out to do when she dragged me to Hudson Tube Saturday night. I *had* screamed my head off and begged for more. Every time I think about that night, my cheeks burn. And I find myself thinking about it all the time. So much so that the Carlos fiasco had shoved the Mace fiasco clear from my mind. Until Monday morning.

I woke up to a pelting rain rattling my windows and the sudden realization that I had no idea how I'd explain losing the choral directors. Not that we ever had them, but I suspected Head Lecherous Jerk would ignore that crucial piece of evidence as I pleaded my case.

I dressed in black from head to toe and headed off to my execution.

~*~

Arriving at my office building, I held my breath as I fought my way through a crowd of nicotine addicts huddled under the small portico that extended above the entrance to the revolving doors. So much for the *No Smoking Within Twenty-five Feet of Entrance* edict posted in bold lettering. I entered the lobby, dripping wet and smelling of the acrid smoke now clinging to my coat and hair.

As I stepped from the elevator, Arlene, Head Lecherous Jerk's secretary, greeted me. "He wants to see you," she said, her face and voice devoid of any hint of what awaited me inside his office.

So much for hoping to slip unnoticed into my cubicle and bury myself in paperwork. I tried to buy myself a few minutes to collect my thoughts and gather my wits. "As soon as I hang up my coat and umbrella."

She shook her head. "He said the moment you arrived." Arlene Flynn was all business. She followed orders to the T and expected others to do the same. In another life she was probably a parochial school nun—the kind who checked shoes to make sure they didn't reflect little girls' undies. According to Uncle Francis, once upon a time anyone sinful enough to wear black patent leather earned an automatic suspension and a one-way ticket to hell.

As I followed Arlene down the hall, I half expected to hear my coworkers chanting, "Dead woman walking." Anger and resentment bubbled inside me. In less than a minute I faced unemployment because I hadn't put out Friday night. Of course, I couldn't exactly use that as an excuse. Besides, Head Lecherous Jerk refused to accept excuses, no matter how justifiable. He expected the promise of a signed contract. Instead, I was about to present him with the lurid vision of tens of thousands of dollars in billings waving *adios*.

For the briefest of moments I considered threatening to sue but dismissed the idea as quickly as it came to me. I had no desire to get embroiled in a lengthy legal battle. If I accepted my walking papers without putting up a fuss, I was bound to receive a good recommendation.

At this point in my career I even had the expertise and experience to set up my own firm and give Head Lecherous Jerk a run for his money. I realized that if I wanted to, I could probably even steal his best accounts, leaving him with nothing but cloggers and ventriloquists. The thought cheered and empowered me.

I took a deep breath, threw back my shoulders, pasted a smile on my face, and opened the door. I wasn't exactly primed for battle with my executioner, but at least I had a plan for the future.

He looked up from his desk and instead of the growl I expected, offered me a huge smile. His tiny green eyes twinkled. His bushy gray mustache bounced up and down as he spoke.

"Congratulations, Ms. Harmony."

I studied him for a moment, bracing for a sneer, a snide remark—something to follow his sarcastic compliment. Instead, he rose from his chair, rounded his desk, and reached for my hand, shaking it warmly. This was definitely not the reaction I had anticipated. "Sir?"

He offered me one of the seats in front of his desk. "You impressed the hell out of Mason Hightower Friday night."

Dumbfounded, I sat down and stared at my boss. I *had* made an impression on Mason Hightower, all right. However, I doubted it was a well-disposed one. The man left my apartment with painfully unfulfilled expectations throbbing between his legs. In my experience, men tended to view such situations and the women who cause them in a less than favorable light.

Still, Head Lecherous Jerk looked far from displeased. He perched one Brooks Brothers clad thigh on the corner of his desk and reached behind to pick up several sheets of paper. "Signed, sealed, and delivered." He waved the pages under my nose. "A courier dropped them off a few minutes ago. We now have the choral directors as an account, and they're all yours. Good work, Polly."

I clenched my teeth to keep my jaw from dropping. My life segued from *Gilligan's Island* to *The Twilight Zone*. One moment I'm expecting to get fired, and the next I'm being handed an account I thought I had lost.

As relieved as I was over not having to face unemployment, I didn't want the account. Not if it meant working with Mason Hightower. After Friday night I didn't want anything to do with the man. My mouth opened, but the words refused to materialize. Instead of turning down the account, I heard myself mumbling a thank-you.

What the hell was I thinking? A minute ago I was ready to tell Head Lecherous Jerk where he could stick Mason Hightower, the choral directors, and himself. However, somewhere between then and now, I lost the courage of my convictions. Or maybe common sense paid me an unexpected visit, convincing me I needed time to sort out my options. Since I wasn't getting canned, didn't it make sense to study those bridges before I burned them?

In all honesty, I doubted I had the drive to start my own business. I had trouble enough dealing with my nearly nonexistent social life. With a fledgling business, I'd eat, sleep, and breathe nothing but work. I was neither that dedicated nor that ambitious. I was also selfish. Maybe I had trouble establishing and keeping a relationship with a guy, but it didn't mean I had given up trying, and that required time and energy.

Mason Hightower still remained a sticking point, though. I could not—would not—work with him under any circumstances, but I needed a viable excuse for passing up the account. "I'm glad he decided to go with our firm, but I think Professor Hightower might work better with one of the other staff members. Someone with a musical background." I forced a sheepish grin. "The truth is, I'm tone deaf, and the choral directors are entitled to an executive administrator who appreciates their music."

So I lied. I'm not tone deaf. I'm no virtuoso, but I did manage to survive eight years of piano lessons without driving my teacher to drink. Head Lecherous Jerk didn't need to know that, though. I'd grasp at any possible straw to avoid working with Mason Hightower.

A puzzled expression settled over Head Lecherous Jerk's face. I guess I didn't blame him. After all, I've never let my inability to draw get in the way of representing the medical illustrators, and my lack of rhythm doesn't keep me from working with the cloggers. As for the ventriloquists, let's just say I'm no dummy. "I'm afraid that's not possible. Professor Hightower specifically requested you. He added it to the contract. No Polly, no account."

Are all men manipulative bastards or only the ones I have the misfortune of meeting? Given his performance Friday night, I seriously doubted Mace could maintain a businesslike relationship unencumbered by an ever-present hard-on. After all, the man had twisted an invitation for coffee into a night of hot sex. Working with him would be pure hell. I'd constantly have to weigh every word. There was no way I could do my job under those circumstances. It wouldn't work.

What was he up to? The man left my apartment hostile and totally unrepentant. I knew all about male arrogance and the lengths some men would go to maintain and defend their pride. Men didn't back down. It was a territorial thing dating back to their caveman roots. They also didn't spend countless hours analyzing their churlish and often infantile behavior, then beg for forgiveness.

Besides, even if my suspicions weren't valid, I wasn't sure I had the backbone to put Friday night behind *me*. My head spun. I needed to get out of Head Lecherous Jerk's office and figure out how I was going to handle this situation. I rose to leave the office but paused at the door. Since I had some hard decisions to make, I needed as much information as possible. "Which of my accounts will you be reassigning?" I asked. "Because if I have a choice, I'd prefer to give up the cloggers."

Head Lecherous Jerk settled himself back behind his desk and turned his attention to another stack of papers. He spoke without looking up at me. "I can't reassign any accounts right now. We're short-staffed at the moment. I have faith in your ability to handle all four clients."

"Short-staffed?" *Since when?*

"I was forced to terminate Nan Osner Friday afternoon," he explained. "My wife caught her snorting coke in the ladies' room during the office party."

Trophy Wife Number Four was hardly a nun. Her reputation as a party girl stretched the length and breadth of Manhattan. Unless she had gone through a religious conversion recently, she still enjoyed her share of designer drugs. More likely she had gotten pissed that Nan had refused to share her nose candy and decided to get even. According to the office rumor mill, she had gotten rid of Trophy Wife Number Three in much the same manner.

Now, thanks to Nan and her run-in with Trophy Wife, I was not only saddled with Mace Hightower, but I hadn't even gotten rid of the cloggers. Life sucked. Big time.

And it was only Monday.

To quit or not to quit? That was the question. And definitely not a decision I wanted to make first thing on a Monday morning, especially after the past weekend. I left Head Lecherous Jerk and headed to my cubicle, wishing I had an office with a door I could close. Part of me was tempted to return home and bury myself under a quilt for the rest of the day, if not the rest of my life.

Did I want to start my own business? No. Did I want to go to work for my parents? No. Did I want to begin all over with another firm? Not really.

The familiarity of my job offered me a certain amount of comfort. I might not care for my boss or most of my coworkers, and I didn't work on the most exciting accounts, but I knew the routine. I did my job, and I did it well. Up until this morning, my career had given me a stability I found lacking in most of the rest of my life. I feared jumping from that proverbial frying pan into the fire. Unfortunately, taking the coward's way out left me trapped in a catch-22 with Mason Hightower.

Halfway down the corridor Jay Steiner stopped me. "Must have been a hot weekend. He wiggled his bushy black eyebrows à la Grouch Marx. His imitation—like everything else about Jay — was second-rate at best. "I had no idea you were *that* good, Polly."

"What the hell's that supposed to mean?" *And who told you?* But I kept that question to myself and leveled him with an icy glare that lost some of its impact when I sneezed. *Great, on top of everything else, I'm catching a cold!*

"*Gesundheit.*" Jay raised his hands and backed up a step. "Hey, no offense, Polly. I just mean…well, it isn't your birthday, is it?" he asked, but both his tone and the lewd expression on his face suggested he knew damn well it wasn't my birthday.

Had Jay seen me at Hudson Tube Saturday night? Had he been lurking in that shadowy corridor, watching as I debased myself with a total stranger? *Oh, God!* I fought to stifle the horror churning away in the pit of my stomach. "No, it's not my birthday," I answered, forcing my voice to remain calm. I sneezed again.

"*Gesundheit.* Again." Jay grinned, his face contorting into a licentious mask. "And if someone had died you wouldn't be here, right?" His words grew singsong, his smile even more lecherous.

"Make sense, Jay, or leave me alone." It was tough tolerating Jay on a good day, and today wasn't a good day. Feigning impatience, I glanced at my watch. "Your point?" I asked, waiting for the bomb to drop.

He glanced down at my umbrella. "Haven't been to your office yet, have you?"

"No."

"Ah." Without any further explanation, he hustled down the hall. "Have a nice day, Polly," he called over his shoulder, "but I doubt it could be anywhere near as nice as your weekend must have been."

I shuddered and sneezed at the same time.

"*Gesundheit!*" he shouted.

My luck grew worse with each step I took towards my cubicle. Ten feet from the entrance I realized the source of my sneezing attack. Roses! I'd know that heady scent anywhere. My sneezes increased to a rapid-fire, nonstop fit. All around me I heard coworkers responding.

"God bless!"

"*Gesundheit!*"

"Bless you, Polly."

I stood at the entryway and through watery eyes stared at the source of my allergic reaction. Three enormous vases of blood-red roses filled the room, one on my desk, one on top of my bookcase, and one taking up a good deal of the available floor space. I groaned.

"Most women have a more positive reaction when someone sends them flowers."

I turned to find Arlene standing behind me, a box of tissues in her outstretched hand. "Thanks." I reached for a tissue. "Most women aren't allergic to roses."

"Too bad." She made a tsking sound with her tongue. "They're so beautiful. Who sent them?"

"Obviously someone who doesn't know me very well." I stepped into my cubicle, plucked the cards from each of the arrangements, and tossed them onto my keyboard. "Please." I motioned to the flowers between sneezes. "Help yourself. Just get them as far away from me as possible."

She stepped inside and lifted the vase from the floor. As she made her way back towards the reception area, I grabbed a box of antihistamines from my desk drawer and headed for the water cooler. At least I now understood the reason behind Jay's innuendoes.

By the time I got back to my desk, Arlene had removed the remaining flowers, but their scent lingered. Although the sneezes tapered off to a manageable few every few minutes, my sinuses throbbed, my head pounded, and my eyes continued to water. I lowered my head into my hands and waited for the antihistamines to start working.

"So who's your secret admirer?" asked Arlene.

I was startled by her return. I hadn't pegged Arlene for an office snoop. Normally she kept to herself at the reception area, attending to Head Lecherous Jerk and ignoring the rest of us.

"Yeah, don't keep us in suspense," said Jay, coming up behind Arlene. Three of his lecherous jerk cohorts pushed their way in behind him. Two female staff members followed. My cubicle, far from expansive to begin with, was now packed wall-to-wall with nosey coworkers, a highly unusual occurrence.

We weren't a close group by any stretch of the imagination. Normally, we kept to ourselves, rarely even going out to lunch with one another. However, the arrival of seventy-two red roses was enough to pique more than a normal amount of curiosity around the office.

Crystal nudged past Bob and Sam. "Hey, what happened to your roses, Polly?"

"She's allergic," said Arlene.

"Gee, that's too bad. They were really gorgeous. So who sent them?"

"I don't know." I lifting the three small white envelopes off my keyboard before anyone decided to swoop down and find out for me.

"Aren't you curious?" asked Arlene. "Open them." Everyone inched closer.

I spun my chair around to keep them from reading over my shoulder and lifted the first card from its envelope.

Looking forward to Saturday. Jeff.

Wonderful! Here I was planning something extremely bitchy, and the guy sends me two-dozen roses. I hoped he got them at a discount from Mr. Shapiro, one of Uncle Aaron's congregants who owned a chain of florist shops throughout the five boroughs. I was dealing with enough guilt as it was.

"Well?" Arlene hovered above me.

I shoved the card back in the envelope. "It's a thank-you from one of my uncle's colleagues. I did him a favor recently."

Arlene raised an eyebrow. I didn't need mindreading powers to interpret her reaction. She didn't believe me for a minute.

"Must have been a pretty big favor." Jay nudged the two men on either side of him.

"Hubba hubba," said Sam.

Bob winked suggestively. "Hey, Polly, I could use a favor or two. Know what I mean?"

I glared at them, three adolescent stooges who, lumped together, wouldn't amount to one decent human being. Jay had a slimy, used car salesman quality to him. He dressed like a throwback from the Disco era, complete with gold chains, and sounded like an extra on *The Sopranos*.

Sam and Bob acted like adult versions of *Beevis and Butthead*, two beer belly morons who had never matured beyond the fourth grade. Worse yet, somewhere out on Long Island lived a younger generation of Jays, Bobs, and Sams, thanks to their fathers' seeds and their mothers' poor judgment. "You're all pathetic. Go find a peep show over on Ninth Avenue if you need a cheap thrill."

The men shuffled their feet and mumbled what might have passed for an apology—if I could stretch my imagination that far, but to my ears it sounded more like I was the one at fault for not having a sense of humor.

An awkward silence ensued until Arlene asked, "What about the other flowers?" She motioned towards the two remaining envelopes. "Who sent them?"

I glanced up at her and the two women flanking her. A combination of curiosity, jealousy, and resentment covered their faces.

I knew little beyond the barest of details about each of these women although I had worked with two of them for several years. As for the newest addition to the office, rumor had it that Arlene, in her late fifties or early sixties, lived with her mother. I had no idea whether or not she'd ever been married. Office gossip claimed she was still a virgin.

Crystal was in her mid-to-late twenties and into body piercing and tattoos, thanks to a boyfriend who practiced on her. She sported a gold loop through one nostril, another in her eyebrow, and at least half a dozen in each ear. Every few weeks she arrived at work with a new addition to the artwork that peppered the visible areas of her arms and legs. I had no doubt other parts of her body were similarly adorned. The men speculated aloud, but I preferred to remain ignorant as to what and where. Fittingly, she handled some of the firm's more avant-garde accounts, including The International Society of Tattoo Artists and The American Aromatherapy Guild.

I figured Nadine for late-thirties. According to bits and pieces I sometimes overheard from phone conversations, she had two troublesome teenagers and a no-account husband who never lifted a finger around the house. Chances were, she had never received roses or anything else other than aggravation from the jerk.

My social life was far from enviable, but none of these women knew that, and given their own circumstances, I could understand why they continued to wait with baited-breath as I opened the second envelope.

Polly Dearest,
It's been nearly three months. Three very long, lonely months. And sufficient time to come to your senses. I'm sure by now you realize how irrational your hasty decision was and regret having made it. You know we belong together. Stop denying your destiny. I'm willing to forgive and forget. Call me.
Yours,
Significant Other

"When hell freezes over," I mumbled, ripping the card into confetti and tossing it into my wastebasket. My destiny was certainly not with a self-centered jerk who couldn't even remember that I'm allergic to roses.

One of the men cleared his throat. I glowered at the group.

"Show's over. Take a hike. All of you. I have work to do."

"Lover's quarrel?" Jay crossed his arms over his chest and made no effort to leave. For that matter, neither did any of the others.

I shoved the remaining envelope into my suit pocket, turned my back and flipped on my computer. Behind me I heard grumbling. I was called everything from a spoilsport to a tight-ass, but after a few minutes, when I continued to ignore them, they all shuffled out.

Alone at last, I withdrew the final envelope from my pocket and opened it. The note was printed on both sides of the card in a very small, precise handwriting.

Dear Polly,

I hope you can find it in your heart to forgive my abhorrent behavior of Friday night. You are a lovely, intelligent woman whom I insulted by treating like a whore. You did nothing to warrant such conduct on my part. The fault lies entirely with me, thanks in part to too much alcohol and the strain of some current personal problems. I beg your forgiveness and offer you my solemn word that this incident will not in any way affect our working relationship, which I hope will be a long and enjoyable one.

Mason Hightower

I stared at the note. Dumbfounded, I read it over several times before slipping it back in my pocket.

FOUR
Revenge, Forgiveness, and the Boomerang Factor

Thanks to Mason's note of apology, I was more confused than ever. His words left me with a sense of emptiness, and although he had taken full responsibility for his actions, somehow I now felt guilty for not having seen past the act itself to a troubled individual in need of comfort.

"Crap!" said Joni later that night after I voiced my feelings. "Don't start practicing pseudo psycho-babble. He's handing you a line because he's scared shitless." She started mocking Mason, "'I'm not responsible for my actions. I have a drinking problem. I'm having troubles at home. My life is a mess. My wife doesn't understand me. My girlfriend left me. My shrink doesn't have time for me. My dog ignores me.' Come on, Polly. You weren't born yesterday. That note and the flowers were damage control. Pure and simple."

"Damage control?"

"Sure. To keep you from saying the wrong thing to the wrong person. He had no idea who you might tell about Friday night and how it might come back to haunt him. The guy's got a rep to uphold, doesn't he? He's some big shot college professor at a conservative Midwest school, right? I'll bet it's even a religious one." She didn't wait for my response. Instead, she winked at me and licked her lips. "You could get him in some deep shit for that stunt he pulled. If you wanted to."

"Polly isn't a troublemaker," said Mitch.

The three of us were sitting barefoot on the floor around Mitch and Joni's coffee table. I had arrived home from work to find a note taped to my door. *Tacos and bitching session upstairs at seven. Mitch.* Sometimes I thought the guy was psychic. He always seemed to know when I needed a strong crying shoulder.

Joni glared at him. "Meaning *I* am?"

"How else do you explain that little stunt you pulled Saturday night?" he asked.

"What stunt? Polly needed to loosen up and have some fun. We went club crawling."

"You set her up!"

"I did not! How could you even suggest such a thing?"

Heat rose to my cheeks, and it wasn't from the half glass of Merlot I had downed so far. I had told neither of them what happened with Carlos, but Carlos apparently had no qualms about complaining to Joni after I ran out on him. For all I knew, knowing Joni and her casual attitude toward sex, she'd gone down on her knees to relieve his discomfort.

As if that weren't enough, Joni had told Mitch all about my fall from grace. At least neither of them knew how good that fall had felt. I continued to keep *that* guilty secret to myself. "It's not her fault," I mumbled into my glass. "I'm a grown woman, responsible for my own actions. And my own lack of good sense."

Mitch scooped browned beef into a taco shell. "Some people occasionally have a lapse of good judgment." He added a spoonful of diced veggies, another of cheese, and a dollop of guacamole. "Others have never acquired any to lapse from." He squirted some sauce over the mixture before raising his head and staring pointedly at his sister.

"I can take care of myself," she said. "You're not my father, you know."

"No. I care more."

The room grew silent. This was a sore spot for both Joni and Mitch. They had no idea who fathered them. For that matter, neither did their mother, having enjoyed herself a bit too much as a groupie back in the day. Mitch was right to be concerned about his twin, though. Joni had inherited her mother's casual attitude towards sex.

Rainbow Hues—born Roberta Eloise Hughes—still believed in free sex and free drugs, regardless of the risk of sexually transmitted diseases and more than one arrest for possession. Although Joni abstained from drugs, both Mitch and I worried that one day she'd wind up in a ton of trouble. Or worse.

"I thought we were talking about my problems tonight," I said after the silence dragged on for too long.

"Well, you can't say I didn't try to solve your professor problem." Joni reached for the bottle of Merlot and topped off each of our glasses. "So maybe Carlos came on a little too strong for you, but don't tell me you didn't enjoy yourself, Polly."

I felt my cheeks deepen to the same shade as the wine. "I don't want to discuss Carlos. Ever again."

Joni shrugged. "Suit yourself, but you'd really have a good time if you only let yourself."

"Joni!" Mitch and I yelled at her at the same time.

"Okay!" She threw up her arms. "So what *is* your problem?"

I leaned my head back against the sofa cushion and stared up at the ceiling. "What isn't my problem?"

Mitch looped his arm around my shoulders. "Tell Doctor Mitch all about it."

I twisted the stem of my wineglass around in my fingers and talked into the deep red liquid. "I thought I liked my job. At least I thought I liked the work I do, but after today, I'm not so sure any more. My boss is an asshole, and so are most of the people I work with. The one account I wanted is going to be a huge pain in the ass, thanks to Mason Hightower, and I don't even get to dump one of the other accounts because Trophy Wife Number Four got the Cocaine Queen fired Friday."

"So quit," said Joni.

I frowned at the wine. "I thought about that, but I'm not sure what I want to do or even if I really want the hassle of starting over somewhere else." Raising my head, I stared first at Joni, then Mitch, and shrugged. "I'm nearly thirty-two years old, and all of a sudden I don't know what I want to be when I grow up."

Joni cast me a withering look. "Hell, Polly! Your folks own one of the largest cosmetics firms in the world. Go work for them, for God's sake!"

"I don't want to! They try to manipulate my life enough as it is. You might think that's cool since your mother doesn't give a flying fig about either of you except when she wants money or needs a trip to Betty Ford, but you have no idea what it's like. I love my parents, but I can only take them in small weekly doses.

And between them and my uncles, even that's getting to be too much."

Mitch nodded at Joni. "Sounds like something happened yesterday."

I polished off half the wine in my glass before answering. "You could say that. Somehow I've gotten myself stuck with the boring cantor for dinner Saturday night. Here."

Mitch raised both eyebrows. "You're cooking?"

I nodded.

"You really don't like this guy, do you?"

"Actually, it's not a bad idea," said Joni. "Polly wants him to stop bugging her. The way she cooks, he'll be running out the door before the main course."

"Very funny." But Joni had a point. I have a reputation for being able to ruin macaroni and cheese, and that's not from scratch. I'm talking the stuff that comes in the blue box where you just add milk and stir.

"How'd you manage to get yourself in that pickle?" asked Mitch.

I glanced across the table and offered Joni a sheepish grin. "I invited him."

Joni's deep aquamarine eyes bugged out. Her jaw dropped. "You didn't!

"I don't get it." Mitch rubbed his hand across his stubble-covered jaw. "Why are you encouraging a guy you're trying to discourage?"

Again I trapped Joni with my gaze, but this time I wasn't grinning. I knew I had guilt written all over my face. "I had this warped idea of revenge. I was going to sic Joni on him to get even for Carlos. Jeff's about as opposite from Carlos as you can get. I figured Joni deserved to be bored to death after Saturday night. And maybe if Jeff saw what my best friend was like, he'd have second thoughts and leave me alone."

I couldn't do it, though. I'm not the vengeful type. In my dreams, maybe. In real life? Not a chance. I wasn't Polly. At heart I was Pollyanna.

"Hell, I don't mind," said Joni. Her lips curled up in a wicked grin. "I'll make him my new pet project—How to Corrupt a Cantor in Twelve Easy Lessons."

"Joni! Uncle Aaron would never forgive me!"

"You won't have anything to do with it, Polly. What time's dinner Saturday?"

I hesitated before answering. "Seven-thirty."

"I'll be there."

"So will I," said Mitch. He glared at his sister. "Someone has to keep you out of trouble and protect this poor guy."

"Good ol' bro," said Joni, "saving mankind from his wild and wicked sister."

"Hmm." Mitch grabbed the taco off his plate and bit into it. "It's a tough job," he said over a mouthful of food, "but someone has to do it." He swallowed and was about to take another bite when he paused and turned to me. "Are you still planning to cook?"

"I suppose. Unless I do takeout."

"Polly the takeout queen. No, I'll cook dinner. Might as well at least get a decent meal out of it."

~*~

Why had I ever invited Jeff to dinner in the first place, let alone right before Christmas? Wasn't my life chaotic enough? I hadn't completed my Christmas shopping and still had end-of-the-year financial and status reports to prepare for the cloggers, ventriloquists, and medical illustrators.

On top of that, I came to work Tuesday to discover that the hotel I'd booked for the cloggers' convention the end of June had gone belly-up. Although the hotel promised they'd reopen under new management in time for the convention, I couldn't take the chance. With the success of *Riverdance* and *Lord of the Dance* over the past decade, the cloggers had seen a fifty percent increase in their membership. Nearly a thousand dancing fools were already registered for their annual get-together, and I needed to find new space for them. Fast.

In between phone calls and e-mails to every moderately priced hotel with large ballrooms from California to Maine, I found myself bombarded with messages from Mason. The ink had barely dried on the contract, but the man was raring to go. He had ideas he wanted implemented, and he wanted everything started immediately. After ignoring the first seventeen e-mails and voicemail messages, I finally shot off a terse e-mail, reminding him that our contractual services began on January 1 and not before. I wished him a merry Christmas and told him I'd be in touch after the holidays. He ignored my post and continued sending suggestions which I routed unread to a folder.

I worked through lunch and well past dinner, but by seven o'clock, I'd closed a deal with a Hilton in Daytona Beach, Florida. Of course, I would now have to reprint all the convention pamphlets, do another mailing, redo press releases, and notify the general membership and speakers, but I had averted a crisis. The cloggers once again had a place to clog. It might not be in Tulsa, as originally planned, but the dates remained the same, and the price was within their budget. Hopefully, no one had booked airline tickets this far in advance.

I stood up and stretched. My butt ached from sitting for hours. My other muscles were stiff from lack of use. My eyes no longer focused thanks to hours of staring at my computer monitor. My throat was sore from the endless phone calls. My stomach complained from too much caffeine and no sustenance other than the Christmas cookies someone had left near the coffee pot earlier in the day. My head throbbed from a combination of my butt, my throat, my muscles, my eyes, and my stomach.

And I still had an evening of Christmas shopping ahead of me. Luckily, all the stores stayed open late this time of year. I flicked off my computer, grabbed my coat and purse, and headed for the elevators.

Halfway down the corridor, I changed my mind and decided to make a pit stop before leaving the building. All that coffee had taken a toll on my bladder. Pushing open the door to the restroom, I came face-to-face with a startled, teary-eyed Arlene.

"Are you all right?"

"Fine." She sniffed and tried to compose herself back into the all-business Arlene Flynn, but her shoulders shuddered as she threw them back and raised her chin. "I didn't know anyone was still here."

"A clogger crisis," I said. "They lost their hotel. I've been on the phone all day trying to book another location for their convention."

She focused on my reflection in the mirror rather than directly at me, dabbing at her raccoon eyes and mascara-streaked cheeks. "Were you successful?"

I nodded. Arlene looked like she needed a friend, but she also looked embarrassed that I'd caught her at such a naked moment. I wasn't sure whether to leave or offer an ear and a shoulder. We stood in awkward silence for a moment. Finally, I nodded toward the stall. "I need to go." I figured if she wanted to talk, she'd still be there when I came out. If not, she'd be gone.

When I finished, she was still standing at the mirror. She had washed her face and was reapplying her lipstick. Her chin-length, gray-streaked brown hair looked like she'd given it a quick brushing. "I was going to get a bite to eat before doing some Christmas shopping. Would you like to join me?"

"You don't mind?" I was extending a lifeline and not simply an offer for dinner. She knew it.

I shook my head. "I'd enjoy the company." Actually, the last thing in the world I wanted was to deal with someone else's problems right now. I had enough of my own, but Pollyanna had once again taken over my body. My parents, for all their damn meddlesomeness, had raised me right. I couldn't turn my back on someone in need.

~*~

Twenty minutes later we settled into a back booth at a small Italian restaurant on Madison Avenue. Neither of us spoke until we placed our orders and the waiter brought us drinks—a strawberry daiquiri for Arlene, a Chardonnay for me. She sipped at hers, and I waited, my fingers wrapped around the stem of my glass.

Finally, she set her glass down and lifted her head. In the dim light I could see the tears floating in her eyes. "Today is my daughter's birthday."

Obviously, this was not a happy occasion for Arlene, but I had no idea why. Not knowing anything about her family, I was at a loss for words. The scuttlebutt around the office pegged Arlene for what used to be known as an old maid. All I could do was stare at her questioningly.

"You didn't know I had a daughter, did you?"

"No, I don't recall you ever speaking about your family to me," I said.

"Or anyone."

I jumped to the obvious conclusion. "Are you and your daughter estranged?"

Arlene laughed a derisive laugh. "You could say that. I haven't seen her since the day she was born."

"She died at birth?" I couldn't imagine how devastating a trauma that might be for a woman—to carry a child inside her for nine months only to lose the baby at the last moment. No wonder she was upset.

"No, I gave her up for adoption."

"Oh."

She bowed her head and spoke into her daiquiri. "I was eighteen years old. A good girl, a God-fearing girl from a good, God-fearing family."

"Everyone makes mistakes, Arlene."

She shook her head. "No, you don't understand. My boyfriend was shipping out to Nam. We only did it once. The night before he left. Four weeks later he was dead, and I was pregnant. He never knew."

An enormous lump suddenly catapulted from my stomach into my throat. I reached across the table and took both of her hands in mine.

Her words came across as a strained whisper. "I couldn't raise a baby on my own." She raised her head and stared at me through watery eyes that pleaded for understanding. "I did what I thought was best for her, but I never stopped loving her."

"I'm sure she knows that."

Arlene shook her head. "No. She blames me."

"You've met?"

Arlene gulped back a sob. Her hands fidgeted with her napkin, twisting it into a tight ball. Tears spilled over her eyelids and down her cheeks, splashing onto the red-and-white-checkered tablecloth. Her words came haltingly. "She tracked me down and called last night. At first I was overjoyed. What a wonderful Christmas present!" She paused to mop her face with the napkin.

I prodded her on. "What happened?"

Arlene's chin trembled. A fresh onslaught of tears filled her eyes. She sniffed them back. "She only made contact to vent her anger. She yelled and screamed at me, told me how much she hated me and how everything that had gone wrong in her life was my fault. When she finished her tirade, she hung up. I never even learned her name or where she lives."

Arlene stared at me from across the table. Her tears continued to flow. Sobs wracked her words. "Times were different. My parents pressured me. It was still considered a stigma. I saw no alternative. I only wanted her to have a happy life. To have two loving parents who could give her all the things I couldn't."

I thought about Joni and Mitch's mother. Flaky as she was, Rainbow had managed to raise her twins on her own. However, Rainbow had the help and support of both an extended commune family and relatives who stepped in and took over whenever she needed them. The actual amount of parenting Joni and Mitch had received from their mother was questionable.

Had Arlene's parents given their daughter the support she needed, she probably would have managed quite well as a single parent. From what I saw, Arlene was a resourceful person. Under the circumstances, however, I couldn't blame her for opting for adoption, and her daughter shouldn't either—no matter what her problems.

Arlene recovered slowly. Sniffing back a fresh wave of tears, she swiped the napkin across her cheeks and blew her nose. "Girls today are so lucky. Life is so much easier for you."

I hardly thought of my life as easy and could rattle off a list of counter arguments, but Arlene needed sympathy, not a debate. "How so?"

She drained her glass before speaking. "You have options my generation never had. You do what you want and don't worry about what other people think."

Her words surprised me. "You were part of the Woodstock generation," I reminded her. "Your generation paved the way for mine."

She offered me a weak smile and a shrug. "Only a small handful. Most of us carried the morality of the fifties with us like a torch. I wasn't daring. I wasn't a troublemaker. I was a good girl who made a terrible mistake. All these years I thought at least I had done right by my baby." She buried her head in her hands. "Now I learn I failed her, too."

I reached across the table and drew her hands away from her face. "Arlene, look at me." I waited until she raised her chin. "You can't blame yourself for that. It's not like you chose the family who raised her, is it?"

"No. Adoptions were tightly sealed back then. Everything was handled by an agency." She paused, then sighed. "I was lucky to get to hold her for a few minutes before they whisked her away."

She closed her eyes. Her voice grew soft. A faraway expression settled over her features, as if she were looking back through time. "She was so beautiful, Polly. So tiny and perfect. She had her father's eyes."

The waiter arrived with our dinners and placed them before us. I glanced down at my veal marsala. Suddenly, I had lost my appetite.

Something grabbed hold of my heart and squeezed and squeezed. How little we knew of each other, those of us who worked together forty-plus hours a week. We assumed so much based on no facts whatsoever.

I waited to speak until after the server departed. "Look, Arlene, what your daughter did was vicious and spiteful, but you can't take responsibility for her problems. We all make our own choices in life. She's a grown woman. If she can't accept her life, she needs to change it, not blame you, her adoptive parents, or anyone else. That's a copout."

Arlene grimaced at her dinner. "I guess she inherited that from me."

"What do you mean? You didn't copout."

"Other women have managed in similar situations. I chose the easy way out. And the least embarrassing way for my parents."

I was quickly developing a deep animosity towards those parents of hers. I hoped I never had cause to meet them. "No, you made a choice—and a huge sacrifice—in the best interests of your child."

Arlene lowered her head and stared at her untouched lobster ravioli and asparagus. She picked up her fork and pushed the food around on her plate as she spoke. "My entire life has been one big copout, Polly. I gave up living forty years ago. At the end of the day I go home to an apartment in Staten Island, the same apartment I grew up in. I still live with my mother. We eat dinner together and share polite conversation. Afterwards we watch television for a few hours. Then we go to bed.

"In the morning the cycle repeats itself. Monday through Friday. Every day the same. On Saturdays I take Mother shopping and to her doctor appointments. On Sundays I take her to church. I have no life of my own. No friends. I gave all that up for one night that forever changed my life. Every day I'm reminded of that." She paused, then added in a near inaudible whisper, "I've never been with another man."

All I could think was *shit*. I bit my tongue to keep the word from escaping through my lips.

I wondered how Jeff felt about older women.

~*~

I never did get any shopping done that night. We stayed in the restaurant for nearly three hours. I ate little. Arlene never touched her dinner but continued ordering strawberry daiquiris until she was quite drunk. After paying the bill, I put her in a cab, shoved a fifty dollar bill into her hands, and told the driver to head for Staten Island. I prayed Arlene remembered her address.

By the time I arrived back at my apartment I could barely climb the steps to the front door. Exhaustion—mental, emotional, and physical—had taken their toll on me. Visions of a hot bath gave me the impetus I needed to spur myself onward.

In the lobby I bumped into Mitch, his arms wrapped around a huge stack of tied newspapers. Tomorrow was recycling day. As a financial analyst and columnist for *The Wall Street Journal*, Mitch read an unbelievable number of newspapers, both national and international, and thus recycled more papers each week than most people read in several months.

He eyed me over the mound of newsprint. "Rough day?"

"You could say that."

"Need to talk?"

I shook my head. "Too tired, but thanks." I let myself into my apartment and headed straight for my bed, kicking my shoes off and discarding clothing along the way. Forget the bath. I no longer even had the energy to turn on the spigots. Still half-dressed, I fell onto my bed and didn't move until seven the next morning.

~*~

I take the subway to and from work most days. The stop is several blocks from my apartment but only two from the office building at the other end. There's a Starbucks on one corner. Most mornings I stop and grab a cup of coffee and a bagel with a *shmear* to go. I'm not a morning person by nature and usually find myself running too late to eat anything before leaving my apartment.

This morning I found Arlene waiting for me inside the coffee shop. She sat at a small round table in front of the window. When she saw me enter the store, she rose, hesitated for a moment, then approached me.

I smiled at her. "Feeling better?" I asked, although I seriously doubted it. Arlene looked like she was suffering from one hell of a hangover.

She bit her lower lip, then took a deep breath before she spoke. "I wanted to thank you for last night. It's not like me to fall apart."

"You had good reason. I placed my hand on her arm. "I'm glad I was there for you."

She lowered her eyes, and I could tell she was embarrassed over last night. She reached into her coat pocket and pulled out a fifty dollar bill. "And I wanted to reimburse you for the cab fare."

I stared at the money, not certain whether or not to accept it.

"That's not necessary."

Arlene pressed the bill into my hands. "It is."

It was common knowledge around the office that I was the daughter of Harmony Cosmetics. After all, Harmony was not a very common last name. Along with believing I had a fantastic love life, my coworkers also assumed I was rolling in money. Although no one ever said anything to my face, I often overheard them conjecturing as to why I worked for Head Lecherous Jerk. For that matter, none of them could understand why I worked at all.

I searched Arlene's determined green eyes and saw that this was a matter of pride for her. She wanted neither pity nor charity. I accepted the money.

She headed for the door.

I reached out for her arm, "Arlene." She turned to face me. "Please don't worry. I won't say anything to anyone."

The corners of her mouth turned up slightly. "Thank you."

~*~

The remainder of the week turned out nearly as stressful and chaotic as Monday and Tuesday. I extinguished three more brush fires, two with the cloggers and one with the ventriloquists, ignored countless sexual innuendoes—thanks to the roses—by various office cretins, and suffered through a very long and boring three hour conference call with the board of the Medical Illustrators Guild as they fought and wrangled over changes to their bylaws.

In between I worked on my year-end reports and continued to disregard numerous e-mails and phone messages from Mason. And I still hadn't found time for any Christmas shopping.

The *coup de grace* to my workweek came from a surprise visit on Friday by Former Significant Other.

FIVE
Like a Bad Penny

"I've been waiting for your call."

I recognized his voice at once. I froze, my fingers poised over my keyboard, but I didn't turn around. *Great. I'm not stressed out enough.* Just what I need to add some excitement to my life—the unwelcome return of Former Significant Other. I closed my eyes and slowly, silently started counting, hoping that by the time I reached ten, I'd shake off the hallucination.

My relationship with Former Significant Other had lasted six months. As it turned out, six months was six months too long. Hindsight is indeed twenty-twenty. Like all the others before him —and don't get me wrong, there haven't been *that* many—I had thought, *This is the one.* Right. So much for my astute perceptions of character.

I opened my eyes and swiveled my chair around. The six-foot-two hunk lounging against the cubicle wall was no hallucination.

Every boyfriend I've ever had falls into the drop-dead-gorgeous-hunk category. Former Significant Other was no exception. From his wavy black hair to his deep blue eyes to the dimpled cleft in his chin, he looked like he stepped off the pages of *GQ*. And he possessed the ego to match those looks.

He waved his cell phone at me. "No call, Polly."

"Very observant. What are you doing here?"

"We need to talk."

"No we don't."

He ignored my answer. Instead, his gaze rove around my small office before returning to me. He frowned. "Where are the roses I sent?"

I opened my mouth to speak. Before I could utter a word, his cell phone rang. He held up his hand. "Hang on a minute." Then he pushed a button, raised the phone to his ear, and turned his back on me. For five minutes he carried on a conversation, conducting business in *my* office. I spun my chair around and went back to my year-end summary of the ventriloquists' finances.

Finally, he ended his call. "Where were we?"

I continued typing. "I was writing a report, and you were leaving."

"No." He shook his head. "You were about to tell me what happened to the roses."

He placed his hand on my shoulder and spun my chair around to face him. His lips curled up into that sexy grin that used to turn my limbs to molasses. It no longer worked. I stiffened.

"You can't stay mad forever, Polly. I've been trying to forget you for months. I can't. Every time I'm with another woman, I think of you. We belong together. In your heart you know that. I want to come home."

Right now the only thing I felt in my heart was a huge case of heartburn thanks to the arrival of Former Significant Other and a cup of coffee that tasted more like battery acid. "So go home. I didn't invite you here."

He sighed. "That's not what I mean, and you know it. I want us to go back to the way it was between us."

His whining tone reminded me of one of the things I disliked most about Former Significant Other—whenever he didn't get his own way, he resorted to the tactics of a two-year-old, wheedling and sniveling until I gave in to him. I noticed early on that it worked incredibly well on various members of his family— especially his mother, who thought he walked on water.

For a while, it worked on me, as well, but it wasn't going to work this time. I'd gotten the man out of my system a long time ago. He wasn't getting back in. "I don't want us to get back together. I've moved on with my life, and you're no longer part of it."

His phone rang again. Without so much as a word of apology, he answered it. This time he talked for a full ten minutes and loud enough that nosey Jay poked his head in to see what was going on. When I waved him off, he continued to eavesdrop in the hallway.

He ended his call. "Now about those roses."

I stood up and grabbed the phone out of his hand. Then I hit the power button to turn the damn thing off. "You want to hear about the roses?" I tried to keep my voice low enough so Jay couldn't hear me. "Fine. Listen up, Mr. Clueless. I'm allergic to roses. Always have been. Always will be. And if you spent half as much time listening to me as you do that goddamn phone of yours, *maybe* you would have remembered that! And maybe you would have put my needs first just once in our relationship instead of always thinking of yourself."

I threw the phone at him. "I'm not playing second fiddle to you, your cell phone, your business, *or* your swelled head ever again. It's over. Got it? Finished. Kaput. Finito. Done. Now go away, and don't come back."

He stared at me, a look of incomprehension pasted across his face. "You don't mean that."

Are all men this dense? "Trust me. I mean every word of it."

He refused to budge. "Why don't we discuss it over dinner tonight?"

"We are not discussing it over dinner tonight or any other night."

"You'll feel differently after a nice romantic dinner." He stroked my arm.

I jerked away.

"I've made a reservation at Prada," he continued in a voice meant to tease me into seeing things his way.

How typical. How thoughtless. I hate Prada. It was one of those new "in" restaurants where people like Former Significant Other went to be seen and hopefully get mentioned in *Scene About Town*. *News flash: Polly Harmony, daughter and heir to Harmony Cosmetics was spotted at Prada last night with up-and-coming techno whiz, Significant Other*. Not likely. The atmosphere at Prada was far from romantic—after all, how could anyone be *seen* in a dimly lit setting—the food was hardly haute cuisine, and the service sucked. You don't go to Prada for food or atmosphere. You go for publicity.

"I'll pick you up at seven," he said.

Before I knew what was happening, he had me in his arms, his lips plastered against mine. Out in the hallway I heard the sound of applause.

"Ah, true love," said Jay.

Once upon a time, Former Significant Other's kisses had curled my toes. Unfortunately, no other part of my body ever responded to him in a similar manner, which was only one of the many problems with our relationship. Now, even my toes ignored his lips. I broke away and shoved him out of my office. "I won't be there when you show up. I have plans." Then I turned to Jay. "And as for you, you lecherous, eavesdropping Peeping Tom, go to hell!"

I returned to my computer and the ventriloquists' end-of-year financial report, but I was so furious that I was incapable of doing anything other than staring blankly at the words on the screen. At exactly five o'clock I grabbed my coat and purse and headed for the elevator.

"Heard you've got a hot date with one of the rose senders," Crystal's singsong voice came up behind me.

"You heard wrong." I tossed the comment over my shoulder, not slowing my pace.

"That's not what Jay said."

I stopped and spun on my heels to confront her. "Jay's an ass. Do us all a favor and ignored the garbage that spews from his mouth."

Crystal pursed her deep purple glossed lips. She now sported a silver stud in the indentation above her chin. I wondered if she had problems with leakage when she drank. "Well, aren't you the touchy one!" She screwed up her face. "I only wanted to say I hope you have a nice time on your date, but forget it."

"I have no date."

"Fine. Whatever." She turned and stalked off towards the restroom.

Damn that Jay Steiner! I stabbed at the elevator button and tapped my toe while I waited, hoping no one else from the office accosted me before I left. On the ride down to the lobby, the pumped in music implored me to have a jolly, holly Christmas, but I felt more like the Grinch. It wasn't fair. Christmas was my favorite holiday. Why was everyone conspiring to keep me from enjoying it?

~*~

I am definitely not my mother's daughter. Shopaholic Mimi Harmony had Christmas down to a science, her purchases completed, wrapped and tagged before the first of December. Here it was, less than a week before the big day, and I still had most of my shopping to do. Every year I vowed next year would be different. Mail order catalogs, their pages decorated with colorful Post-it notes—a different color for each family member and friend—covered my coffee table. But in typical Polly-the-Procrastinator fashion, I'd never gotten around to placing a single order. Now it was too late. I braced myself for an evening of hostile crowds and long lines. So I wouldn't enjoy myself much. I'd still rather spend Friday night maxing out my VISA at Sharper Image than breaking bread with Former Significant Other.

And did I ever max to the max! If Sharper Image gives out a Best Customer of the Year Award, I'm definitely a shoe-in. I never could figure out that fascination men have for gadgets, but this evening I was grateful for it. I stood at the checkout counter four hours later, laden down with gifts for everyone on my list—my father, my uncles, Mitch. Even Mom and Joni, who although not gadget gaga like the men in my life, did succumb to certain sybaritic pleasures fulfilled by various computer-controlled gizmos. All I can say is, God bless Sharper Image, and God bless their holiday gift-wrap service.

I stared at the six large shopping bags lining the gift-wrap counter and groaned. Too bad they didn't have a delivery service as well. In hindsight, perhaps gift certificates might have made for a wiser choice.

Dad got the prize for both heaviest and lightest gifts. Having gotten the exercise bug recently, his gifts included a mini-stepper for the office—mini in size but not weight, unfortunately—and an electronic pedometer for his morning jogs.

For each of my uncles I purchased a binocular-type device that measures distance from the golf tee to the hole and an electronic indoor driving range. Last year I bought them indoor putting ranges. Now they could play an entire round of golf without leaving the office.

My uncles often complained they got better results during counseling sessions held on the golf course rather than under the church or synagogue roof. Uncle Emerson claimed swinging a golf club loosened tongues. Uncle Cal said defenses and walls dropped in direct proportion to handicaps. Now they could all golf-counsel their parishioners no matter what the weather.

For Joni, the slave to fashion who owned twelve pairs of Manolo Blahnik stilettos, I found a pair of gel-lined, therapeutic socks and a deluxe foot spa.

Mitch, the quintessential audiophile, was getting a motorized, lighted CD storage rack. Unfortunately, Sharper Image didn't have a CD department. I'd have to schedule a trip to Virgin Records sometime before Christmas to pick up the newest George Winston.

My mother was the most difficult person on my list. You'd think with all her newfound hobbies and outside interests, she'd be easy to shop for. No way. There was never anything easy about Mom, and lately she was getting worse. Dad claimed it had to do with what he called *the change*.

Here I was, suffering from mental anxiety. Mom was suffering from menopause. All of a sudden, it occurred to me that many of life's problems began with "men." How fitting was that?

One of Mom's major complaints of late—other than my lack of mate and grandbabies for her to spoil—was constant hot flashes. I may not have successfully found said mate to produce desired offspring for her, but I did find a personal climate-control system for her to wear around her neck. The gadget claimed to warm you in the winter and cool you in the summer. At this stage of her life, Mom required no warming, but I was hoping the cool setting did the trick for her.

My other gift for her was a sound soother, a digital doohickey that played recordings—most dealing with some sort of falling, babbling, tripping, or cascading water—guaranteed to relax the most hyper of souls. I bought this as much for dad as Mom. If she didn't calm down soon, I was afraid she'd drive him crazy—or give herself a mental breakdown. Another of those "men" words.

Maybe it had something to do with the enormous sum of money I dropped in his establishment, but the store manager, eyeing my six large shopping bags and two hands, offered to hail me a taxi. I wasn't about to refuse.

Within minutes I was settled into the back seat of a Yellow Cab, my six shopping bags stored in the trunk.

"You look like you bought the store out," said the cabby as we headed downtown.

"Just about."

He chuckled. "*Tis the season to go in hock. Fa la la la la.*"

I couldn't remember the last time I rode in a cab with a friendly, talkative driver—let alone someone who spoke unbroken English. I glanced at his picture ID. Jeremy Chadwin. I also couldn't remember the last time I rode in a cab that wasn't driven by someone wearing a turban and named Mohammed or Ishmael.

"Jeremy Chadwin." I read his name out loud. "So what's your story? Out-of-work actor? Moonlighting med student? Failed dot-com entrepreneur?"

He glanced up at me in his rearview mirror, and I could see his brows knit together and the corners of his mouth dip down. "You mean because I'm driving a taxi for a living, and I'm not an immigrant? You have something against honest labor, lady?"

His antagonistic tone took me by surprise. "No, of course not."

"Then maybe you have something against foreigners."

"I didn't say that. I'm not a racist, and I didn't mean to sound condescending. It's just that I haven't had an English-speaking cab driver in a long time."

"I see." He nodded his head in a way that further roused my suspicions.

I leaned forward and glanced down at the pile of books scattered on the floor in front of the passenger seat. "Grad student?"

He slowed for a red light and turned to face me. Flashing neon from the store windows around us twinkled reflectively in his dark eyes. He had a kind face, a bit seasoned and roughly hewn, a face that looked as though it were filled with the wisdom of a man who'd already experienced a good deal of life. Where's your evidence, counselor?"

"On the floor beside you."

He glanced down at the thick texts filling the space. "Oops."

The light turned green. He stepped on the gas.

I could barely make out one of the titles in the dim light. "*Psychoanalysis, Evolutionary Biology and the Therapeutic Process*? Not exactly light reading."

"Guess you caught me. I'm picking up a little extra cash while I work on my dissertation. Teaching stipends only go so far in this city." He stopped at another light and stuck his hand through the pass-thru slot in the Plexiglas that separated us. "Jeremy Chadwin, at your service."

I accepted his hand and shook it. "Polly Harmony."

"So Polly Harmony." He turned back but kept one eye on the rearview mirror as he drove and spoke, "Are all those gifts for your husband and kids, or are you, please Lord, unattached and available?"

I laughed. "You don't waste any time, do you?"

"It's not that long a cab ride. So?"

"So?"

"Any special someone in your life right now?"

"Do you try to pick up all your passengers?"

"There was this octogenarian this afternoon. She was willing, but I didn't think I could keep up with her, so I decided not to pursue it."

"All this and a sense of humor, too."

"I'm doing everything I can to stack the deck in my favor, but you still haven't answered my question."

I stared at the back of Jeremy's head. Was I crazy? He could be a serial killer for all I knew. Maybe the text books were his MO I glanced up into the mirror. He grinned, and a herd of butterflies started stampeding in my belly. "I should have my head examined."

"I know a few good shrinks," he offered.

"I once dated a therapist. He spent the entire night psychoanalyzing me."

"I never mix business and pleasure. Besides, I'm not licensed to practice yet."

I leaned back in my seat and sighed. "Give me your number. I'll think about it."

When we arrived at my apartment, Jeremy insisted on carrying my shopping bags up to the door for me, then refused to accept any money for the cab fare. "Guilt is a great motivator." He closed my fingers around both the cab fare and a piece of paper with his phone number on it. "Now you'll feel obliged to call me. Soon."

He jogged down the steps and back to his cab but waited until I unlocked the outer door and got both myself and my packages inside before he pulled away from the curb. I stared at the piece of paper he'd pressed into my hand. I'd wait until after the holidays, but I fully intended to give Jeremy Chadwin a call.

I was feeling pretty good as I let myself into my apartment. Considering the way my day had started, it ended on an up note. Other than a few minor gifts, my shopping was finished, and I'd met an interesting guy with definite date potential.

My euphoria lasted only until I swung open the door and discovered Former Significant Other waiting on the other side. He stood in the middle of my living room, his arms crossed over his chest. "Where have you been?" he demanded. "We had a reservation at Prada hours ago."

I couldn't believe it. "How the hell did you get in here?"

"I used my key."

I never thought to get his set of keys back when I asked him to leave. Dumb me. I guess I assumed he'd toss them. "Give them to me." I held out my hand.

"Where were you?" he asked again, ignoring my outstretched palm.

I glanced down at the six Sharper Image bags at my feet, then scowled at him. "At an orgy."

"Very funny, Polly. I can't believe you forgot about our date and went shopping instead."

Had I seen this self-centered side of Former Significant Other when we first met, I could have spared myself a lot of time and aggravation, but either he'd kept his conceit closely hidden, or I'd been oblivious to his major flaws—hopefully, not out of desperation, but who knows? If love is blind, where does that leave lust? Deaf, dumb, *and* blind? Considering both the love and the lust died early in our relationship, I now considered myself a firstclass chump with a big fat *sucker* stamped across my forehead.

I knew there was no point in arguing with Former Significant Other. He lived in his own reality, a world that revolved exclusively around him and totally removed from the rest of the galaxy.

I crossed the room and picked up the phone. "I'm calling the police." I tried to maintain my cool, but inside I was seething. "You have ten seconds to hand me those keys and leave this apartment before I do."

He chuckled. "Polly, darling, you know you don't mean that."

I started counting. "One...two...."

"Come on, sweetheart, you're just upset because I didn't beg you to take me back right away. I know how that cute little brain of yours works. Your feelings are hurt, and I understand that, but you hurt me, too, and I had a lot of thinking to do about us."

I seriously doubted he'd spent the past few months pining

away over our aborted relationship. More likely, he hadn't found anyone else to take my place, and he was getting desperate. Former Significant Other had enjoyed the cachet that his association with a Harmony brought him. My family knew people with money to invest. His business had grown and flourished because of my connections to those people. "Three...four...."

He stepped closer, his arms outstretched. "Polly, Polly. We belong together, baby. Forever. I'm your destiny, and you're mine. You'll see I'm right if you only give us one more chance."

He sounded like he was reciting some prepared speech. *My destiny?* Oh, brother! What did I ever see in this bozo? I hit the nine-button on the phone. "I'm not kidding. Bother me again, and I'll file a complaint and get a restraining order against you."

"Don't be ridiculous, Polly." He grabbed the phone from my hand.

That was the last straw. All pretense of civility on my part flew the coop. I now saw Former Significant Other for the passive-aggressive control freak he was. It was time to get down and dirty. "And I'll make sure everyone knows," I added. "I don't think that will sit very well with all those high-profile clients of yours."

That did it. Nothing mattered more to Former Significant Other than the reputation he'd carefully culled as a mover and shaker of the movers and shakers. His business and prestige all hinged on his ability to rub shoulders with the elite and coax them into investing large sums of money in his various hi-tech ventures. One well-placed mention in the society columns—and as the daughter of Harmony Cosmetics, he knew I had the means —and bye-bye Golden Boy, hello Social Pariah.

He stuck his hand into his jacket pocket and pulled out a set of keys. "Someday you'll regret this." He placed both the keys and the phone in my hand. It wasn't a threat. I could hear the remorse in his voice. He knew he'd lost. Without another word he left my apartment.

~*~

"I don't know if I felt worse for him or myself," I told Joni the next day. With list in hand, we were searching the aisles of The Food Emporium for the items Mitch requested for the meal he planned to prepare that evening. "After Former Significant Other left, I had this strange emptiness inside me. Like I was the last single woman on the face of the earth, and I'd just turned away the last available man—even though I didn't want him."

"There you go again. Polly Pathetic. Former Significant Other was a loser and a user. You can't seriously feel bad about kicking him out."

"I don't, but there is something to be said for being a twosome. Someone to come home to at night. Warm your bed. Laugh at your jokes. It's nice knowing that you always have a date on Saturday night, and you never have to leave your apartment."

"Date? You're describing a life sentence."

I reached for a jar of extra virgin olive oil, stared first at Mitch's list and then the label, and frowned. "How can something be *extra* virgin?"

Joni snorted. "You're asking me?"

"Right. Stupid question." I placed the olive oil into the shopping cart. "Anyway, I don't see what's so wrong with wanting to be half of a whole. I'm tired of searching for Prince Charming. I'm beginning to think all those damn fairy tales we dreamed over as kids are lies. Prince Charming doesn't exist and never did."

"Fine. I agree. Fairy tales are bogus, but that doesn't mean you should settle for the likes of someone like Former Significant

Other."

"No, of course not." We continued down the aisle in search of the specific brand of angel hair pasta Mitch wanted. Joni maneuvered the cart around other shoppers. I scanned the shelves. The Food Emporium carried an entire aisle's worth of pastas but apparently not the one Mitch requested. "Are you sure you're brother isn't gay?" I finally asked in frustration after failing to find Mitch's choice.

"What? Mitch-the-Stud? Are you crazy?"

"Well, have you ever known a straight guy who loved to cook as much as he does and is so anal about food brands. Where the hell is this stuff?"

Joni grabbed the paper out of my hands. "Let me see that." I pointed to the item in question on Mitch's list. "Fresh pasta. He wants fresh pasta, not dried. We have to go over to the refrigerated section."

"Stupid me!"

"Hey, you're the idiot who invited the guy for dinner, remember?"

How could I forget? What in the world had possessed me to ask Jeff to dinner this evening? I didn't even like him. In his own way Jeff Jacoby was as condescending and self-righteous as Former Significant Other. Was this a new trend in my social life? Or worse yet, a rut? "I need to learn to think on my feet better and not blurt out the first stupid idea that crosses my mind."

"Serves you right for wanting to get even with me for Carlos." She grabbed a container of fresh angel hair and tossed it into the cart. "You're too damned inhibited Polly. You need to loosen up and enjoy life more."

I picked up a bag of spinach and threw it at her. "With jailbait?

No thank you."

"Carlos is twenty-two."

"Oh, excuse me."

"A very mature, experienced twenty-two," she said with a sly wink and a knowing grin. "Too bad you didn't stick around to find out."

I didn't even bother to comment. After all, I'd acted like a very *immature*, desperate thirty-one-year-old that night. So maybe we cancelled each other out. Either way, I'd like to put the whole nightmare behind me, but Joni continued to bring it up every chance she got, almost as if she somehow knew my darkest secret and kept baiting me to admit it.

I only hoped Joni kept her mouth shut about Carlos during dinner. The last thing I needed was for Jeff to go blabbing to Uncle Aaron about his wanton great-niece. I had visions of my uncle the rabbi conspiring with my uncle the priest to send me off to some convent in a remote corner of Albania.

~*~

An hour later and nearly a hundred dollars poorer, we lugged the contents of two laden shopping bags back to our apartment building. As I unloaded the items onto my kitchen counter, I decided I'd made one of the bigger mistakes of my life by inviting Jeff to dinner. "This is ridiculous." I surveyed the gourmet delicacies spread before me. "I'm trying to discourage the guy, not encourage him. Why am I going to all this trouble?" I reached for the phone. "I'm calling Jeff and canceling."

"No!" Joni grabbed the phone from my hand. "Don't you dare. I've given up a Saturday night to meet this dweeb that's got the hots for you. Besides, I'm looking forward to having some fun tonight."

"That's exactly what I'm afraid of. What the hell was I thinking?"

"Don't get so mental, Polly. It's not like I'm going to give the guy a lap dance on your couch."

"Do I have your word on that?"

"Absolutely. Besides, you said he's pushing forty, right? Forget it. Men reach their sexual peak in their early twenties. I want a guy who can get it up and keep it up." Her eyes twinkled; her mouth twisted into a lascivious smirk. "All night. After all, it's the only thing they're really good at or good for."

Maybe I'd enjoy life more if I could adopt Joni's easygoing attitude regarding sex and men. Joni's motto was, *Always yield to temptation, because it may not pass your way again*. I've tried, but it doesn't work for me.

Joni's right when she points out that I have sexual hang-ups, but as I discovered from my Carlos escapade, a conscience is what hurts when all your other parts feel so damn good. Besides, I'm hung up on still wanting that damn fairy tale. And I'm scared to death of waking up one day to find I'm facing menopause and still sharing my bed with only my dreams. "I don't want to become Arlene," I said.

Joni froze, a grape halfway to her open mouth. Her face grew serious. I'd told her about my revealing dinner with the company secretary. She wrapped her arm around my shoulders. "None of us do, honey."

Tears gathered behind my eyes, and I hated myself for my own weaknesses. "Sometimes I feel like I have one foot in that life already. Will I still be alone five years from now? Ten years from now? My mother's right about one thing. My clock *is* ticking down. No matter how I laugh it off, the truth is, I want the dream,

Joni. I want a husband and kids, but I have this fear that either I'll have to settle for someone I don't love or wind up all alone. I don't know which would be worse."

"You have time. We both do."

I pulled away and stared at her. "You?" I'd never considered that Joni, the ultimate good-time party girl, might also want the dream.

She shrugged and looked away. "Maybe. Eventually. Someday."

Well, well, well.

~*~

At seven-ten that evening Jeff rang my doorbell. "He's early," I muttered, my hands submerged in a sink full of sudsy water. Mitch had assigned me cleanup detail. He didn't trust me with so much as peeling a carrot.

Mundane KP tasks like the aforementioned peeling—as well as dicing, slicing, and chopping—were assigned to the more experienced and less klutzy Joni, who unlike me, had never confused her finger for a white radish.

"We're having fish this evening," said Mitch after reminding me of the radish incident and my trip to the emergency room last summer when I had to have my left index finger stitched back together. "No red wine. No blood."

Joni tossed a handful of chopped chives into the salad bowl and grabbed a dishtowel. "I'll get the door." I watched as she sashayed across the room in a pair of Manolo Blahnik strappy red sandals and a skimpy purple Donna Karan slip dress that left little to the imagination. I glanced down at my own outfit, a pair of pleated navy wool pants and a bulky blue and white snowflake pattered knit sweater.

Mitch caught my scowl. "I told her she was a little overdressed," he whispered in my ear, "but you know Joni." He wore a pair of stone washed jeans and a burgundy button-down shirt. His ecru cashmere sweater came off as the apartment had heated up from his cooking.

Yeah, I knew Joni. "Underdressed is more like it." I gazed up at Mitch. "I feel like such a bitch. Poor Jeff. How can I do this to a guy whose only crime is liking me? He doesn't stand a chance against her."

"I'll keep a tight rein on her. Don't worry."

Joni pressed the button by the front door, buzzing Jeff through the outer entrance. Swinging her hips seductively to *Round 'Bout Midnight*, from the Wynton Marsalis CD she'd earlier loaded into my player, she waited until he knocked at the apartment door.

"I'm not a very nice person," I said.

Mitch bent down and kissed my cheek. "You're a wonderful person. Just a bit confused at times and a really, really lousy cook."

"Thanks. I think."

Mitch laughed.

I glanced back over at Joni. "I hope Jeff has a strong heart."

Jeff knocked. Joni swung the door open, and the potent aroma of roses flew into the room. My nose reacted immediately. I sneezed. Bubbles rose from the sink and drifted towards the stove.

"Bless you." Mitch grabbed his pan of sautéing morels a moment before the soap descended on them. I sneezed again. And again. The kitchen filled with floating bubbles. Mitch rushed to cover the mushrooms and the lobster bisque simmering on a back burner. Then he grabbed the bowl of salad and the loaf of French sourdough bread sitting on the counter. Juggling both in his arms, he carried them a safe distance from the bubble fallout.

"Roses." Joni stared at the large bouquet that pretty much concealed Jeff. "Shit!" She pushed him out into the hallway, "Hi, Jeff. I'm Joni, and you and I need to talk." With that she slammed the apartment door behind them.

"You think it's safe to leave them alone out there?" I asked Mitch between a series of sneezes.

He shrugged. "If they're not back in five minutes, I'll go rescue him."

My mind immediately leaped to Holland Tube and Carlos. I knew from experience that a lot can happen in five minutes—especially around Joni. Jeff was on his own for the time being, though. My hands dripping from soapy water and my nose dripping from roses, I hurried off to the bathroom in search of an antihistamine.

Mitch couldn't find Joni and Jeff, though. After five minutes, he stuck his head out into the hallway. No Jeff. No Joni. No roses.

"Maybe they went upstairs," I suggested.

Mitch stepped back into the apartment and shrugged. "He's a big boy. I suppose he can take care of himself."

I wasn't so sure. We were talking about Joni here, after all. Jeff didn't stand a chance if she was up to something. And Joni was always up to something.

The minutes ticked away. "Dinner's ready," said Mitch. "It's going to get overcooked."

I glanced at my watch. Joni had abducted Jeff nearly fifteen minutes ago. "Let's give them a few more minutes."

Joni finally returned with Jeff in tow ten minutes later. He looked both mortified and extremely uncomfortable. I hoped it was from embarrassment over the roses and not anything Joni had said or done, but knowing Joni, who knew? She looked far too innocent for Joni, even though her scantily clad body was practically draped over him.

"I'm sorry, Polly." Jeff peeled himself away from Joni and held his arms akimbo. "I had no idea you were allergic to roses."

"No permanent damage done," I assured him. I then made introductions. "I guess you've already met Joni, and this is her brother Mitch."

The men shook hands the way men do when they're sizing each other up and getting a feel for the lay of the land. Or right before the bell rings and the match begins. I could understand Jeff's suspicious curiosity. After all, I'd invited him to dinner at my apartment. Most men would take that to mean a twosome. Unless of course, you were into group things, and I doubted such an idea would even cross Jeff's mind.

Mitch's sudden predatory stance baffled me, though. "Mitch and Joni are my best friends," I added, but my words sounded lame.

All Jeff said was, "I see."

In the pit of my stomach I felt the beginnings of a long evening. A *very* long evening.

It wasn't.

After the initial awkwardness, the evening progressed better than expected. Joni behaved herself—as much as Joni is capable of behaving. On more than one occasion she *did* position herself as close to Jeff as possible without sitting directly in his lap, and her conversation included more than one outrageous innuendo and crass joke, but much to my surprise, Jeff seemed to find her amusing.

"It's definitely me," I whispered to Mitch. We were in the kitchen preparing coffee—well, actually, Mitch was preparing the coffee since he claimed I always burned the grounds. I was getting out plates and utensils for dessert. "Around me, Jeff gets tongue-tied. And if I spoke like Joni, he'd launch into a lecture." I motioned across the room. "Look at him. With Joni he's a regular chatterbox."

"Maybe it's because when he looks at you, he sees wife potential. The wives of community leaders don't use four-letter words—at least not in public or among strangers at dinner parties."

"So you're suggesting he sees Joni as the evening's entertainment?"

"Something like that." He poured the coffee into four glass mugs. "Hand me the whipped cream."

I retrieved the bowl of cream he'd whipped earlier. "Joni isn't a threat to this fantasy he's created in his head about you and him," said Mitch.

"I suppose."

"You almost sound disappointed." He added a dollop of cream to the top of each mug. "I thought you didn't want a relationship with him."

"I don't. We have nothing in common." But neither did Jeff and Joni and yet, around Joni, Jeff acted like a normal guy. "What is it about me that I bring out the awkward dork in the man?"

Mitch shrugged. "So you do. Big deal. It's not like you have that effect on every guy you date. You don't click with Jeff. And since you've made it clear that you don't want to click with him, why all the angst?"

Why indeed? I found Jeff dull and conservative. I wanted to discourage his attentions. Yet here I was annoyed that I'd gotten exactly what I wanted. Maybe there was something to Freud's famous question, *What do women want?* What exactly did I want?

When Jeff remembered the dinner included others beside him and Joni, he spent most of his time picking Mitch's brain about financial trends and investments. I sat back and observed my two best friends and my dinner guest like an outsider peering through a window at a party I wasn't invited to. I should have felt relief. I didn't.

~*~

When the evening finally broke up, I walked Jeff downstairs. "Your friends are very interesting," he said.

Interesting is one of those words people use when they mean something altogether different but don't want to hurt anyone's feelings. I didn't challenge him, though. I had something to say, something that I'd put off for too long because I'm basically a coward, and contrary to my initial reasons for hosting this evening, I really didn't want to hurt Jeff, merely discourage him. "You're a very interesting person, too," I began.

His eyebrows raised, and he cocked his head slightly. "I sense a 'but' coming on."

"I'm sorry, Jeff. You're a nice guy, and I'd like to keep you as a friend, but...." I smiled slightly. "You're right. There it is."

He chuckled and shook his head. "You don't have to say anything further, Polly. I knew the moment your friend opened the door this evening that there could never be anything between us. A woman interested in developing a relationship with a man doesn't invite a couple of chaperones to the party."

"The chemistry isn't there, Jeff."

"I know."

I didn't expect that. "You do?"

"You're a beautiful woman, Polly. Charming. Intelligent.

Everything a man could want in a life-mate."

"Now *I* hear a 'but' coming."

He laughed. "But we both know it would never work out between us. I wanted it to. I kept rationalizing away our differences, forcing myself to believe I could make it work if only I tried hard enough. I wanted you to forsake your passions and share mine, but that was very selfish of me. I'm sorry I put us both through that."

"I'd like to remain friends." After all, if we parted on less-than-friendly terms, my Saturday's at Uncle Aaron's synagogue could become quite awkward.

He bent over and brushed my cheek with his lips. "I'd like that, too." He opened the door and stepped out into the crisp December night.

And that was that.

SIX
Mimi Does Christmas and Polly Does Carlos...Sort Of

I skipped church the next morning. It was Uncle Cal's week but also his year for my parents and me to attend his Christmas Eve service the next night. I figured he'd understand. Besides, I only had a day to finish my shopping, since Head Lecherous Jerk expected us to show up for work on the twenty-fourth.

I was halfway down the street when I heard a horn honking and someone calling my name. "Hey, Polly Harmony! Want a lift?"

I spun around, trying to figure out who'd called and from where, when a yellow cab made a U-turn and pulled up beside me. "Are you stalking me?" I asked Jeremy.

"Are you paranoid?"

"You tell me. There are eight million people in this city and at least half as many taxis. What are the chances of our being on the same street at the same time?"

Jeremy scratched his head. Two perfectly shaped dark brown brows knit together in a pseudo-thoughtful pose. "You have a point, but if you need reassurance, I just dropped a fare off down the street. We could track him down and have him vouch for me."

"And how do I know he's not your accomplice? You could have plotted this entire coincidence."

"You are paranoid!"

I laughed. "Who me? I'm just your typical, cynical New Yorker."

Several horns blared behind him. "Get in. I'm blocking traffic."

I hesitated for a moment. "First, swear you're not a stalker or a serial killer."

Jeremy made the sign of the cross over his heart. "On my saintly mother's family Bible, I swear I will not lay a finger on your very sexy body." He winked, then added. "At least not yet."

I opened the back door and jumped in. "Was that a proposition?"

"I certainly hope so." He stepped on the gas. "Where to, sweet Polly?"

"First set your meter, Jeremy. You're not my personal chauffeur."

"Chivalry is definitely dead," he muttered. Then with an over-exaggerated sigh, he reached across the dashboard and flipped the meter on.

"I thought you moonlighted to make ends meet? How do you expect to pay your bills if you start driving me around for free?"

"Don't be so logical. Where to?"

"Times Square."

"You're kidding, right?"

"Actually, no. I have to buy some tacky gag gifts. What better place?"

Jeremy turned onto Park Avenue and headed uptown, then glanced into his rearview mirror and wiggled his eyebrows. "I love a woman with a sense of humor. How about meeting me for lunch later?"

"Don't you have to work?"

"What? Cabbies can't take lunch breaks?"

After a few more minutes of banter, I agreed to meet Jeremy at a little deli on Forty-eighth Street at twelve-thirty. This wasn't a Robert DeNiro movie, I reminded myself. Jeremy seemed like a nice guy—a guy I'd like to get to know better, and lunch at a crowded midtown deli sounded safe enough.

I also couldn't help noticing that he looked even better in daylight than he had under the glare of nighttime neon and oncoming headlights. Jeremy possessed the kind of features that make women drool. Each was perfectly sculpted but out of wood rather than polished marble. The resulting composite produced a rakish, rather than pretty boy, face. The mischievous glint in his milk chocolate eyes, his shaggy head of toffee-colored hair, and the quirky way his lips twisted when he smiled, all enhanced his appeal.

~*~

The deli was jammed, but Jeremy had commandeered a booth and waved me over when I arrived. "Bought out another store, I see," he said by way of greeting. He rose and took my shopping bags from me, placing one in the corner of each booth seat. Then he helped me off with my coat and hung it on a hook at the end of the booth.

The gesture took me by surprise. I tried to remember the last time a date behaved so gentlemanly. I couldn't. My uncles held doors and coats for me. So did my father. But they were of past generations. Guys my age? I don't think it would ever have occurred to any of them.

"Guess I got a little carried away. I wait until the last minute, then go overboard."

"Big family?"

"Not too big. You?"

The waitress came over and handed us menus. "Beverage?" she asked me.

"Coffee, please."

"And a refill," added Jeremy, pointing to the empty cup sitting in front of him. After the waitress left, he answered my question. "My family is normal size, I suppose. Parents, a couple of siblings, a few nieces and nephews, assorted aunts, uncles, and cousins. One grandparent still alive. Most of them live out on Long Island. A few of the more successful ones have moved up to Connecticut."

"My family is a bit less traditional," I said.

"How so?"

The waitress returned with my coffee and a pot. I waited to answer while she refilled Jeremy's cup and took our orders—a BLT club for him, a turkey on rye for me. When she left, I gave him the two-minute History of Harmony, beginning with both sets of Romeo and Juliet grandparents and ending with me, the last of the line.

"There's definitely a paper in that," he said when I finished. "Too bad we didn't meet before I started writing my thesis." He sat back and crossed his arms over his chest. "So, considering this eclectic family of yours, can I assume the gag gifts are for them?"

"Along with everything I bought Friday night, except for a few gifts for friends."

"Get me anything? We're friends."

"Forward, aren't you?"

"Hey, it's New York, babe. You don't get anywhere unless you hustle."

I had to agree with that, but I got the upper hand when I leaned across the table and pulled a small gift-wrapped box out of the top of the bag sitting next to him. "As a matter of fact..." I handed him the box.

Jeremy turned a deep shade of reddish-purple, a color that definitely clashed with the orange and black plaid shirt he wore. He began to stammer. "I didn't mean...Polly, you shouldn't...I...."

"Don't get all flustered, Jeremy. It's only a little nothing. I saw it and thought of you. I figured you wouldn't let me pay for my own lunch, considering I have to twist your arm to accept cab fare, so...." I shrugged and began to feel the heat rise to my own cheeks.

Suddenly, I was back in fifth grade, hoping Ryan Fitzpatrick liked the Valentine I'd spent painstaking hours crafting for him. As it turned out, Ryan hadn't appreciated my efforts, and for the next several months I suffered through endless teasing from all the boys in Mrs. Sternbach's class. "Just open it, will you?"

"If you insist." Jeremy slipped off the gold ribbon, tore away the red foil paper, and lifted the lid. He removed the coffee mug from the box and studied it for a moment. I held my breath, waiting for his response. Then his face broke into a wide grin, and he burst out laughing. I exhaled.

"'Neurotics build castles in the sky,'" he read. "'Psychotics live in them. Psychiatrists collect the rent.'" He turned his gaze on me, his eyes twinkling. "I love it! Thank you." He placed the mug on the table between us, "But maybe I'd better not take it into the office once I have my own practice."

"Sensible call."

"So what about all those other gifts." He nodded his head in the direction of the shopping bags. "Equally caustic coffee mugs?"

"Along with a few T-shirts and sweatshirts. My mother is the quintessential shopper. I found a sweatshirt for her that says, 'Veni, Vedi, Visa: I came. I Saw. I Shopped.'"

"For your sake, I hope she has as good a sense of humor as her daughter."

"She does." Except when it comes to my lack of husband and children, of course. Mom saw nothing funny in that, but I was hardly about to impart *that* tidbit to a man I barely knew.

"What else did you buy?"

I decided against telling Jeremy about the T-shirt I found for Joni. I wasn't ready to explain Joni to Jeremy, and a shirt that read, *I'm one of those bad things that happens to good people* definitely required an explanation.

Instead, I told him about the mugs I bought for my uncles. "They golf together once a week. The mugs say, 'If it goes right, it's a slice. If it goes left, it's a hook. If it goes straight, it's a miracle.' Perfect choice for golfing clergymen, don't you think?"

Jeremy agreed. "And for your father?"

"Dad's a little kid at heart. He still loves going to amusement parks and riding roller coasters. I found him a sweatshirt that says, 'Growing Old is Inevitable; Growing Up is Optional.'"

The waitress brought our order, and for a few minutes we concentrated on our sandwiches. Then Jeremy broke the silence, "So what else did you buy? There's more in those shopping bags besides four mugs and two sweatshirts."

"Nosey, aren't you? Didn't anyone ever tell you that curiosity killed the cat?"

He grinned again. I really liked the devilish look that sparkled in his eyes and the way his mouth tilted up in challenge when he smiled that way. There was a definitely charming quality to Jeremy Chadwin. The kind of charm that easily cajoles the stripes off a zebra or makes a normally sensible girl lose all semblance of control. I didn't care. I felt myself falling and decided to let go and see where I landed.

"But satisfaction brought him back," he said.

"With one less life," I reminded him.

"What's one life when you have eight more at your disposal?"

"But with that attitude, you could find yourself with only one life left. Then what? Anyway, the rest of the gifts wouldn't interest you. Half a dozen CD's, some aromatherapy candles, things like that. Boring girl stuff mostly. Nothing funny."

"I don't know. Depending on who you bought the aromatherapy candles for, they could be *very* funny."

Jeremy's wit intrigued me. I had known my share of therapists and shrinks—former classmates, friends of my parents, church and synagogue members I'd met and socialized with on occasion. Plus a date or two that I'd rather forget. Never had any of them shown the slightest glimmer of a sense of humor. Most spent their time analyzing conversations and events *ad nauseum*, always searching for that deeper hidden meaning. They bored me to death, but Jeremy seemed as different from them as summer is from winter.

I didn't want the afternoon to end, but I felt guilty keeping Jeremy off the streets. I doubted he'd be driving a cab if he didn't really need the extra cash. The city was jammed with last-minute shoppers and tourists trekking to Radio City Music Hall and Rockefeller Center. Jeremy was losing considerable income as we dawdled over lunch. "I really need to go," I finally said.

He signaled the waitress for the check and handed her a twenty and a ten. Then he helped me on with my coat, slipped on his, and grabbed my shopping bags. "I'll take you home," he offered as we wound our way through a maze of crowded tables and around a package-laden floor toward the exit.

"Thank you, but I have some other errands to run first. You go back to work." He studied me as we walked down the block. Was he trying to determine whether or not I was telling him the truth? He didn't challenge me.

We continued walking until we came to his cab, parked in a loading zone two blocks from the deli. "Aren't you afraid of getting a ticket?"

"Nah. My brother's an NYPD district captain."

"How convenient."

Jeremy changed the subject. "You haven't called me yet," he said.

"It hasn't even been two full days. I didn't want to sound desperate."

"Are you going to?" His voice held a hint of challenge. His face took on a look of anxious anticipation, like a little boy waiting impatiently for the rest of the household to awaken so he could open his Christmas presents.

"I had planned to wait until after New Year's."

"Got a date for Saturday night?"

"No."

"Now that's a crime that needs rectifying. Have dinner with me. I'm much better company than a movie rental."

"I don't know. Depends on the movie, doesn't it? I've seen some pretty good ones."

"But you have nothing to compare them to. You've never spent a Saturday evening with me. How about if I pick you up at seven? Consider it research." He grinned that wickedly sexy grin of his and waited for an answer.

How could I refuse? The man was charming me right off my feet. "All right. Research at seven."

He handed me my shopping bags and hopped into his cab. "See you Saturday, Polly. And Merry Christmas."

"Merry Christmas."

~*~

"He's perfect," I told Joni later that evening. "Charming, witty, thoughtful, intelligent, *and* gorgeous. About six feet tall, milk chocolate eyes, hair the color of toffee candy, and a smile that makes you forget the world."

"And you obviously have." She surveyed the piles of wrapped presents strewn across my living room floor. We were doing our best to organize them into as few shopping bags as possible for easy transport.

Every year Uncle Aaron rented a car for Christmas Eve. He, Joni, Mitch, and I first picked up Uncle Emerson's booty—he joined us later in the evening after conducting his own Christmas Eve service—and the four of us drove to my parents' home in Summit.

My mother had adopted Joni and Mitch as surrogate children soon after the three of us met. She always included them at holiday gatherings. Joni and Mitch usually begged off from minor celebrations like Hanukkah, though. Having been brought up— or not brought up—by Rainbow and assorted other surrogates, they were still often overwhelmed by Mimi's smothering brand of motherhood. However, they always joined us for Christmas and

Easter.

Mom even tried to include Rainbow one year after she unexpectedly showed up in New York right before Christmas. Rainbow arrived with little decorated bags of marijuana as presents for everyone—including my uncles. Mom had a conniption fit. "I was a flower child, too," she said, after flushing the contents of the bags down the toilet, "but I grew up. A long time ago."

"I've already suggested Uncle Aaron rent a full-size car," I told Joni. "We'll manage."

"I'm not talking quantity. I don't see your Santa's List gifts."

"Oh, shit!" Many of the families in Uncle Francis' parish, immigrants and single-parent households for the most part, struggled to make ends meet. Each year the families made up wish lists for Santa. Members of Uncle Cal's, Uncle Emerson's, and Uncle Aaron's more affluent congregations each chose a family and fulfilled their wishes.

I was always overwhelmed by how little the families requested—a warm coat, a new set of bed sheets, a newspaper or magazine subscription. In the past I'd always added a few frivolous items, things they'd never buy themselves, like bubble bath for a harried mother of three who held down two jobs or a stuffed animal for a toddler with few toys. "I can't believe I forgot!"

"Where's your list?"

I grabbed my purse and rooted around inside it. "Found it!" I waved a piece of paper in the air.

She glanced at her watch. "Grab your coat. The stores are open until eleven. We've got about three hours to save your ass. I'll be right down." She flung open my living room door and bounded up the steps two at a time. "You must be in love," she called over her shoulder. "I've never known anything or anyone to kept do-gooder Polly from shirking her charitable duty."

In love? Me? With Jeremy? I didn't even want to contemplate the possibility, but I'd be kidding myself if I refused to admit I *was* looking forward to Saturday night.

~*~

My mother does Christmas like Macy's does the Thanksgiving Day parade. Once a year we put up with her over-the-top transformations and actually enjoyed all the sparkle and tinsel and evergreens that covered every square inch of the house. It was tradition.

Unfortunately, now that she considers herself semi-retired, Mom allows her decorating bug to consume her three hundred and sixty-five days out of the year. She transforms the house for every holiday, from Presidents' Day to Arbor Day. Christmas has lost its uniqueness. Like a kid who ate the entire box of chocolates at one sitting, there can be too much of a good thing.

I tried not to dwell on that as I entered the brightly lit house on the hill, though. This was Christmas. As I stepped across the twinkling threshold, all the problems of the last few weeks lifted from my shoulders. I forgot about Head Lecherous Jerk and all the little lecherous jerks at work. I shrugged off the unexpected and unwelcome return of Former Significant Other. I dismissed the recurring vision of Mason Hightower standing in the middle of my living room with nothing but a hard-on and a pair of G-clef patterned socks. I even tried to free my mind of Carlos and his magical fingers—not an easy task considering the very thought of those fingers still sent shivers of pleasure up my spine.

And the kid with the magic digits stood at the fireplace, sipping an egg nog!

I blinked, hoping the stud casually leaning on the mantle only bore a striking resemblance to Carlos. No such luck. It was Carlos, all right. Straight down to his half-buttoned black silk shirt and skintight black jeans. "What the hell is he doing here?"

Joni looked just as puzzled. "I haven't a clue." I glared at her. "Honest, Polly. I didn't invite him."

I scanned the room. Every year instead of delivering our Santa's List gifts on Christmas day, Mom went one step further and invited the families for Christmas Eve dinner. This year's dinner included the family she and my father had sponsored, the family I had sponsored, and the family Joni and Mitch had sponsored.

Obviously, Carlos, the budding Tommy Hilfiger beefcake, belonged to one of those families. Judging from the pregnant girl clinging to his bicep, I was willing to bet he was the absentee father of mine. I also wondered how much of that modeling check he'd received had gone to supporting the girl and the baby balanced on her hip. "What's Carlos' last name?" I asked.

"I'm not sure."

"It wouldn't by any chance be Jones, would it?

"Maybe. Why?"

I waited to answer. Behind us, Uncle Aaron and Mitch carried in an armload of gifts and overnight bags from the car, depositing everything in the hallway. When they returned to the car for another load, I whipped out the Santa's List from my coat pocket and read it to her. "'Tiffany Clinton, seventeen years old. One child, Jesse Jones, fourteen months. Pregnant with second child.'

"I'm willing to bet Carlos, or Craig, or whatever he's calling himself this week, is Jesse's father. *And* the father of the one on the way."

"That sleaze ball!" Joni threw her purse on top of a pile of packages and stormed towards the living room.

Knowing Joni's family history, I understood her anger. She had an extreme bias against men who sowed their seed on the run. All the same, I had to diffuse her righteous indignation. Now was not the time for a confrontation. I grabbed her arm. "No. Not here. It's Christmas. Don't spoil it for Tiffany and little Jesse."

Joni stepped back into the foyer. "You're right, but wait until I get my hands on a certain piece of his anatomy the next time he shows up at Holland Tube. I'll make him wish he'd become a priest."

The thought did little to lift the pall that had settled over my Christmas good cheer. "And don't breathe a word of this to Mitch," I warned her as we headed upstairs to deposit our coats. "He already knows more than enough about that night, thanks to you." At times like this, Mitch's latent white knight took over, and the last thing I needed was to have to explain Carlos to my parents or Uncle Aaron.

I hoped Carlos had enough smarts to keep his mouth shut throughout the evening. Joni, I could swear to secrecy, and although she might spill the beans to Mitch, I knew I could trust her to keep her mouth shut around my parents and uncles. Carlos, on the other hand, was a great unknown.

Joni and I headed back downstairs and began to mingle, introducing ourselves to my mother's guests. We found Uncle Aaron and my father attempting conversation with my parent's Santa's List family, an elderly couple who spoke broken English. The woman, Mrs. Martinez, wore double hearing aids and used a walker that was barely wide enough for her massive frame. Her husband, a little sliver of a man, squinted sideways through rheumy eyes, one hand cupped to his ear to catch whatever words he understood.

"He needs a hearing specialist and an eye appointment," I whispered to my father.

He wrapped his arm around my shoulders and gave me a hug. "Already in the works."

"And a membership at Weight Watchers for her?"

Dad shot me one of those behave-yourself-Polly glares, the kind I hadn't received since junior high when he caught me forging Mom's name on a note to get out of gym class. But knowing Dad, he'd had the same thought, and he knew I knew it. After all, we swam in the same gene pool. Besides, he was fighting too hard to keep from laughing.

Dad had written the gym excuse for me when I told him how Regina Koltzner kept picking on me for still being a baby and wearing undershirts instead of bras. Then he got Mom to take me shopping. I glanced down at my chest. After all these years I still received pleasure in knowing snot-nosed Regina graduated high school still wearing a 32B, while I had matured into a cleavage-producing 36C.

Joni and I drifting over to Mitch and the family he and Joni had sponsored. The Cabrerra family consisted of Mr. Cabrerra, a disabled day laborer who hadn't worked in nearly six months due to a construction site accident, his wife, and their three school-aged children.

The kids stood politely beside their parents, not saying a word, but their gazes kept roving in the direction of the piles of brightly wrapped gifts surrounding the Christmas tree. They were in for a treat. Joni and Mitch had gone overboard, nearly buying out F.A.O. Schwartz, for the five and six-year-old girls and their seven-year-old brother. The children would have to wait until tomorrow morning, though. Mom always sent the families home with their gifts unopened so they could experience Christmas morning in their own homes.

After a few minutes of conversation with the Cabrerras, Joni and I could no longer put off dealing with Carlos. We crossed the room to where he still stood in front of the fireplace, the glow from the hearth only adding to his stud muffin, sexy good looks.

He gave no indication of recognizing either of us. I wasn't sure whether to be angry or relieved, but I wasn't going to let him get the upper hand. "You must be Tiffany." I extended my hand to the young girl. "I'm Polly Harmony, and this is my friend, Joni Hughes."

Tiffany lowered her eyes and smiled shyly. I could barely hear her whispered, "Hi." Out of the corner of my eye I caught a puzzled-looking Carlos studying me as if the sound of my voice had triggered some latent memory.

"And this is Jesse?" I asked, pretending to ignore Carlos. "He's adorable."

"Thank you," she murmured.

"Are you the father?" asked Joni, directing a hostile glare at Carlos. He shifted his gaze to her. Recognition dawned. Color drained from his face.

"This is Jesse's daddy Craig," said Tiffany. She smiled adoringly at Carlos.

"Funny," said Joni. "I could have sworn you were that new Tommy Hilfiger model." She turned to me. "You know who I mean, don't you, Polly? That young piece of ass who struts his stuff at Holland Tube. What was his name? Carlos?"

"Yes, I believe so," I said.

"Craig, did you say? Well, I'm glad to hear I'm mistaken,"

continued Joni, speaking to Tiffany but continuing to stare pointedly at Carlos, "because *Carlos* is a real prick. I hear he's making tons of money from his modeling but hasn't shared a dime of it with his family. His girlfriend and her kids have to rely on charity to make ends meet."

"Maybe you heard wrong," said Carlos, jutting out his chin ever so slightly.

"Did I?" Joni offered him a too-sweet smile. "Perhaps you're right. I'll have to ask him the next time he *dares* to show up at Holland Tube."

I latched on to Joni's arm and nudged her away. "We'd better go see if Mom needs help in the kitchen." I flashed Tiffany a smile. "Nice meeting all of you."

"Well, I think he got the message," said Joni as we headed towards the kitchen.

"Good thing Tiffany is too dense to have gotten it, also. What were you trying to do, start a domestic incident in my mother's living room? You promised me you wouldn't confront him tonight."

"I didn't."

"Right."

"Hey, Polly! That scumbag deserves to squirm. I'd like to see what happens when Tiffany discovers those tight buns flashing down at her from some billboard in Newark. He won't be able to keep his secret from her then."

"No, he won't." I frowned, the future so obvious. "He'll walk out on her and the kids for some hot Victoria's Secret model. He'll become the darling of the gossip columns, and Tiffany and her kids will be forgotten in some homeless shelter."

"Maybe you and I should make damn certain that doesn't

happen."

"And how do we do that?"

Joni grinned what could only be described as an avenging smirk. Mitch wasn't the only white knight in the Hughes household. His sister had a real soft spot for fatherless kids and an ice-cold heart for men who abandoned their offspring. In all fairness, her father—whoever he was—never knew his seed had dallied with Rainbow's eggs. Rainbow herself was clueless as to Joni and Mitch's father's identity, but that didn't matter to Joni.

"We start by having a little talk with your Uncle Francis," she said. "With the right amount of persuasion, we can at least ensure a portion of Carlos' income goes directly to Tiffany and the kids."

I liked her idea. And Uncle Francis was exactly the avenging saint to aid Joni, the avenging angel. "We can talk to him later tonight. He's doing the earlier family mass at St. Benedict's this year. He should arrive around the time we get back from Uncle Cal's church service."

~*~

My mother served a dinner spread that probably rivaled anything Wolfgang Puck ever created for an Oscars banquet. Throughout the festivities, I occasionally glanced over at Carlos, sitting at the opposite end of the long dining room table. He sat sullenly, saying little to either Tiffany on his left or Mr. Cabrerra on his right. For the most part he ignored little Jesse, except when he caught me staring at him. Then he morphed into The Devoted Daddy, grabbing the startled child off his mother's lap and bouncing him so hard that poor Jesse upchucked his turkey and sweet potatoes all over his father's silk shirt.

"Two points for the kid," Joni whispered into my ear.

I grabbed my napkin and pretended to stifle a coughing fit to keep from laughing out loud.

The party broke up shortly after the last crumbs of apple pie were consumed. Mom sent each Santa's List family home with enough food for tomorrow's Christmas dinner as well as the remainder of the week. As they headed out the door, I heard Joni say, "See you around, *Carlos*." I turned in time to see his tanning salon skin blanch the same sickly gray as the stain that now covered his expensive silk shirt.

~*~

Once we returned from Christmas Eve services at Uncle Cal's church, we waited for Uncle Francis, Uncle Emerson, and Uncle Cal to arrive at the house. Soon after, my father dragged my mother off to bed, and Joni and I waylaid Uncle Francis as he helped himself to a turkey sandwich in the kitchen. Sensing a conspiracy in the works and not wanting to be left out, my three other uncles and Mitch hovered around the kitchen table until we finally had no choice but to include them.

They all listened with great interest to our abbreviated tale of Craig—alias Carlos—the Scum Bucket Wayward Father and Tommy Hilfiger Hunk. Mitch, of course, knew the details we deliberately omitted, but he kept a straight face, averting any direct eye contact with either me or his sister, when Uncle Cal asked how I had come to know Carlos.

"We met at a nightclub in Manhattan a few weeks ago," I mumbled. At least I wasn't lying to him.

Uncle Francis turned to me. "This wouldn't have anything to with that evening you didn't want to discuss, would it, Polly?"

Heat suffused my neck and cheeks. From Uncle Francis' expression, I figured the color of my face now rivaled the bright red of my Christmas sweater.

"I thought so." He shook his head. "That damn kid's been a thorn in my paw for years."

Talk about an unexpected jolt! And here I thought I was about to get Classic Lecture Number Twelve: Less-Than-Lady-Like Behavior-for-a-Woman-Your-Age.

"You know him?" asked Mitch.

Uncle Francis snorted. "I've been trying to straighten that boy out for years—ever since I caught him and his buddies helping themselves to the sacramental wine in the church basement. Believe me, six drunken altar boys is not a pretty picture. And even harder to explain to the visiting Bishop. Since then, Craig's had several run-ins with the law. Everything from shoplifting to grand theft auto, all before he turned sixteen. Salvatore Esposito, his juvie officer, and I struck up a lasting friendship thanks to Craig Jones."

Uncle Aaron reached across the table and patted Uncle Francis on the shoulder. "We all have our failures, Francis. Don't flog yourself."

"I suppose, but now he's dragged that bubble-brained Tiffany Clinton down with him and keeps getting her pregnant." Uncle Francis sighed; his shoulders sagged, the weight of the world sitting heavily on his wise, wrinkled face. He shook his head in disgust. "Seventeen years old, no common sense, no high school diploma, and already a second child on the way. Just like her mother. The cycle never ends."

"Does he still report to that juvie officer?" asked Uncle Emerson.

"No. Craig's over eighteen now," said Uncle Francis. "Why?"

"Just an idea," said Uncle Emerson, "but maybe your friend could exert a little pressure on Craig. Get him to agree to have the modeling agency garner part of his wages for Tiffany and her kids."

Uncle Francis' eyes lit up. "He served time for breaking and entering last year and was released on parole a few months ago. I'm sure Sal could find out who his parole officer is. Maybe even get him to agree to help."

Uncle Cal spoke for the first time. His commanding baritone immediately captured the attention of everyone in the room. When he spoke, he sounded like a Supreme Court justice handing down a verdict. And his words were as carefully thought out. "We need a plan, though. Judging from what you've told us, Francis, if the money is simply turned over to Tiffany, it will wind up back in Craig's hands."

The other three uncles nodded in agreement.

"The money should go to pay for job training and day care," I said. "Tiffany needs the skills to help herself."

Uncle Aaron cleared his throat. "I hate to throw a wet blanket on all your good intentions," he said, "but if you do get a portion of Craig's income turned over to Tiffany—and I'm not even sure you can legally do that—you still won't have any control over how the money's spent. Remember the old adage, you can lead a horse to water, but you can't make him drink."

"I prefer another old adage," said Uncle Francis. "Trust in the Lord."

I really loved my uncles. I had no idea whether or not they had the law on their side in this little scheme of theirs, but it didn't matter. They had God in their vestment pockets. Carlos didn't stand a chance.

SEVEN
Jay's Comeuppance and Gottlieb the Bear

The remainder of Christmas week dragged on, each day feeling like a full week. Jay "The Lecher" Steiner found countless opportunities to interrupt me in my cubicle or waylay me in other parts of the office. His behavior grew increasingly obnoxious, even for Jay.

Then I realized that with each conversation, instead of speaking to me, he was talking to my breasts! At first I thought it was my imagination, but as one day spilled over into the next, I became increasingly convinced that imagination had nothing to do with it. The man was definitely ogling me every chance he got.

If he had glued his eyeballs to Crystal, I might have understood it. Crystal dressed provocatively, exposing as much thigh and cleavage as she could get away with, the better to show off her boyfriend's artistic masterpieces. I didn't. Not wanting to encourage the adolescent fantasies of the office boors, I always dressed for work in fairly conservative suits and separates. I kept my blouses buttoned nearly to the neck, my sweaters loose rather than formfitting.

"What is your problem?" I finally screamed at him after he had interrupted me for the fourth time in less than an hour Thursday morning.

"Problem?" he asked, feigning innocence. "I have no problem. As a matter of fact, I'm quite healthy and plan to stay that way, thank you." With that he cocked his head, grinned in the direction of my left breast, and backed out of my cubicle. "See you later, Polly."

"Not if I can help it." After he left, I checked my blouse. I wasn't missing a button. No stain marked an indelicate spot. My breasts weren't engorged; my nipples weren't erect. *What the hell was going on?*

I bumped into Nadine on a trip to the ladies' room before heading out for lunch. "Have you noticed anything odd about Jay's behavior?" I asked.

"You mean more than normal?"

"He keeps staring at my boobs," yelled Crystal from a closed stall.

"Come to think of it," said Nadine, "I have noticed him gawking at my chest a lot lately."

Nadine hid her average figure behind multiple layers. Never warm enough, she constantly complained about the office temperature, even when the rest of us walked around bare-armed and perspiring during summer brown-outs. "Mine, too," I said. "So what's he up to?"

The toilet flushed, and Crystal joined us at the bank of sinks. After giving her hands a cursory rinse, she pulled a mascara wand from her purse and added another thick coat to her lashes. I noticed she now bore a tiny yellow star tattooed on her temple alongside her right eye. I wondered if it was a Christmas present from her boyfriend, the tattoo artist. I also wondered if she had ever read Ray Bradbury's *The Illustrated Man*. Pretty soon Crystal wouldn't have a square inch of unadorned flesh left on her body. "Maybe he's picked up a new fetish," she suggested.

"Can you all of a sudden pick up a fetish?" asked Nadine. "I thought you were born with them, like birth defects." She turned to me for confirmation of her theory.

"I haven't got the faintest idea," I said. "All I know is I'm getting really pissed off."

"Like that's going to do any good." Crystal snorted. "What're you going to do, Polly, file a complaint with Head Lecherous Jerk?"

"Good point," said Nadine. "It's the same old shit, Polly. Ignore it. We all know he's got the maturity of an eight-year-old. He's like my kids. The more I nag, the more they do what I'm nagging them to stop or don't do what I'm nagging them to do."

"I suppose you're right," I said. "I'd still like to know what he's up to, though."

"Maybe nothing," said Nadine. "He's Jay. That's reason enough to act obnoxious."

~*~

When I returned from lunch, I found a copy of *Time* magazine on my keyboard. *Heard you talking earlier. Check out page seventeen*, read the scrawled note on the lime green Post-it attached to the cover. It was signed with only an "A." A for Arlene.

I flipped to page seventeen and found an article titled, *Men Say Goodbye to an Apple a Day; Hello to Lust*. I sat down and read the article, the results of a German research team that claimed ogling a woman's breasts for ten minutes a day could increase the average man's life expectancy by five years. *Better than a daily thirty-minutes workout at the gym for cutting the risk of both stroke and heart disease*, claimed the scientist who headed up the study.

I picked up my phone and dialed Nadine's extension. "Conference in the ladies' room in five minutes," I told her. "Bring Crystal." Then I went off in search of Arlene.

Five minutes later I showed Nadine and Crystal the article in *Time*. "I think it's time we gave Jay a taste of his own medicine."

Crystal literally growled. "Okay, tell me how to rig the laser printer to stun. I promise to aim low. Like maybe about six inches below his belt." She sighted an imaginary semi-automatic. "Pow! Pow!"

Nadine giggled at Crystal's Rambo stance, then turned back to me. "Maybe Polly has a slightly less violent idea in mind. Something that won't land us all in jail, hopefully?"

I laid out my plan.

"Hey, Polly, I'm impressed." Crystal eyed me with a new respect as she lightly punched my upper arm. "I didn't think you had it in you."

I took this as a left-handed compliment but didn't protest. I needed her cooperation. I needed everyone's cooperation and full participation for my plan to work. I told them so. "We all have to agree."

"I'm in," said Nadine.

"Wouldn't miss it for the world," said Crystal.

I turned to Arlene. "You in?"

"I don't know." A deep blush colored her cheeks. "It's kind of embarrassing, don't you think?"

"Yeah, for Jay," said Crystal. "That's the whole God damn point."

"I'm not sure I can do it," admitted Arlene.

"Sure you can," I encouraged her. "You won't be alone. We'll be right beside you."

She took a deep breath, bit down on her lower lip until it turned white, and stared at each of us one at a time. Crystal glared at her; Nadine's eyes begged. I offered her what I hoped she'd take as an encouraging smile. Finally, she nodded. "Okay."

Jay didn't stand a prayer.

~*~

The four of us devised a schedule for a full-frontal attack—pun intended. Every fifteen minutes, round the clock, one of us found an excuse to poke our head into Jay's office. I began the assault. Arlene, Crystal, and Nadine hovered in the corridor, out of sight but not earshot.

"You have a minute, Jay?" I entered his cubicle, a perimeter module three times the size of mine. A Playboy bunny calendar hung on one side of the entrance, placed on the wall opposite the desk. Miss December, wearing little more than a Santa cap and a provocative unspoken invitation on her lips, kept an eye on Jay as he worked. Tacky plastic figurines, many with chauvinistic messages, lined his desk in front of his computer monitor. A window behind the desk looked out on an impressive view of a brick wall. On the narrow sill, out of Jay's view as he worked at his desk, sat a small, cheaply framed photo of his wife and three kids.

"For you, sweetheart, always." Jay smoothed what little hair he had left back with both palms. His face, alight with one of his trademark leers, zoomed in on my chest, but I had blocked his view with a stack of papers I clutched against my body. He frowned almost imperceptibly before motioning me to the chair opposite his desk. "Have a seat."

Instead of taking the offered chair, I rounded his desk and propped my hip against the corner so I could look down on him as I spoke. *Way* down. Using my free hand, I pulled a sheet of paper from my stack and placed it at the edge of his desk. "I'd like to go over some of these figures with you." I leaned over to gain the maximum view of my quarry.

While focusing on his fly, I stole a quick glance up at his face. Jay had followed my gaze to his crotch. His brows knit together. I continued speaking, ignoring his puzzlement and the deepening color that rose from his neck up to his face. "I've been going over the projected budget for the choir directors. Because of their size, I think we need to outsource production of their monthly newsletter in order to maximize our manpower hours."

I waited a moment for Jay to respond. The seconds ticked away. He remained silent, his expression growing from confused to dazed. "Jay?"

"Uh...." Tiny beads of perspiration broke out across his brow.

"Are you listening to me, Jay?" Again, I spoke to his groin.

He uttered a pathetic sounding moan, then clasped his hands tightly over his fly. For the first time in days he spoke to me and not my breasts, but instead of meeting his eyes, I continued to stare into his lap.

"Huh?"

"I want to outsource the newsletter production," I said to his white knuckles. The hard-on he couldn't control pressed his hands upward. I smiled at the movement.

"Whose newsletter?" His voice cracked. A trickle of perspiration made its way from his temple to his jawbone before disappearing under his collar.

I heard a sharp laugh come from the direction of the corridor. I ran the tip of my tongue over my lips. "The choir directors. Are you all right, Jay? You look a bit... uncomfortable."

He pushed his chair back and stood. With shaking hands, he grabbed the edge of his desk, pressing his body into the Formica top. "Um...sure. Fine. Yeah. Okay. That sounds like a good plan." He reached for the sheet of paper I had placed on his desk and held it in front of him like a shield. "I'll check you out."

I played with the top button of my blouse. "You mean you haven't seen enough yet?" Then, I lowered the papers for the first time.

"I mean your figures. I'll check out your figures. Your math."

I wet my lips once more, stood, and headed for the corridor. Pausing at the exit to his cubicle, I turned back. "See you later," I told the bulge in his pants.

~*~

Fifteen minutes later we all gathered outside Jay's office once more as Crystal entered with a question. She came on even stronger than I had. We kept our onslaught up all day, thus keeping Jay up all day.

Whenever one of us heard him leave his office, we followed. He spent a good deal of time in the men's room. We waited at the entrance and tossed him knowing winks when he came out. Sometimes we spoke to him—or rather, his dick. At other times, we merely stared. We sent him pornographic e-mails and got a friend of Crystal's to make anonymous phone-sex calls to him every few hours.

Jay took to walking around with his hands cupping his groin to mask his constant state of arousal, but that only made matters worse. Bob and Sam took notice, and he became the butt of their pubescent sex jokes.

We were relentless. By Friday afternoon, Jay broke. We sat him down in the conference room and forced him to sign a statement swearing he'd never again ogle, touch, tease, or harass us in any way, shape, or form. He already knew the penalty for non-compliance, and he knew the first time he broke the pledge, we'd start all over—with a vengeance.

~*~

"Men are such weaklings," said Nadine. We had decided to celebrate our victory at Grunts and Peons, a trendy midtown bar that catered to the after-work office crowd.

"Yeah," agreed Crystal. She raised a glass in toast. "To Polly for coming up with a brilliant idea." She shook her head and stared at me as if seeing me for the first time. "You really are full of surprises."

I took that as a compliment and clinked my glass of Merlot against her Red Dog. "And to all of you for going along with it. My plan wouldn't have worked without your cooperation."

"I can't remember the last time being at work was so much fun. I'm almost sorry he caved so soon." Nadine turned to Arlene. "And you were magnificent."

"Yeah," agreed Crystal. "Who'd a thunk it."

I smiled at Arlene. She blushed into her whiskey sour, her fingers fidgeting with the stem of the glass. Once she'd overcome her initial trepidation, she dove in like an actress attacking a juicy stage role. And because she was the least likely of all of us to act in such a flagrant manner, her performance had the greatest affect on Jay. "It was fun, wasn't it?"

Probably the only fun poor Arlene had experienced in a long

time.

"Well, I don't think we'll have to put up with any crap from Jay for a while," I said.

"Or any of those other infantile jerks," added Nadine. "I think they all got the message."

"Yeah," said Crystal. "Don't mess with us! We fight dirty." She raised her beer bottle, and we all followed with our glasses.

"And we fight to win," added Arlene. She polished off her drink and slammed the glass onto the table. "Damn, that felt good," she said. "What do we do for an encore?"

I had an idea, but now was not the time to discuss it with her.

~*~

On my way home, I passed Joni a block from our apartment. She rushed by, not seeing me. "Where are you off to in such a hurry?" I yelled, grabbing her arm to stop her. She definitely wasn't dressed for a date. At least not a Joni-type date. She wore a long black herringbone wool skirt under a navy three-quarters stadium coat. A pair of low-heeled suede ankle boots replaced her trademark Manolo Blahniks. Her long blonde hair, normally falling seductively across her face like a nineteen-forties movie star, was pulled back into a sedate bun. On her head, she wore a blue plaid cashmere scarf that crisscrossed at her neck, the ends tucked into her coat. And although I couldn't be certain, because the sun had set and she ran off so quickly, I could swear she wore no makeup. I almost didn't recognize her.

"I'm late for something." She wriggled out of my grasp. "Talk to you later."

"Stay out of trouble," I called after her. Which was like telling a Manhattan rat to stay out of the curbside trash.

~*~

The next day Joni came downstairs to help me root through my closet in search of the perfect outfit for my date with Jeremy. As I tried on one ensemble after another, I told her about my vicarious emasculation of Jay Steiner. Her eyes blazed with delight. She flopped onto my unmade bed. "Now you finally get it."

I stared at my image in the full-length closet mirror, shook my head, and started stripping—for the seventeenth time. "Get what?" I stepped out of the wine-colored velvet princess dress. "Too fancy," I muttered, tossing it onto an ever-growing pile of discarded clothes that littered my bed and spilled over onto the floor.

"The power high! It's all about control." She planned a little control of her own this evening with a trip to Holland Tube. Or as she put it, she intended to bust a few Carlos balls in case his tightly clad ass dared to show up at the club. "There's no other rush like it."

She had a point. Arlene's transformation from Tillie Titmouse to Xena, Princess Warrior, was proof enough of that. "Speaking of control," I asked, "what exactly are you planning to do tonight? I thought we promised to leave Carlos to my uncles."

"No reason why I can't help God and his earthly servants, is there?" Her voice sounded far too sweet and innocent, and she spoke while folding one of the sweaters I'd rejected and tossed on my bed. Joni wasn't into folding her own clothes half the time, let alone mine.

I almost felt sorry for Carlos. Almost but not quite. In truth, I hoped he did show up, and Joni made him squirm. Literally. As far as I knew, Jay only cheated in his head and with his words. Carlos cheated with his mouth.

His tongue.

His hands.

And other parts of his body I didn't want to think about.

"So where were you off to in such a rush last night?" Anything to change the subject and get my mind away from Carlos and his various body parts.

Joni scooted off the bed. Turning her back to me, she placed the sweater in my open bureau drawer and began folding another. "I'm taking a course. I didn't want to be late for the first night of class."

Throughout grad school, Joni had complained she couldn't wait to finish and never intended to set foot in another classroom for the rest of her life. She wasn't exactly what you'd call the scholarly type, even if she'd never received less than an A in any subject. Joni and Mitch's seed supplier must have been a pretty bright guy because his offspring were near-geniuses. And we all knew they didn't inherit *that* trait from Rainbow. "Interesting. In what?"

"Um, just some technical garbage for work. Boring, really. Computer crap, mostly."

I didn't press, but I also didn't believe her. I'd known Joni too long. She was definitely up to something.

After trying on nearly every piece of clothing in my wardrobe, I finally settled on a calf-length flared camelhair skirt and an ivory shaker knit sweater that I accessorized with a thin gold chain necklace and hoop earrings. I had no idea where Jeremy planned to take me for dinner, but knowing his financial situation, I doubted he'd chosen anything four star. At least, I hoped he hadn't.

Joni scowled at my outfit. "You look like you just stepped off the pages of a Talbot catalog."

"So what's wrong with that?"

"Nothing if you're on your way to a Junior League tea or a PTA meeting. At least wear my Manolo alligator sandals."

"In thirty-three degree weather? Thanks but no thanks. I'm wearing my brown suede boots."

"That's the trouble with you, Polly. You're too damn practical."

"Maybe so but at least my toes won't turn blue from frostbite."

She glanced at my clock radio. "Well, I'm out of here." She skirted around several heaps of clothing and headed for the door. "Have fun. I expect a full report tomorrow."

~*~

As I began straightening up my bedroom, I looked forward to an enjoyable evening. Me. Jeremy. A quiet little bistro somewhere in Little Italy, maybe. A bottle of wine. A hot embrace. An even hotter kiss....

The outer doorbell rang, tearing me from my reverie. I dashed into the bathroom and gave myself a spritz of Blue Rhapsody before hurrying to the living room to buzz him in. A moment later he knocked at my apartment door.

I swung open the door. I was expecting Jeremy. I got the shock of my life. "My God, it's a bear!"

Jeremy laughed. "No bear. Just Gottlieb."

The bear—and it was a bear, no matter what Jeremy said— charged. A moment later, I was flat on my back, pinned by a monster with bad breath. Nose to big black ugly nose, we eyed each other. Enormous hairy paws pinned my shoulders to the floor. He lowered his head and sniffed me, dragging his big black, cold, wet, ugly nose against my skin. I shuddered with fear. Drool spilled from the corners of his mouth and trickled down my neck.

I cringed.

He yelped.

I yelled.

Then he opened his mouth and attacked my face with a huge slurping tongue. "Yuck! Get him off me!"

"Gottlieb, sit!"

He did. Right on my chest.

"Not there, you crazy mutt. Here." Jeremy yanked at the behemoth's collar, freeing me of its weight.

I gulped in a lungful of air and clambered to my feet. Steadying myself against the door jamb, my adrenaline pounding, I first glared at my attacker and then his master. My mouth opened, but the words refused to come out.

"I guess Gottlieb got a little carried away." Jeremy's face broke out in a sheepish grin. He chuckled. "I think he likes that perfume you're wearing."

Great! Wait until Mom finds out the pheromones in Blue Rhapsody drive four-legged animals wild.

Jeremy's expression grew sober when I continued to glare daggers at him. I suppose he expected me to laugh along with him, but I found nothing funny about the situation. "Are you all right?" he finally asked.

"For someone who's just been mauled by a bear? Sure. I'm fine. Wet but fine." I swiped at my cheek with the sleeve of my sweater. Instead of wiping away goop, I only succeeded in plastering bristly black and brown hairs to my skin—the same bristly black and brown hairs that now covered my sweater.

I glanced down. My skirt had fared no better. Three hours planning what to wear, dressing, doing my hair and makeup—all destroyed in one fell swoop by a two-hundred-pound slobbering giant. I grimaced at Jeremy and pointed to the monster at his feet. "That *thing* could have killed me!"

"Nah." He bent down and wrapped his arm around the beast in question. "Gottlieb's as gentle as a lamb. He just got a little excited over meeting you."

"Exactly what *is* Gottlieb, and why is he here?"

"Jeez, Polly, he's only a dog. Two parts St. Bernard. One part Mastiff. One part Newfoundland."

I eyed the ursine monster in question. No way was Gottlieb *only* a dog. "And four parts bear," I added, tossing a scowl in the culprit's direction. He responded with a slap of his tail that reverberated along the planks of my hardwood floor.

"I'm sorry," Jeremy repeated. "He's been cooped up a lot with my schedule the way it is. And besides, I wanted you to meet him. Once you get to know him, you'll love him." He ruffled the dog's fur. "Won't she, boy?"

Gottlieb barked. Again, his tail pounded the floor, this time with enough force to rattle the dishes on my drain board. *Highly unlikely.*

I don't dislike dogs, but Gottlieb—no matter what Jeremy claimed—was no dog. Horse maybe. Whatever, the animal belonged on a farm or in a zoo, not a New York apartment. "I need to change." I indicated towards the drool and dog hair that covered my face, my sweater and my skirt.

"Take your time," said Jeremy. "We'll make ourselves at home."

"Don't get too comfortable," I told the dog as I passed him on the way to my bedroom. Gottlieb lowered his head onto his paws and whimpered.

Jeremy stroked his fur. "She didn't mean to hurt your feelings, boy." Both dog and master looked up at me with pleading eyes.

Oh, brother! This wasn't turning into the romantic date I'd envisioned. I stripped off my skirt and sweater and dumped them in a corner with the rest of the clothes for the dry cleaner.

Jeremy had arrived in a pair of jeans and a blue hound's tooth check flannel shirt. I guess I didn't have to worry about dressing for dinner. I pulled the jeans I'd worn earlier out of the hamper, grabbed a clean knit turtleneck and headed for the bathroom to recomb my hair and wash the slobber off my face and neck.

I returned to the living room to find Jeremy and Gottlieb curled up on my sofa. Remote in hand, Jeremy flipped through the channels on the TV. Gottlieb chewed the corner of one of Mom's needlepoint pillows—the one that read, *Welcome Friends*. I snatched it out of his mouth. "The sentiment doesn't apply to beasts."

Gottlieb growled his disappointment.

Jeremy ignored the interplay between me and his monster. His attention was riveted to a sports commentary on CNN. I reached over, grabbed the remote out of his hands, and switched off the television.

"Ready?" he asked. He jumped to his feet. Gottlieb followed, tipping over my coffee table in the process.

So much for the crystal Christmas bowl Uncle Cal had given me only four days earlier.

Jeremy gaped in horror at the pile of broken glass scattered among the pinecones I had placed in the bowl. "I hope that wasn't expensive."

I frowned at the remains of my gift and sighed. "No, it's only Lalique."

"Oh, good."

I rolled my eyes and shook my head. Someone had once told me you can tell a lot about a man by the way he treats his mother. I was quickly learning you can also tell a lot about a man by the pet he keeps and how he relates to it. My high hopes for any relationship with Jeremy were crumbling faster than a stale muffin. "Let's go. I'll clean it up later." I wanted to leave before Gottlieb the Bull-in-a-China-Shop-Dog did any further damage to either me or my apartment.

"I thought we'd have dinner at Hound Dog Café," said Jeremy as we stepped out into the chill night.

"I've never heard of it."

He directed me over to a chartreuse Volkswagen beetle parked in front of a fire plug. "I've got three hundred thousand miles on this baby," he bragged, noting the astonishment on my face.

"Impressive," I muttered. "My parents had one back in their hippie days, I believe." Actually, I could have cared less about the age of the rust-pocked car. I was more concerned as to how he planned to squeeze the three of us into it.

Jeremy unlocked the door and moved the passenger seat forward. "In you go, boy." Gottlieb jumped in, taking up every square inch of the small backseat. His upper body blocked most of the tiny elliptical rear window. His head skimmed the roof. Jeremy replaced the seat and held the door for me. "Your turn."

Once we pulled away from the curb, Gottlieb leaned forward. He placed a huge paw on the back of each bucket seat and sandwiched his head between the small space separating my seat from Jeremy's. Hot doggie breath hit me like a blast of air from a sidewalk subway vent. Jeremy reached over and scratched Gottlieb's head. The dog yapped his pleasure in my left ear. Doggie drool dribbled down the sleeve of my coat.

Gottlieb was in heaven.

I was in hell.

"Why Gottlieb?" I asked as we headed uptown. I really didn't care about the dog's name, but I knew if I didn't tamp down my anger and engage Jeremy in small talk, I'd wind up giving him a piece of my mind. And at present my mind was filled with every expletive in the book. "That's a very unusual name for a dog."

"I named him after a neighbor that lived next door to us when I was a kid. The moment I saw Gottlieb, he reminded me of Mrs. Gottlieb."

"She was a big, fat, ugly drooler?" I asked.

Jeremy glanced over at me. The passing streetlights reflected the hurt in his eyes. "She was lovable and kind. Every year she baked gingerbread houses for all of the kids on the block."

A little voice inside me suggested I shouldn't continue to disparage Gottlieb in front of his master. Given a choice between the dog or me, I had a feeling which Jeremy would choose. And it wouldn't take him a New York minute to decide.

Which brought me to another decision—one I hated to make but knew *I* had no choice. I couldn't compete with the hairy, four-legged beast breathing down my neck. Tonight was the beginning and end of my relationship with Jeremy Chadwin.

~*~

Having come to that conclusion, I merely shrugged when we arrived at our destination, and Gottlieb followed us into Hound Dog Café.

I expected an Elvis-themed restaurant. Silly me. Hound Dog Café catered to dog lovers and their companions. A cacophony of woofs, barks, and yelps mingled in the air along with people-talk. Dog posters lined the walls. In each of the four corners, wide screen televisions alternately played the spaghetti scene from *Lady and the Tramp* and various clips from *Lassie*, *Rin Tin Tin*, *Scooby Doo*, *A Hundred and One Dalmatians*, and several other movies and television shows I didn't recognize.

The larger dogs ate from dishes placed on the floor, but many of the smaller dogs sat on chairs, joining their human counterparts to eat at the table. Some wore napkins wrapped around their necks like bibs on a baby, their masters fussing over them as if they were children.

The host led us to a table at the far end of the restaurant. "Isn't this a great place?" asked Jeremy. He nodded a greeting to several other diners as we passed.

"Definitely unique."

"No, actually, there are quite a few restaurants throughout the city that now cater to four-legged family members. Gottlieb likes the menu here best, though." We took our seats. Gottlieb settled his huge rump on the floor between us and leaned his black jowls on the plastic tablecloth. I inched my chair away from him.

The way Jeremy coddled his dog, I shuddered to think how he'd raise his kids. Then I remembered all the spoiled brat offspring of the psychologists I knew. No, Jeremy and I definitely had no future.

The butterflies he initially produced in my stomach had morphed to queasy green worms. From the corner of my eye, I watched as Gottlieb drooled on the table and wondered how I was ever going to keep my dinner down.

Ten minutes later, when our food arrived and the mutt dove into his platter of kibble burgers, I knew I couldn't. "I'm sorry," I pushed my plate aside, threw my napkin onto the table, and rose. "I can't do this."

Jeremy stared across the table at me, his forkful of T-bone poised halfway to his open mouth. "Are you feeling ill, Polly? Do you need to go home?"

I grabbed my coat off the back of my chair and slipped into it. "This is all perfectly normal to you, isn't it?"

"What?"

I waved my arms to encompass the room. "This. People and dogs eating together."

"What's wrong with it?"

"Everything!" I shook my head. "Look you're a nice guy, but this isn't normal, and I can't deal with it."

"Polly, sit down, please. Let's talk this over."

"There's nothing to talk about, Jeremy."

"You're willing to walk out on a relationship before it ever has a chance to get off the ground?"

"We don't stand a prayer of a chance." I stabbed a finger in the air towards Gottlieb. "Not with your obsessive attachment to that...that slobbering beast."

The culprit in question pricked his ears, raised his head, and yowled at the insult. Jeremy reached over and patted his head, murmuring soothing words until Gottlieb turned his attention back to his food.

Jeremy speared me with a glare. "Maybe you're the one with the problem. A hatred of animals is often a sign of more deep-seated problems."

"Is that your professional opinion, Dr. Chadwin?"

"It's your hang-up, not mine."

"I see." I swung my purse over my shoulder. "Well, I obviously failed your little psychological test this evening. Maybe you should consider becoming a dog psychologist because you certainly respond better to animals than you do people. Have a good life."

I turned and marched out of the restaurant without a glance back. Jeremy made no effort to stop me. I didn't expect him to.

In all honesty, I couldn't blame Jeremy completely. I thought back to our first meeting and all the early signs I chose to overlook—his initial antagonistic tone, his later pushiness. And then there was his chosen profession. I should know to stay away from shrinks and almost-shrinks. We're like oil and water.

It's not that I have anything against therapy. I know there are many people who benefit by it. I just hope I'm one who never needs it, because in my experience, I've yet to meet a therapist who wasn't as screwed up as his patients.

So maybe I'm not a dog person. Or any type of pet person, for that matter. Does that make me a bad person? I don't think so. And I resent being made to feel like I'm one by a man who treats his dog like a human. That, in my mind, is sick. And downright creepy.

I walked to the corner and hailed a cab. The driver wore a turban. I glanced at his license. Abdullah Bin Ibram. No highbrow texts littered the floor or front passenger seat. With a welcome and much needed sense of normality surrounding me, I gave Abdullah my address and settled back for the ride downtown.

The taxi pulled up to the curb in front of my apartment building at the same time Mitch rounded the corner. He waved a greeting, then waited at the bottom of the steps while I paid my fare. "I thought you had a big date tonight."

"I struck out."

"Me, too." We started up the steps. "She told me we lacked chemistry."

I gave him a playful punch to his shoulder. "You're not losing your touch, are you, Mitch?"

"Nah." He reached into his pocket for his keys. "We had plenty of chemistry up until this evening." He unlocked the outer door and held it open for me.

I stepped into the small lobby. A welcoming blast of heat from the cast-iron steam radiator greeted me. "So what happened?"

"There was this big shot Hollywood producer at the party we were attending." He shrugged. "Need I go on?"

"At least you lost her to another guy. I lost out to a mutt—the biggest, ugliest mutt that ever walked the face of the earth."

Mitch draped an arm over my shoulder. "Want to talk about it?"

I nodded. I really needed a friend at the moment, and Mitch was one of the best friends I'd ever had. "He seemed so nice. So normal."

"They always seem normal at first, then you get to know them."

"Maybe I should have Mom needlepoint that on a pillow for me." I stepped out of Mitch's embrace to unlock my door. "I think I need a constant reminder."

"We all do from time to time." He stepped across the threshold and immediately zeroed in on the broken crystal and pinecones still scattered across the floor. "What happened here?"

"Gottlieb. A four-pawed giant monster. I'll bet he even lets that hairy beast sleep in his bed!" I shivered at the thought. And to think hours earlier I'd fantasized about my own naked body snuggled under the covers beside Jeremy. "I'm not into threesomes, thank you very much! Or bestiality." I grabbed a couple of magazines off the floor and used one to scoop the broken glass and pinecones onto the other.

Mitch bent down to help, carefully picking up the larger chunks of glass and the pinecones. "He wanted you to have sex with his dog?"

I might have laughed if I weren't so hurt and angry. "I don't think Jeremy's *that* sick, but who knows? The way he treated that monster, anything's possible."

I stormed across the room to the kitchen area and dumped the remains of my Lalique bowl into the trash. Mitch followed, adding his handful of jagged chunks. "I really liked that bowl." We both stood over the trash can and stared down at the remains of my Christmas present.

"Maybe you can find a replacement."

"Yeah, and maybe at the same time I can shop around for another guy who will only wind up breaking my heart and not my crystal."

Mitch hugged me. My stomach rumbled. "You didn't eat, did you?"

"I tried, but I guess I'm too much of a princess. I sort of lost my appetite when Jeremy's dog joined us at the table." I yanked open the refrigerator door and surveyed the contents. Four near-empty shelves stared back at me. "Have you eaten?"

"You mean you actually have something edible in there?" He bent over my shoulder and peered into the fridge. "Hmm. How old is this?" He reached in and withdrew a poorly wrapped, package of cheese. Fuzzy green mold dotted its surface. "I don't think so." He tossed the cheese into the trash. "Let's go to my place. I'm not up for a trip to the ER tonight."

~*~

Mitch and I were still talking when Joni dragged herself into their apartment a little after two in the morning. "Looks like someone had a good time tonight," said Mitch.

She hugged her arms around her chest and offered us a dreamy smile. "Hmm."

"Did you see Carlos?" I asked.

She kicked off her shoes, flopped down on the sofa, and tucked her legs under her. "He never showed. The scummy coward."

"Meet someone new?" I asked.

Joni shook her head.

I turned to Mitch. "Do you get the impression she's being deliberately evasive here?"

Mitch eyed his sister. "Definitely."

"Well, I'm glad at least one of us didn't strike out tonight," I said.

Joni's eyes grew wide. "What happened, Pol?"

"Reason Number Thirteen. Never go out with a guy who brings his dog along on the first date."

"He didn't!"

"He certainly did." I then proceeded to tell Joni about Gottlieb the hairy Bear-dog, the chewed pillow, the broken Lalique bowl, and Hound Dog Café. "And the creep actually had the audacity to accuse *me* of having a problem!"

"At least you found out right away. Think how much worse you'd feel if he hadn't brought the monster around until after the fourth or fifth date."

"I suppose." I knew Joni was only trying to make me feel better, but it didn't help. I stood and yawned. "I think I need to go to bed. It's already tomorrow."

"Which uncle do you visit tomorrow?" she asked.

"None. Five Sundays this month. I'm sleeping in."

"Why don't we all go out for a late brunch?" suggested Mitch.

"Sounds like a plan." I hugged them both. "Who needs anyone else, right?"

"Right," said Mitch. "We have each other."

As I headed back downstairs, I realized that Joni hadn't offered any words of agreement to Mitch's declaration.

EIGHT
The Seven-Minute Date Craze

Einstein had it all wrong. Time is neither relative, nor a constant. Had he participated in speed dating, his theories would never have seen the light of day.

Every year Uncle Emerson's congregation holds a gala ball and charity benefit on New Year's Eve. One of his congregants is a trustee of the Metropolitan Museum of Art. Somehow, this resourceful man manages to reserve the Temple of Dendur for the event each year—without paying the hefty rental fee. No one knows how. No one dares to ask too many questions.

For the first time in years I didn't have a date for the evening. Neither did Mitch, having recently been dumped for the Hollywood producer. We decided to go together.

Joni preferred attending stag. "You never know who you might meet," she said. "Why be hampered by a guy on your arm when there's a much more interesting specimen standing across the room?"

It was hard to argue with her logic, but I wasn't as outgoing as she. I liked the security of a guy on my arm, even if he was a friend and not a lover.

Apparently, Joni had no trouble finding a plethora of interesting specimens that night, because once the three of us arrived, Mitch and I immediately lost track of her.

A gathering such as this attracts the New York *in* crowd. Media moguls and network broadcast journalists rub elbows with dot.com billionaires—the few that are left—, Wall Street gurus, Broadway stars, single-name-only models, Hollywood queens, dethroned queens, gossip queens, and drag queens.

Normal topics of conversation heard around the pool range from local politics to recent vacations on private islands to who's sleeping with whom or who recently checked in or checked out of the Betty Ford Clinic and who else was there. However, this year many of the conversations revolved around The Seven-Minute Date, the Manhattan version of speed dating.

After my recent string of bad luck with the opposite sex, I had to admit, the idea held a certain appeal. But could you really get to know someone in only seven minutes?

I thought about all the blind dates I'd endured over the last decade or so, going all the way back to junior high when Mom got a call out of the blue one day from her old college roommate. She'd married a man with a son from a former marriage—a son just my age.

His name was Jerry Kronrott. He was short and fat, with ears that stuck out from his head and a face covered with acne. He lived and breathed *Star Trek*. Of course, his new stepmother failed to mention any of this to Mom when the two of them decided I should invite Jerry to the ninth grade Harvest Dance.

I refused to speak to Mom for a full week afterwards and still won't date anyone who watches *Star Trek* reruns. Seven minutes with Jerry Kronrott would have been six minutes and fifty-nine seconds too long, but definitely preferable to spending an entire evening with him.

So when Uncle Emerson approached me at the buffet table, I listened with interest.

"What do you think about this Seven-Minute Date thing?" he asked.

"Do I look that desperate?"

"No, of course not." But I noticed he didn't look at me as he spoke, a sure sign of a pastoral lie. "I want to try it at the church. I thought maybe you could help me?"

"Sure, why not?"

According to the buzz making its way around the room, the entire concept started with a rabbi and the singles group at his synagogue. Apparently, I wasn't the only unattached person in Manhattan turned off by trying to meet someone online or at a club or bar. And forget about workplace romance. I wasn't into lecherous jerks.

So what else did that leave? Espresso bars? Contrary to popular fiction and television sitcoms, most coffee houses in Manhattan were frequented by out-of-work gay actors, nannies with their charges, caffeine-addicted teeny-boppers, and the already-attached on their way to or from the nearest health club. Those of us who lived in The Big Apple knew that *Friends* existed only in TV reruns.

What did I have to lose? As Mom constantly reminded me, my healthy egg producing days were numbered and my womb was shrinking at an alarming rate—at least alarming in her over-reactive mind. No doubt, she had formed a pact with my gynecologist to secure this information.

Although I didn't think nearly thirty-two was the same as one foot in the grave, I had to keep reminding myself that Mom came from the don't-trust-anyone-over-thirty generation, even if she had passed the big three-uh-oh herself long ago. Amazing how she tended to forget that minor fact—along with most of her other youthful indiscretions.

"What did you have in mind?" Mitch asked Uncle Emerson as the three of us wandered off in search of an empty table.

I was surprised by his interest. Mitch never had any trouble getting dates, but maybe he, too, was growing frustrated with the whole dating game crapshoot. His last few girlfriends hadn't remained around much beyond the getting-to-know-you stage. Sometimes they walked. Sometimes Mitch walked. He always shrugged it off, though. After all, guys liked playing the field and dreaded getting tied down, right?

Or maybe that was simply another urban legend, a myth men perpetrated for fear of revealing their true feelings. That Y chromosome was a sneaky little bugger, after all. I glanced over at him. Did a hearth-and-home guy lurk behind that playboy mask of his?

Both Joni and Mitch worked hard at downplaying their unorthodox upbringing. Shunted back and forth between communes and reluctant relatives most of their lives, they'd never known a normal childhood, but neither ever complained about it. And somehow they both survived to become sane, productive members of society with very few hang-ups, considering the odds against them.

Mom thought otherwise, though. That was why she'd taken them under her wing. For all her quirkiness, my mother had an uncanny knack for knowing when someone needs rescuing and nurturing. She'd swooped down on Joni and Mitch the moment she met them. Neither had complained.

According to Mimi Harmony, self-proclaimed expert on everything, both Joni and Mitch needed to find the right life partner and settle down. For that matter, so did I, as Mom constantly reminded me. But whereas her edicts concerning my love life—or lack of it, as she was prone to point out—ran the risk of turning into a hostile war of words between us, her commentaries about Joni and Mitch produced no such rancor. That was because she never forced them to listen to her diatribes —only me.

When I questioned her on this, she told me it was the price I paid for her genes. Mimi believed she didn't have the right to lecture anyone who didn't swim in her own genetic soup. Lucky me. I was compelled to doggie paddle my way through well-meaning advice on a near-daily basis.

I tried to picture Joni-the-Free-Spirited-Nymph presiding over a toddler play date in a Westchester colonial. My imagination didn't stretch that far. On the other hand, as I stole another glance in Mitch's direction, I found it less difficult to conjure up an image of him pushing a jogging stroller along a path in Central Park. For all her busybody manipulations, maybe Mom had it at least half right.

As we ate, Uncle Emerson laid out his plan. "We can advertise at places where singles go," he said. "Put flyers up at gyms, bookstores, coffee houses."

"Laundromats in upscale neighborhoods," I suggested. "Most

singles don't have washers and dryers. And don't forget Facebook and Twitter."

"Good ideas."

"How will you control the numbers?" asked Mitch. "You could wind up with way too many people, and what if you get half a dozen women all in their early to mid-twenties and forty-seven male septuagenarians? This could turn into a logistical nightmare."

"We limit the ages and require a pre-registration," said Uncle Emerson.

Mitch nodded. "Could work."

"It's working all over town," said Uncle Emerson. He waved his arms to encompass all of Dendur. "We could host a series of evenings. Different age groups for each." He winked at me. "Who knows? Maybe we'll even get our little Polly married off this way."

I sputtered into my glass of champagne. "Well, thank you very much. So you've crossed over to the enemy's camp, I see. Is there anyone along the Eastern seaboard Mom hasn't recruited in her effort to find me a husband?"

"I believe there's a guy up in Bangor, Maine she hasn't been able to reach yet," said Mitch. "I understand he doesn't have a telephone."

I scowled at him. "Very funny. How about if we find someone for you, and what about you?" I asked, turning to Uncle Emerson.

"Actually, I was considering a gay Seven-Minute Date night." He said this with a completely straight face. I knew he was serious. He'd been in a committed relationship for many years until his partner died suddenly from a massive heart attack last year. His voice grew distant, his eyes watery. "But not for me. I'm just not ready to move on yet, Polly."

I patted his hand. "I understand." Everyone in the family missed Arthur.

He placed a hand on top of mine. Three of my four uncles had suffered great losses over the past few years. Seven years ago Uncle Aaron lost Aunt Harriet to cancer. Two years later, Uncle Cal lost Aunt June to a drunk driver running a red light. Last year it was "Uncle" Arthur. Only Uncle Francis, by virtue of his celibate status, had gone unscathed, but that hadn't diminished the anguish he suffered over the losses of his "brothers." When one of my uncles grieved, they all grieved.

Uncle Emerson recovered quickly, shrugging off his sorrow and planting a smile on his face. "We should plan for Valentine's Day," he said. "That's such a depressing day for so many in my flock."

I could relate to that. Valentine's Day. Never in the history of mankind had the merchants of America banded together in all their perverse glory to inflict so much pain on so many innocent souls whose only sin was to be dateless on February fourteenth.

My own hatred of Valentine's Day dates back beyond the Ryan Fitzpatrick fiasco in fifth grade. It goes all the way back to kindergarten when my constant nemesis, Regina Koltzner, received twice as many valentines in her decorated shoe box as I did in mine.

In hindsight, I'm certain she stuffed her box with cards of her own making since she also wound up with twice as many valentines as anyone else in the class. However, this logic escaped my five-year-old brain, especially since I was the only one Regina ever bothered to tease.

Throughout my adult life, I've spent more than my share of Valentine's Day evenings curled up with a movie rental and a carton of Chinese takeout, reliving my many Valentine's Day humiliations. At least these days I have a Netflix subscription and can avoid the embarrassment of joining the other losers lined up in the Blockbuster checkout line.

Frankly, I can think of no finer justice than lining up every florist and Hallmark retailer in the country in front of a firing squad of archers. Let them suffer the same death as the holiday's namesake.

"I don't know," I said, coming back to the topic at hand. "Isn't sponsoring a Seven-Minute Date on Valentine's Day a bit like rubbing salt in a wound?"

"What do you mean?" asked Uncle Emerson.

"You might as well call it The Seven-Minute Date for Losers. You're reinforcing the fact that here it is Valentine's Day, and they don't have a date."

"Is that how you see yourself, Polly? A loser?"

I stared at him. His lined face and soft hazel eyes held nothing but concern, but I hated when Uncle Emerson put on his counseling cap. I turned to Mitch for validation. "You know what I mean, don't you?"

"I understand what you're saying," he said, "but I don't think it's necessarily true. We could put a positive spin on it."

"How?"

"By playing up the fact that we know these people are choosy, like you, Polly. Not losers." He offered me a wink and a grin.

"Damn right, I'm choosy." I slammed my hand on the table and stuck my tongue out like a five-year-old at Uncle Emerson. "So there! Stuff that in your therapy hat."

Uncle Emerson leaned back in his chair, folded his hands across his chest, and smiled one of those damn therapist smiles as if to ask, *And how does that make you feel?*

I lifted my glass and growled into my champagne. Counting to ten, I reminded myself that he was my uncle, he meant well, and I loved him. I just wished he, along with the rest of my well-meaning family, would stop trying to marry me off. "You know, there's no crime in being single," I told him.

"Did I say there was?"

I growled again. Then, to add insult to injury, my mother came marching over to our table.

Other than a brief greeting once we arrived, I had managed to avoid Mom, Dad, and the rest of my uncles all evening. The Temple of Dendur was pretty much standing room only, and it was easy to hide behind all the Armani tuxedos and sequined Versace gowns. My luck, apparently, had run out.

"What are you two young people doing sitting there in a corner? Get up! Go mingle!" She turned her attention to Uncle Emerson. "You're not helping."

"Actually, Mimi, I was."

"What? By hiding them out of sight?" Her voice grew loud and shrill. Several people nearby turned to stare at her. "At this rate I'll never get grandchildren!"

"You'd better go find my father," I whispered to Mitch. Mom had gone off the deep end—again. There was only one way to bring her back to reality—shock treatment.

I stood and confronted her. "I'll tell you what, Mom. If that's all you care about, why don't you go pick out someone for me." I waved my arm at the crowded room. "Doesn't matter whom. I'll take him home, screw his balls off, and nine months from now, you'll have a grandchild."

"Polly Faith Harmony!" Mom turned a deep reddish-purple.

Behind her, Uncle Emerson fought to stifle a belly laugh.

I smiled sweetly. "Yes?"

"That's disgusting!"

I grabbed a glass of champagne from a passing waiter and handed it to her. "Chill, Mom. I was only kidding."

Her scowl told me she doubted my words. I didn't care. She had it coming. The day Mimi entered menopause, she'd ceased to think of me as a daughter. Now I was only a grandchild incubator.

I suppose I shouldn't have been so harsh. Mom was going through a rough period. Her raging hormones exacerbated her normally high-maintenance, but usually lovable, personality. I wished I weren't an only child. It would have been nice to have a few siblings to share the burden right now. I wrapped my arms around her and kissed her cheek. "I'm sorry, Mom. You know I love you."

"I know." She sniffed and kissed me back. "And you know I love you, too, don't you? I'm only thinking of your happiness, dear. I hate seeing you alone."

"I know." I wasn't too keen on being alone, either, but now was not the time to admit that to my mother. She might grab the mike from the emcee and start auctioning me off to the highest bidder.

And people at my office wondered why I didn't work in the family business.

~*~

With the onset of the new year, Mitch and I set about helping Uncle Emerson organize his Valentine's Day Seven-Minute Date extravaganza. I did so with mixed feelings, uncertain what to expect from such an event or how I'd react to my various blind *dates*.

Mitch, on the other hand, dived in headfirst, enjoying every step of the planning phase, no matter how small or tedious. He looked on the event as a great adventure—one he fully anticipated enjoying. Or so he said. Numerous times.

Too many times, come to think of it.

I began to suspect that much of his enthusiasm was for my benefit. Had he taken Uncle Emerson's quip about marrying me off to heart? Mitch didn't need a Seven-Minute Date to find eligible women. His track record proved that. Yet, he devoted every available hour to making certain Uncle Emerson's event was a smashing success. For me?

Joni chose not to join us. "Sounds awfully forced, if you ask me."

Mitch and I were sitting side-by-side at his computer, designing a flyer for the event. Joni was on her way out. For a change. "Besides, guys are going to tell you what they think you want to hear no matter where you meet them. It's no different than sitting down next to someone at a bar. Everyone's looking for the same thing."

"Says cynical you."

"Come on, Pol. At least at a bar you can get up and leave after a minute or two if the guy drools in his beer. With this kind of setup, you've got to stick around and smile for seven minutes."

I nursed a glass of Cabernet. "Some of us are looking for more than only a quick lay."

Joni smirked as she stopped at the desk and grabbed the glass out of my hand. "I never said I wanted it quick. Where's the fun in that?" She helped herself to a long sip before handing the glass back to me and heading for the door. "Anyway, you've already experienced a drooling dog, and I have better things to do with my time than interview a bunch of losers."

Mitch and I turned from the monitor and glared at her over our shoulders. "Present company excepted, of course," she added with a chuckle.

"Of course. And exactly where have you been spending all your free time lately?" asked her brother. "Polly and I hardly ever see you any more."

Joni and I normally crashed after work in her apartment or mine at least three times a week, but I'd barely seen her since before Christmas. What I hadn't realized was that apparently, neither had her brother.

"I've been busy."

"Doing what?"

"Things." She grabbed her purse and coat. "Gotta run." With that she was out the door.

"What's going on with her?" I asked Mitch.

"Beats me. She's been acting weird for weeks."

"Define weird."

He thought for a moment. "Not like Joni. I can't explain it."

Neither could I, but I had to agree with him. Joni wasn't acting at all like Joni. "You have any idea where she runs off to every night?"

Mitch shrugged. "I don't think it's a club or anything. Not the way she's dressed."

I had noticed Joni's change of wardrobe. Wild had given way to sedate. She wore her skirts longer, her shoes flatter. Loose turtlenecks had replaced tight plunging necklines. She'd swapped her dramatic makeup for a freshly scrubbed, ingénue look. Frankly, I thought she looked terrific. She just didn't look like Joni.

"Do you think she's met someone?" I asked.

"If she has, she's keeping him a big secret. I'll tell you one thing, though, wherever she goes, she's usually back early and hasn't brought a guy home since before Christmas."

There was only one explanation. The theme from *The Twilight Zone* echoed in my head as the thought took hold. "That's not Joni. Joni Hughes, my good friend and your sister, had been abducted by space aliens and replaced by a poorly cloned imitation."

Mitch grabbed the glass of wine out of my hand. "That's it. You're flagged."

~*~

Mitch and I weren't able to convince Joni to join us, but I wasn't going to take no for an answer from Arlene. I had decided to make her my New Year's project. Instead of sitting around bemoaning the sorry state of my own love life, I planned to concentrate on dragging Arlene out of her self-imposed exile from life. After all, I wasn't Mimi Harmony's daughter for nothing. Those rescuing genes of Mom's swam laps in my genetic pool, as well.

With Arlene, though, I knew I'd have to employ a bit of reverse psychology if I were going to get her to agree to participate in The Seven-Minute Date.

I started by inviting her to lunch the next day.

"I need your help," I told her as we headed for a local deli around the corner from our office. The place was known for two things—not having changed its décor in over four decades and its nasty employees, but the sandwiches were decent and the prices reasonable. For Manhattan.

As we hurried down the street, the January wind whipped at my back and nipped at my exposed cheeks. "Damn, it's cold," I muttered.

"Is it Jay again?" she asked.

"No." I yanked open the deli door. Welcoming warmth and a surly hostess bundled in several bulky sweaters greeted us. I waited until we were seated and the hostess had handed us our menus before continuing. "This is personal."

I knew Arlene still felt awkward over her breakdown in the ladies' room and subsequent confession to me. I saw it in her eyes whenever we interacted. I was privy to a deep, dark secret of hers, and that made her anxious. I had no doubt it even caused her sleepless nights. I had to win her confidence and convince her that I would never divulge her secret to anyone. Maybe by disclosing a deep, dark secret of my own, I could even the playing field. I also hoped it would get her to accept my invitation.

"How can I help you?"

"Have you ever heard of The Seven-Minute Date?"

Arlene nodded. "I saw something about it on one of the morning news shows."

A waitress appeared with two glasses of water. "What do you want?" she asked.

Arlene ordered an egg salad sandwich on whole-wheat toast. I chose a chicken Caesar salad.

The waitress left, and I continued. "My uncle is a minister. He's planning a Seven-Minute Date at his church for Valentine's Day, and he roped me into helping him." I picked up my spoon and twirled it around in my fingers. "The thing is..." I glanced up at Arlene. "He expects me to participate in the event, too."

"And that's a problem?"

I took a deep breath. "I'm very nervous about it," I confessed. "I'm no good at blind dates. I really hate being put on the spot, and having to make small talk with perfect strangers, gives me heart palpitations."

I smiled ruefully and plunged on. "The truth is, Arlene, I'm really pretty much of a wallflower. I don't have an outgoing personality in situations like that. I hate parties of any kind. This whole Seven-Minute Date thing absolutely terrifies me."

Arlene looked skeptical, but in truth, much of what I told her was fact. "Polly, you're one of the most confident young women I've ever met. Look at how you handled Jay."

"That was different. I know Jay. It's strangers I have a hard time with."

"Then why did you agree to do it?"

"My uncle caught me at a weak moment, I guess. I should have turned him down, but...well, if you were to meet Uncle Emerson, you'd understand why I couldn't. He's awfully hard to say *no* to. Now I'm stuck. I have to go through with this." Also a true statement.

"I don't understand how I can help."

"The thing is, I'd really feel a lot better if I had a friend to go with me, someone who'd agree to take part in the whole thing, too. It would make me feel so much less self-conscious."

"But there'll be plenty of other people involved in this, won't there?"

"Of course, but no one I know." Okay, so I finally lied. I'd have Mitch there. And all my other uncles planned to show up to support Uncle Emerson, but Arlene didn't have to know that.

I saw the light dawn in her eyes. "You want me to go with you?"

"Oh, would you, Arlene? I'd be eternally grateful." I held my breath.

The waitress reappeared with our lunch and slapped a plate in front of each of us. Arlene stared blankly at her egg salad sandwich.

"I don't know, Polly. I'm not sure I could go through with something like that. Besides, isn't it for people your age?"

"And older. There's going to be one area set up for singles thirty through forty-five and another for those forty-six through sixty."

"I see." Arlene pondered for a moment. "I wouldn't have to commit to anything afterwards, would I?"

I sensed her wavering. "Of course not. That's the whole idea. After seven minutes you part company. If you're interested in each other, you exchange phone numbers. If not...." I shrugged.

"I haven't had a date in a long time."

"Actually, I'd prefer not to think of this as a date." I grinned sheepishly. "I think I'll get through it better if I don't."

"No one would have to know about this, would they?"

"You mean like people at work?"

Arlene nodded.

"God, no. That's the last thing I want. Promise me you won't breathe a word of this to anyone."

Arlene laughed. "Trust me. This is our secret. The last thing in the world I want is to hand Jay or anyone else ammunition to use against me."

"Then you'll do it?"

"I'll do it, but only because it's you, Polly, and I owe you."

I reached over and squeezed her hand. "Arlene, you have no idea how much this means to me. Thank you so much. You're such a wonderful person."

She blushed. Poor Arlene. When was the last time someone had complimented her? Certainly that alone was worth a little white lie on my part. She fumbled with her sandwich before taking a tiny bite.

I took a forkful of my Caesar salad and silently toasted my own cleverness. My plan had worked.

NINE
The Seven-Minute Hour

Two interviews into The Seven-Minute Date, I began to agree with Joni's assessment of the entire damn thing. I had come prepared with a series of questions to ask my *dates*. Bachelor Number One, a six-foot plus specimen with shaggy dark brown hair, closely cropped beard, blue eyes, and a killer smile, struck out before I had a chance to begin my inquiry.

Me: "Hi, I'm Polly."

Him: "Hi, I'm Justin, but you can call me Riker."

Me: "You go by your last name?"

Him: "No, it's because everyone says I look like him."

Me (somewhat puzzled): "Look like whom?"

Him (somewhat surprised): "Riker. Will Riker."

Me: "I'm afraid I'm not familiar with him. Is he someone I should know?"

Him (incredulous): "Will Riker. You know, the first officer on *Next Generation*?

Me: Next generation of what?

Him: *Star Trek*!"

Me (with a huge sigh): "Oh."

For the next six minutes and thirty-five seconds, I closed my ears and feigned interest while Bachelor Number One droned on about himself.

When the timer buzzed, signaling the end of our *date*, he stood, reluctant to leave. "You never told me anything about yourself," he said. "Polly? Wasn't it?"

I offered him an overly sweet smile. "I hate *Star Trek*."

Bachelor Number One left in horror. Bachelor Number Two sat down. He was shorter than Bachelor Number One by at least half a head and a good twenty pounds heavier—mostly around his middle. He wore his receding, long black hair tied back in a ponytail that fell below his shoulders. A row of diamond studs ran the length of both of his earlobes. A blue-white crystal dangled from a thin leather strap tied around his neck.

He didn't bother to introduce himself. His face held no expression.

I smiled. "Hello."

He ignored my greeting. Instead, he pulled a piece of pink quartz out of a brown suede pouch hanging from his belt and placed it on the table between us.

"What's that for?"

"I'm checking your aura." He clasped his hands together under his chin, narrowed his gaze, and stared resolutely at the rock for nearly a minute. He sighed. Then he scrutinized me with the same intensity. After another sigh—this one heavier than the first—and a shake of his head, he turned his attention back to the rock once again. Finally, he glanced up at me. A deep frown covered his face. "Sorry."

He stood and placed the rock back in his pouch. "Wrong aura. It would never work out between us." He turned and walked away.

I sat back and scanned the room. At all the other tables couples were engaged in animated conversations. Even Mr. *Star Trek* had found a like-minded space alien to capture his attention. He sat mesmerized, a huge grin plastered across his face as the woman opposite him chatted away. Maybe I did project the wrong aura.

Or maybe, as Joni had suggested, these guys were all a bunch of losers. I wouldn't have wanted Mr. *Star Trek* or Mr. New Age Crystal Gazer if either had groveled at my feet, pledging their undying fealty until the end of time and beyond. Perhaps the other women in the room were not as choosy.

I glanced at the clock. Three minutes and thirteen seconds to go. I closed my eyes and waited for the buzzer to sound the end of the second round.

"Don't tell me you struck out, too?"

My eyes flew open. Mitch hovered over me, an amused grin on his face. "What do you mean, *too*? I saw you chatting away with some blonde on the other side of the room."

"She chatted. Or chattered, actually. Like a magpie. Nonstop." He sat down opposite me and propped his elbows on the table. "I've never heard anyone say so much about nothing in such a short period of time. Talk about lung capacity! The woman barely came up for air."

"I did notice she was rather well-endowed."

Mitch chuckled. "I thought that was a guy thing. Aren't you

women the ones who claim personality and sense of humor are more important than big breasts?"

"They are."

"So?"

"Really, Mitch, the woman could give Dolly Parton a run for her money. How could I *not* notice?"

"All right. Score a point for the feminist across the table."

"Thank you." I sat back and folded my arms across my chest. "Now let's discuss your bad manners, Mitch. From very recent personal experience, I can tell you that getting up and walking away before your allotted seven minutes is up, is a real kick in the teeth, no matter how boring your date is."

"Actually, she left. I was determined to tough it out, but she was only interested in bagging herself a surgeon—preferably cosmetic."

"I'm not even going to touch that one."

"No need. Great minds think alike. Anyway, when she discovered I wrote a financial column for *The Wall Street Journal*, she excused herself to powder her nose."

"Tacky bitch."

"So what happened to your date?"

"Apparently, my aura is all wrong. He didn't want to waste his time."

Mitch screwed up his face and looked at me as if I were pulling his leg. "What the hell's an aura?"

"I'm not quite sure, but I think it's got something to do with crystals and New Age mumbo-jumbo. All I know is mine's wrong. At least according to him."

"What's wrong with it?"

"Beats me. He didn't stick around long enough to tell me."

I didn't admit that the rejection bothered me, though. After two strikes, I was beginning to feel like a perennial wallflower. The evening began to remind me of those horrible school mixers I used to suffer through in junior high. Late to physically blossom, at thirteen I looked more like a nine-year-old, and there is nothing worse than being different from your peers at that age. Kids are cruel. Especially when Regina Koltzner is their ringleader.

One Friday night a month, I'd clutch a paper cup full of sickeningly sweet fruit punch and try to make myself invisible as I stood in a corner of the school gym and watched everyone else having a good time. If only I'd been allowed to disappear into the highly polished woodwork, the evenings might have been somewhat bearable. Unfortunately, at every dance, some well-meaning teacher-chaperone would notice me standing alone and take pity. Then she'd force one of the boys to ask me to dance.

This always made me feel as though I were being attacked on two fronts at once—mortified by the teacher for singling me out, humiliated by the boy who didn't want to dance with me. Whoever the chosen dance partner, he never felt any qualms about telling me so as he tried to dance as far away from me as possible and still fulfill the teacher's order.

I got even with all those boys, though. A few years later when I finally did transform from an ugly, flat-chested duckling into a gracefully, well-endowed swan, I refused to give any of them the time of day. And I made it clear why.

Unfortunately, that, too, boomeranged on me, and I became known as a stuck-up, tight-assed snob. Sometimes you can't win.

All of a sudden I felt like I was back in junior high, standing on the fringes, excluded from the fun. Maybe we never truly lose all of those early insecurities that made our childhoods a living hell.

We just push them to some dark corner of our subconscious where they bide their time, waiting to spring back to life when we're most vulnerable. And at the moment, I was feeling *very* vulnerable.

The buzzer sounded. Mitch stood and stretched. "Well, better luck with Round Three."

I stifled a yawn but wasn't as successful in curbing the smirk that sprang to my lips. Mitch hadn't mentioned anything derogatory about his first *date*. I had no doubt his last one was an aberration. After all, even a hunk like Mitch strikes out once in a while—as his recent uncoupling with the starry-eyed Hollywood wannabe proved. He'd do fine the remainder of the evening.

Mitch drew women the way billionaires draw gold-diggers, and in the back of my mind, I still couldn't help but think he was only participating in the evening out of friendship for me. Mitch didn't need The Seven-Minute Date to provide him with a social life. His track record was still well on the plus side. Unlike mine. "Yeah, good luck to you, too," I told him, but I doubted he'd need it.

Bachelor Number Three sat down. "Mark Burman." He extended his hand. He looked downright glum. Maybe he'd struck out with his first two *dates*, also.

I shook his hand. "Polly Harmony."

"So, Polly Harmony, how did you get roped into taking part in this crazy thing?"

"My uncle organized it."

He nodded. "Legitimate excuse."

Did this mean I'd passed the Loser Elimination Test? If so, what about him? "And you?"

"My in-laws blackmailed me into coming."

"Your *in-laws*?" I didn't bother to hide my shock. I hoped he was joking, and this was merely his way of trying to find out if I had a sense of humor, but he looked dead serious. Actually, he looked plain dead—as if someone or something had drained all the life from him, and he was merely going through the motions of living. His entire body sagged. Every movement seemed an excruciating effort.

"I suppose I should explain," he mumbled.

"Please do."

"I'm a widower. My wife died of a cerebral aneurysm a little over a year ago. Her parents think it's time I got on with my life."

"I see." I sensed The Seven-Minute Date rapidly morphing into The Seven-Minute Therapy Session. "And you don't?"

He ran his hands through his closely cropped salt-and-pepper hair and sighed. "What's the point? I could never love anyone the way I loved my Courtney."

Strike three.

For the remainder of the seven minutes I listened to a laundry list of Courtney Burman's outstanding qualities and why no other woman would ever measure up to her.

As Mark droned on, my gaze wandered around the room. Uncle Emerson had taped lace-edged red hearts and cardboard cupids around the walls of the church assembly room. Smiling faced cherubs mocked me from every direction. At least it felt that way. I realized I was growing increasingly paranoid as the evening dragged on, but after three disastrous *dates*, I had good reason.

Uncle Emerson had set up a table of snacks—a sparkling cider punch and heart-shaped sugar cookies—near the archway that separated the assembly room from the dining room where the second group of *dates* was taking place. Arlene and Uncle Cal stood by the punch bowl. They were sipping punch and carrying on what appeared to be a lively conversation. Both wore cheerful expressions.

To the outside world, Uncle Cal had taken Aunt June's death with stoic acceptance of God's will. Only those of us in the family knew how deeply he still continued to grieve.

Uncle Cal is a perfect example of the old expression, *physician heal thyself*. As a clergyman, he spends a good part of his time counseling grief-stricken members of his flock. He shows great compassion and patience in helping them deal with their loss. But after my aunt's death, he erected an invisible barrier between himself and everyone else. Only I, my parents, and the other uncles ever see the lighter, fun side of him any more.

I was surprised to see him enjoying himself with Arlene. His posture was relaxed, rather than the stiff bearing he normally assumed around others. And he was smiling. Maybe after all these years, he was finally ready to move beyond his own grief.

And what about Arlene? Why was she chatting away with Uncle Cal instead of interviewing *dates*? Had she already given up on the evening? Although I would have derived a good deal of pleasure in knowing other women were striking out as badly as I was, I didn't want Arlene to be one of them. There has to be some justice in the world.

If I were my mother, I'd march right up to Uncle Cal and tell him to let Arlene get back to her table, but I'm not as brazen as Mom. Not by a long shot. Most of the time this is a good thing. At least I think so, but tonight I wished I had inherited a few more of Mimi's *chutzpah* genes.

Mark finished his eulogy at the sound of the buzzer ending the third session. As he rose to leave, I stopped him with a question, more to satisfy my own curiosity than anything. "Why did you come this evening?"

His eyes filled with puzzlement; the corners of his mouth turned even farther downward. "I thought I told you. I had no choice. My in-laws forced me to come."

"Yes, but how?" I knew it was none of my business, but under the circumstances, I couldn't understand why he'd bowed to such pressure. Since I had to sit and listen to him for seven minutes, the least he could do was explain why he'd subjected me to such a tragic tale.

He started to speak, then appeared to think better of it and merely shook his head. "They don't understand. No one can possibly understand." And he walked away, taking the mystery with him.

I watched as he headed for the exit. Whatever the blackmail, he'd obviously fulfilled his obligation with only three *dates*.

In a rather perverse way, I envied Courtney Burman. I'd never known undying love from a man. Come to think of it, as I reflected back over a decade of aborted relationships, I'd never known *any* kind of love from a man. True, some had parroted the words from time to time, I always knew the sentiment didn't match the sentence—sometimes even as it was being uttered.

Before anyone else sat down at my table, I bolted for the powder room. I needed a break. Bachelors Number One and Number Two had been bad enough, but Number Three had really thrown me for a loop. I hadn't registered as the designated shrink for the evening, and I felt uncomfortable in the role.

As I stood in front of the mirror, contemplating my rotten luck, Arlene entered.

"How's it going?" I asked.

She bit her lower lip and giggled like a teeny-bopper. Color infused her cheeks. She'd taken a long lunch break that day—

unusual for Arlene who normally took all of five minutes to down a sandwich at her desk. She returned ten years younger. Someone had transformed her utilitarian, no-nonsense, gray-streaked hair into a sassy, sophisticated, blonde-highlighted feather cut. The results had taken ten years off her face.

She bubbled with enthusiasm. "I can't believe how much I'm enjoying myself. And to think, I nearly refused to come with you! I'm meeting so many nice men. And several have asked for my phone number. Do you believe it?"

"Arlene, that's wonderful!"

"It feels so strange. After all this time...." Her words trailed off. Her expression suddenly changed, her enthusiasm deflating as quickly as a pinpricked balloon. Fear and uncertainty replaced giddiness. She stared at her reflection in the mirror and nervously fingered her new hairdo. "How am I ever going to explain this to mother?"

"Arlene, you're a grown woman. You don't need your mother's permission to go on a date."

"I know. It's just that.—"

"She still treats you as though you're eighteen, unmarried, and pregnant."

Arlene grimaced. "Yes."

"Don't you think it's about time she stopped punishing you for a decades' old mistake? And high time you stopped taking that punishment?"

"It's not that easy, Polly. You don't know my mother. She's never embraced the idea of forgive and forget. She's more into eternal damnation for sinners."

"Isn't that a bit presumptuous of her? That's up to God, not your mother, and He *is* into forgiveness. Ask any of my uncles."

"God doesn't have to share an apartment with Hermione Flynn."

I didn't see why Arlene did, either, but I tabled that argument for another day. "True, but I know you, Arlene, and someone who has the courage to bring Jay Steiner to his knees can stand up to anyone. Including your mother."

"You have a way of making it all sound so simple."

"It is simple. Just do it."

"Just do it? You've been watching too many sneaker commercials, Polly." All the same, her face grew thoughtful.

I hoped she take my advice. I knew Arlene had the backbone to stand up to her mother, but I couldn't force her to do it. "It's time to start living again, Arlene."

"Maybe you're right." She reached for one of my hands with both of hers and gave it a soft squeeze. "You missed your calling in life, Polly. You should have been a therapist."

I rolled my eyes and groaned.

~*~

A few minutes later, I sat back down at my table and braced myself for Bachelor Number Four. Based on my three previous experiences, the odds were against me. Still, I plastered a pleasant smile on my face and called forth what little of Pollyanna was left inside me on the slim chance that Alexander Pope was right, and hope really does spring eternal.

Bachelor Number Four approached wearing a pleasant smile on his face and no crystals dangling from his neck. I took this as a positive sign. "You're Polly, aren't you?" he asked as he settled into the chair opposite me.

"Yes, have we met?"

"Not officially. I've seen you occasionally at Reverend

Harmony's church. He's mentioned you a few times. Keeps wanting to introduce us, but we never seem to be all together in the right place at the right time." He extended his hand. "I'm Neil Pearson."

Neil Pearson? His name sounded vaguely familiar, but I have this habit of blocking out any conversations where one of my relatives is trying to fix me up with someone. Invariably, when an uncle plays Cupid, I wind up suffering the consequences. Jeff Jacoby was only the most recent in a long line of relative-induced, blind or semi-blind dates that herald all the way back to various church and synagogue socials during my adolescent years.

"I've heard so much about you," Neil continued.

I'll bet he had, but he also had a very sexy smile that was definitely starting to push a few buttons. Maybe instead of three strikes and Polly's out, the fourth time would be the charm. I crossed a few mental fingers and plunged ahead. "Then you definitely have the advantage. Mind if I ask you a few questions?"

"Not at all. Shoot."

"Okay. These may sound a bit odd, but I've had a strange night so far."

He nodded in sympathy and tossed a quick glance to his left. "I know what you mean." I followed his gaze across the room to a table where Mitch's Dolly Parton clone sat, her mouth moving at lightning speed.

I took a deep breath and plunged forward. "How often do you watch *Star Trek* reruns?"

Neil furrowed his brow and wrinkled his nose. "I don't. Is that a problem?"

I couldn't help but smile. "Not at all. Do you believe in personal auras, consult crystals, or practice any other New Age philosophy?"

"No. No. And no. Do you?"

"Definitely not. Final question: Are you planning to spend your time telling me about the love of your life that for one reason or another is no more?"

Neil snorted. "Hardly, since I haven't found her yet." He leaned forward, placed his elbows on the table, and steepled his hands in front of his mouth. "I don't suppose you'd like to explain these strange questions, would you?"

"My three *dates* so far this evening. The first was a diehard *Star Trek* fanatic, the second used a chunk of crystal to examine my aura, and the third mistook me for a grief counselor."

Neil roared with laughter, catching the attention of several people at nearby tables. "You definitely inherited your uncle's sense of humor. Now that we've gotten that out of the way, how about telling me something about you, Polly Harmony? Other than the fact that you obviously have no fondness for *Star Trek*, anything New Age, or anyone who uses his seven minutes to talk about...exactly what did he talk about?"

"His dead wife."

Neil's expression grew serious. His light gray eyes darkened to smoke, and small lines highlighted the corners of his mouth where his smile had faded to a frown. "Jeez. What did you do?"

"What could I do? I sat and listened."

"That was very nice of you. It must have been an extremely awkward situation."

It was, but I didn't deserve his praise. In truth, I'd felt put-upon and downright bitchy as I forced myself to sit through Bachelor Number Three's ramblings. But I hadn't gotten up and walked away—unlike the way Bachelor Number Two treated me, or the way Mitch's overly endowed surgeon hunter had treated him. So maybe I did deserve a partial brownie point—or even a full one.

And maybe I should have paid more attention to Uncle Emerson when he tried to tell me about Neil Pearson. Bachelor Number Four quickly changed my opinion of the evening, making me forget all about the debacles otherwise known as Bachelors Number One, Two, and Three.

I studied Neil as he spoke. Although he said he'd recently celebrated his thirty-sixth birthday, his boyish enthusiasm—not to mention his tousled black hair and impish grin—made him look quite a bit younger.

When he mentioned that he worked as a broker on Wall Street, I asked him if he knew Mitch.

Neil nodded, then frowned. "Are you telling me I have competition?"

"He's my upstairs neighbor. We're good friends."

His frown grew into a scowl. "How good?"

"Mitch and his twin sister have been my best friends for ten years."

"So he's what? Like a cousin?"

"More like a brother."

Neil relaxed. His smile returned. "Okay. I won't have to kill him then."

"What!"

He laughed. "Gullible, aren't you? It was a joke, Polly. Mitch is a great guy. We've met several times."

And I'd met too many strange men so far this evening. How did I know Neil Pearson wasn't an enforcer for the Mafia? "I'm not sure I like your sense of humor, Neil."

"Which is why I'm a stockbroker and not doing standup over

at *Caroline's Comedy Club*." He reached for his wallet. "Would it help if I whipped out my Amnesty International membership card as proof of my nonviolent leanings?"

I decided to give him a second chance—after he produced the aforementioned member-in-good-standing card. I wasn't taking any chances.

When the buzzer sounded, announcing the end of the seven minutes, I also gave him my phone number.

~*~

"So what did you think of Neil?" Uncle Emerson plopped his long frame in the chair Neil had vacated moments before. He straddled the seat, stretched his legs out into the aisle, and leaned back, clasping his hands behind his head. A wrinkled Ichabod Crane with a paunch, Uncle Emerson always preferred sprawling out across a plush carpet to the confines of a metal folding chair.

"He's nice."

He beamed. "I had a feeling about you two."

"We just met. Let's not start planning the wedding ceremony yet, okay?"

Uncle Emerson leaned forward, hovering over me like a panting puppy dog. "But you will go out with him?"

I planted a kiss on his leathery cheek. Everyone should be as easy to please. "If he calls."

"He will."

Whether by divine intervention or clerical coercion, I surmised, wondering whether Uncle Emerson would pull an Uncle Aaron and I'd show up in Summit for Sunday night's dinner to find Neil Pearson standing in my parents' living room.

~*~

The brief break between dating periods came to an end. Uncle

Emerson left, and Bachelor Number Five sat down. One look at his chosen attire for the evening, and I knew I was in for an interminably long seven minutes.

Who in his right mind shows up for something like this wearing torn jeans and a Guns 'n Roses T-shirt? Mike "The Mane Man" Keivus—so named, he explained, for his unkempt mane of blue-black hair that skimmed his breastbone—also sported a three-day growth of beard on either side of a scraggly goatee, a silver choke chain around his neck, and a leather studded band strapped to his wrist.

Part of a tattoo peaked out from underneath the sleeve of his shirt. Too bad Crystal has a boyfriend. They'd make a smashing couple.

When I was in high school, I had an English teacher who forced us to memorize passages from Shakespeare. We never analyzed those speeches, never dissected them and discussed the meaning behind the words. Only memorized. A new piece every Monday; an oral quiz on Friday. And the class was supposed to be *Honors* English. I often wondered if Mrs. Bustard forced her lower track classes to memorize pages of *The Cat in the Hat* or *Green Eggs and Ham*.

Things that are drummed into us in our youth have a nasty habit of pitching camp and never leaving. That's why the beginning of one of those Shakespearean selections came to mind as I sat and listened to Bachelor Number Five discuss the similarities between Beethoven and Heavy Metal.

"If Beethoven were alive today, he'd write Heavy Metal instead of symphonies." Mike fingered his goatee and paused, staring at me as if waiting for some kind of agreement or acknowledgement.

"Fascinating." I stifled a yawn and forced my eyelids to keep from drooping as I stole a glance at the clock. *Tomorrow and tomorrow and tomorrow creeps in this petty pace from day to day to the last syllable of recorded time*. Only three minutes had crept by at a decidedly petty pace. It seemed more like three hours.

When the buzzer sounded, Mike suggested we cut out and head to his place for a *private recording session*. I declined.

I also declined to give him my phone number when he asked. "I don't think our tastes in music are compatible," I explained somewhat apologetically. I smiled, bit down on my tongue, and refrained from adding the myriad of sarcastic comments fighting to spew forth from between my tightly pursed lips.

The remainder of the evening brought me face to face with the sorriest collection of losers I'd ever had the misfortune to meet.

Bachelor Number Six looked and whined like Woody Allen. He was also as opinionated. Maybe he *was* Woody Allen, although he introduced himself as Morton Seeb and denied knowing how to play the clarinet when I asked.

I decided Bachelor Number Seven was related to Bachelor Number Two. He wore magnets strapped to all his pressure points and owned an alternative pharmacy that specialized in homeopathic remedies.

Bachelor Number Eight made Mike Keivus look like he'd stepped off the pages of *Esquire*. At least Mike had taken a shower at some point in the past forty-eight hours. I doubted Bachelor Number Eight had bathed in the past month.

Bachelor Number Nine's major goal in life was to visit every major league baseball stadium, every NFL football stadium, and every NHL hockey arena in both the United States and Canada before he turned forty. I wondered why he left out basketball but refrained from asking. I was already hearing far too much about the life of a jockaholic, even though I'm a diehard Mets fan.

"And how do you expect to support yourself during this odyssey?" I asked when he came up for air.

He winked at me. "I invested heavily in dotcom stock and sold out before the crash and burn. Made a bundle."

"So why come here?" I asked. "You don't have time to get involved in a relationship with anyone."

His answer shocked the hell out of me. "I'm looking for someone to go with me."

I told him to look elsewhere.

Bachelor Number Ten showed up with his ribbon-adorned Lhasa Apso, Snookums, under his arm. Enough said.

Then there was Bachelor Number Eleven who looked like he stepped off the cover of an historical romance novel. Unfortunately, the illusion he created died the moment he opened his mouth. Bachelor Number Eleven was far from the brightest crayon in the box.

Finally, there was Bachelor Number Twelve. He brought his mother, a domineering harridan who made me thankful for Mimi. She conducted the interview—or rather interrogation—while he sat quietly alongside her. I must have passed muster because she agreed to let him go out with me. However, when I asked if she planned to chaperone our dates, she changed her mind, informing me that if I didn't learn to curb my waspish tongue, I'd never catch a man.

In my mind I could see Joni holding her sides and laughing hysterically. *I told you so. I told you so. I told you so.* Thank heaven for Neil Pearson's appearance. Bachelor Number Four turned out to be the only bright spot in the entire evening. One out of twelve wasn't such a great statistic, but it sure beat striking out.

TEN
Looking Before Leaping is Hard Work

Joni didn't disappoint. Between Mitch's experiences and mine at The Seven-Minute Date Extravaganza, we had her rolling on the floor. "I can't stand this!" Tears streamed down her cheeks as she hiccuped to catch her breath. "You're making it all up."

"Trust me. If I had that vivid an imagination, I'd be a bestselling author, not an office drone dealing with the likes of Head Lecherous Jerk and his minions."

Mitch rubbed his jaw. "I don't know, Polly. Writing careers are launched on far less talent every day of the week. This evening had enough material in it to write a book, a screenplay, *and* a sit-com series."

Joni clapped her hands together. "Sure! You could call it *Mitch and Polly Visit the Wonderful World of Dateland*."

Funny how she'd left herself out. "What about *Joni, Mitch, and Polly Visit the Wonderful World of Dateland*? You've experienced your share of interesting men over the past few years."

"That would give it an X rating," said Mitch. "The major networks wouldn't touch it. Only cable. The book would have to come in a plain brown wrapper, and our promotional tour would be limited to Howard Stern. It might not have as much sizzle, but we'd make more money with a PG rating."

Joni stuck her tongue out at her brother. "Despite what Mr. Conservative thinks, I lead a healthy sex life, not a wild one."

Mitch raised both eyebrows. "Since when?"

"Since none of your business, Bro."

"Bitch."

"And you say that like it's a bad thing?"

I jumped up and positioned myself between them before they came to blows. "Hey, you two! Time out! It's late, and I'm not in the mood to play referee at a fist fight between my two closest friends."

"Polly's right." Mitch reached out and dragged Joni into his arms. She capitulated—reluctantly, allowing him to wrap her in a hug. "I'm sorry. It's just that I've been worried about you lately. You've gotten awfully secretive." He exhaled forcefully. "We used to share everything. What the hell's going on with you, Joni?"

She stepped out of his embrace. Chewing on her lower lip, she glanced back and forth between us as if trying to make up her mind about something. "Look, I'm not ready to talk about it yet, but everything's fine. I promise."

I studied her outfit, a pair of camel and brown tweed wool pants, an ivory cashmere turtleneck with matching pearl-buttoned cardigan, and a pair of low-heeled suede pumps. If I didn't know any better, I'd have thought she raided my closet. "Aliens," I mumbled under my breath to Mitch. "Definitely alien abduction."

Joni turned on me. "What's that supposed to mean?"

I lifted my glass of wine to my lips and smiled sweetly at her. "You tell me your secret, and I'll tell you mine."

~*~

Uncle Emerson didn't pull an Uncle Aaron the following Sunday. We had no surprise guests for dinner, but I did have to sit through an evening akin to the Spanish Inquisition with my mother playing the role of Torquemada. Mom outdid The Grand Inquisitor without resorting to racks, thumbscrews, or any other form of physical torture, though. She didn't need to. She had a far more powerful weapon—her mouth.

"I want to hear all about this young man you met the other night. The one Uncle Emerson knows."

Word travels fast in our family. Especially when it deals with me and my so-called social life. No doubt Uncle Emerson called Mom the moment he got home Valentine's night to fill her in on my *date* with Neil.

"Really, Mom!" I rolled my eyes and tossed a pleading cry for help in my father's directions. He shrugged haplessly and spun around to busy himself washing romaine and endive leaves at the sink. "I spent all of seven minutes with him. Those are the rules. Seven minutes for each *date*. No more. He may not even call me."

"So you call him."

"If he's interested, he'll call. I'm not calling him."

Mom sighed. I recognized the tone. It was her where-did-I-go-wrong sigh. "He asked for your phone number?"

"Yes."

"He'll call."

"Maybe he was only being polite."

"He'll call." She turned her attention back to her bouillabaisse, stirring it once before lifting the wooden spoon and taking a sample taste. "Needs a pinch more salt, Howard." She stretched her arm out behind her. My father grabbed the salt shaker off the counter and deposited it in her upturned palm.

Without missing a beat, Mom sprinkled some salt in the pot and launched back into her interrogation. "So what's this Neil do for a living?"

"He works on Wall Street."

Mom frowned. "A yuppie tycoon? What does he do besides count his money?"

Mom hated people who generalized, stereotyped, and jumped to conclusions, but it never prevented her from doing so. "I don't know, but he belongs to Amnesty International."

She brightened. "It's a start. And he goes to Uncle Emerson's church, right?" When I nodded, she knit her brows together and struck a thoughtful pose, tapping the side of her cheek with an index finger. "He can't be a corrupt capitalist pig, then. Emerson wouldn't have wanted the two of you to meet."

I glanced around my mother's state-of-the-art kitchen in her multi-million-dollar home in one of New Jersey's poshest suburbs. Mom never felt the slightest qualms about enjoying all the money she and Dad made from Harmony Cosmetics because she gave so much of it away. She expected other corporate tycoons to do the same and really got pissed off at those who didn't follow her example.

"Just because someone works on Wall Street, doesn't mean he's rolling in money, Mom."

She eyed me as if I'd lost a few sprockets in my brain. "Show me one who isn't. How do you know he belongs to Amnesty

International?"

In the soap opera of my life, sometimes I need a program to keep up with Mom's rapid-fire scene changes. "Because I accused him of being a Mafia hit man."

"Polly Faith Harmony! No wonder you're still single, and I don't have any grandchildren. You chase men away with ravings like that."

Second verse, same as the first. I wish Mom would learn another song.

Dad reached out and placed his hands on her shoulders as if trying to keep her from springing a gasket. "Relax, Mimi. She was joking." He signaled me over Mom's head.

"Yes, of course. Only a joke, Mom."

She scowled at me then spun around and confronted Dad, waving the wooden spoon inches from his nose. "This is your fault, Howard."

"Now how do you figure that?"

"She inherited her sense of humor from your side of the family, not mine."

Dad roared with laughter. "You're telling me Aaron and Francis have no sense of humor? That'll be news to them."

Mom's face pinched up. She forced a heavy sigh through flared nostrils and stamped her foot. "Oh, you know what I mean!"

"I love it when you get all hot under the collar, woman." He captured her cheeks with his palms and her lips with his mouth. Mom sighed an altogether different sigh from the one she used on me. She wrapped her arms around Dad's neck and sank into his chest.

"Okay, I'm out of here." It was nice to know my parents still had the hots for each other after thirty-two years of marriage, but

I didn't need a graphic display. Not when my own love live was so pathetic. I headed for the living room and the less steamy companionship of my four bachelor uncles. I'd much rather listen to stale ecclesiastic jokes than watch my parents make out any day of the week.

As I exited the kitchen, I uttered a silent prayer, hoping that Neil called me. I needed some steam of my own. It had been a long, cold, lonely winter so far, and my thirty-second birthday was fast approaching.

I shuddered to think how Mom would decide to celebrate *that* milestone if I still wasn't dating anyone when the big day arrived. Billboards with my picture and phone number on the New Jersey turnpike? A giant neon sign in Times Square? Full-page ads in every major newspaper along the Northeast corridor from Boston down to Washington?

Knowing Mom, she already had a plan of action set to implement if necessary. After all, she was getting more and more desperate over my single status, which resulted in her lack of grandkids. And she obviously had little faith in my ability to remedy the situation on my own.

I wondered if I should swallow my pride and call Neil Pearson.

~*~

Every once in a while, my belief that God really doesn't have a sadistic sense of humor is reaffirmed. After all, who but God could stand up to Mimi Harmony when she set her mind to something?

My prayers were answered. Neil called later that week and asked me out for the following Saturday evening—a day before my birthday. If after that night, we parted knowing we'd made a mistake, I'd at least make certain none of my relatives found out for twenty-four hours. Birthdays are hard enough to swallow. I didn't want the added burden of defending my nonexistent social life while I sliced the cake and opened presents.

To that end, the first thing I did after hanging up from Neil was call Mom to let her know she could cancel the billboards and newspaper ads. I wasn't taking any chances. She wasn't amused. Over the phone line, I heard one of those long sighs that needs no interpretation. She followed up her dramatic exhalation with some pointed references to my warped sense of humor and her long-suffering status.

Sarah Bernhardt move over.

Dad says I goad Mom, and maybe he's right. I know at times I come across as overly sarcastic—especially when I'm put on the defensive. It's one of my many faults. Sometimes, I can't help myself, though. Mom needs to lighten up. She's driving me crazy.

I've had this recurring nightmare lately. In it, I'm finally married. Every morning I wake to find Mom hovering over my bed. As soon as I open my eyes, she shoves a thermometer in my mouth. After a few minutes, she takes it out, reads my temperature, and says, "It's a good day to conceive. Have some sex." Then she stands there and watches to make sure we do it right.

I'd like to see Freud interpret that one.

~*~

Meanwhile, another nightmare resurfaced. Mason Hightower came to town.

The college choir he directs had been invited to perform at a benefit concert at Alice Tully Hall at Lincoln Center. Mace repeatedly reminded me of this in his daily e-mails, strongly suggesting that as executive director of the organization he presided over, it behooved me to attend the function.

Listening to a group of college students sing a selection of obscure Nineteenth Century American ballads and rounds, didn't exactly rank high on my list of ways I'd prefer to spend a Thursday evening. However, since several other officers and board members of The International Society of Choral Directors would also be present for the event, I could hardly turn down the invitation.

As of the first of the year, the choral directors were on the books as a client, and Mason Hightower was officially a pain in the butt I could no longer ignore. He monopolized my time as though he were my only client, not one of four. By rights and contract, he was entitled to two hours of my time each day.

Unfortunately, the International Society of Choral Directors had been run for the last several years by the retired wife of one of its members. Two hours a day didn't begin to come close to the time I needed to straighten out the mess she'd created.

At the same time, Mace kept generating ideas for improving the organization, the newsletter, the annual symposium—you name it. I admired his enthusiasm and desire to expand and improve his organization, but I grew to dread his e-mails—or even worse—his phone calls. Without appearing rude, it was very difficult to get him to shut up.

I finally had to lay down the law on Tuesday afternoon. Mace was due to arrive in town the following day. I'd already received two previous phone calls from him that morning. I listened politely for a few minutes, then interrupted when he segued into a monologue about some fascinating—his word—bit of minutiae he'd unearthed while researching a paper on an obscure sixteenth century French composer I'd never heard of. "Look, Mace, this is all very interesting, but if you don't let me get some of my other work done, you'll be assigned another executive director."

"I don't want another director, Polly. I want you. It's in our contract."

"The contract stipulation isn't worth an overripe fig if I get fired."

That's when he played his trump card, and I realized, too late, that I'd been royally manipulated. "Have dinner with me tomorrow night. We can go over everything—brainstorm a few ideas about the organization, prioritize the agenda, create a timetable for implementing various changes. And you can catch me up on the progress you've made organizing our records. Shall we say seven at my hotel?"

Fool me once, shame on you. Fool me twice, shame on me. Finding Mace naked in my living room was bad enough. I wasn't about to step foot into his hotel room unless I brought along a division of marines. "Six at my office. I'll order in some takeout for us."

He voiced his disappointment but finally gave in when I refused to budge. "All right." He exhaled dramatically. "Six o'clock at your office, but forget the takeout. I'll have the hotel fix up a box dinner for us."

~*~

Mace arrived several minutes before six with a hotel employee in tow. "Jean Claude will set up and serve," he informed me as he shrugged out of his topcoat. He deposited it on the empty chair in my cubicle.

I raised an eyebrow at the oversized picnic cooler in Jean Claude's arms. My idea of a working dinner consisted of pizza on paper plates and cans of soda. Under the circumstances, an elegantly catered dinner for two struck me as surreal. Maybe I should have expected it, though. From what I'd learned of Mason

Hightower, the man never did anything halfway. "Went a bit overboard, didn't you?"

Mace tossed me one of his rakish grins, the kind that brought out his dimples and transformed him from *American Gothic* farmer to Indiana Jones. I donned my steel-plated armor. I had no desire to travel down that road again.

His voice, deep and thick like brandy, tried to scale my outer perimeter defenses. "There's no reason to deprive ourselves of a fine meal. Where should Jean Claude set up our dinner?"

I had to admit, whatever was in that cooler, it certainly smelled good. As usual, I'd existed most of the day on nothing more than a constant infusion of caffeine. My mouth began to water. My first line fortifications fell to the succulent aromas.

I grabbed my laptop and a stack of files and escorted them down the hall to the conference room. Jean Claude set the box on the floor, removed a white Damask linen tablecloth, and spread it out across one end of the long conference table. Next came china, crystal, silverware and a pair of candlesticks. After he lit the candles, he held out a chair for me. "Mademoiselle?"

"Well what have we here? A little after-hours seduction in the workplace? Shame on you, Polly."

Heat rose to my cheeks, not from embarrassment but from anger. My head whipped around. Jay Steiner stood in the doorway, a wide leer spread across his arrogant face.

Most days, everyone clears out of the office as close to five o'clock as possible. Just my luck, Jay, normally one of the first down the elevator, had decided to stay late. The cynic in me knew it had nothing to do with his own workload. Jay had obviously overheard my earlier phone conversation with Mace.

I motioned to the computer and files at the far end of the table, then narrowed my gaze and spoke to his crotch. "We're having a working dinner. If you and *Dick* would care to join us, I'm sure the professor has some financial questions you can answer for him."

Jay got the message—loud and clear. His leer disappeared. The color drained from his face. Trying to dig up some ammunition to use against me wasn't worth the risk of another full-frontal assault from the office Double X Chromosome Brigade. After his very public humiliation some weeks back, he still avoided the women in the office as much as possible.

He stepped back out into the hall, tripping over both his feet and his words. "Sorry. Can't. Just leaving. Parent-teacher conference this evening." He glanced at his watch. "Gotta run." And he did. Spinning on his heels, he raced down the hallway.

I choked down a chuckle. Jay at a parent-teacher conference? Highly unlikely. After all, this was the man who kept his family's picture on the windowsill behind his back so he didn't have to look at them. I'd lay down odds that he didn't even know what grades his kids were in, let alone their teachers' names.

"Who's Dick?"

I turned my attention back to Mace. "Excuse me?"

"Dick. You spoke as if there were two people there, Polly. The gentleman was alone."

I settled into the chair Jean Claude still held for me and finally gave in to the urge to laugh. "Dick is Jay's assistant." That was all the explanation I planned to give Mace, no matter how perplexed his expression grew.

He shrugged and took the seat opposite me.

Jean Claude removed a bottle of Riesling and a corkscrew from the cooler. I stood and reached for the wine. "Why don't we save this until after we've gotten through all our paperwork?"

Mace had alluded to a drinking problem in his letter of apology, blaming it for his bare-naked behavior in my apartment. Although I was giving him another chance, if only on a professional level, I didn't want to risk a repeat of that night. Not in an empty office.

He glanced at the bottle, the corners of his mouth sinking almost imperceptibly. Our gazes locked for a long moment. Finally, he sighed, then nodded. "Perhaps, you're right. We'll save the wine for later."

Jean Claude served our dinner—a baby greens salad, salmon Wellington with white asparagus, and apricot mousse for dessert.

Mace behaved like a perfect gentleman throughout the meal. Still, I felt the need to direct the conversation back to business whenever he strayed off the subject and into an amusing anecdote. My businesslike attitude reminded him that this wasn't a date. I wanted no misinterpretations this time. No unspoken signals.

He understood. His expression grew melancholy, like a little boy who'd suddenly come to accept that there really is no Santa Claus. "I blew it for good last time, didn't I?"

"It would never work out, Mace. I don't think it's fair to either of us to expect otherwise."

He stole a glance down the table to the still-corked bottle of Riesling. The man had problems. Whether alcoholism headed the list or was the panacea that masked more deep-rooted troubles, didn't matter. As engaging as he could be, I wasn't about to get sucked into whatever quagmire Mason Hightower doggy-paddled around in. I had more than enough reasons to keep this relationship on a purely professional level.

When we finished our meal, Jean Claude cleared the conference table, packed up the cooler and departed, leaving the bottle of wine, the corkscrew, and two glasses.

I spread out my files, flipped on my laptop, and continued with the purpose of our meeting. By nine-thirty we'd covered every issue Mace had raised in his numerous e-mails, and I'd given him an overview of my progress in straightening out the organization's records.

"Well, that about does it." I gathered up the papers spread across the table, tamped them into a neat stack, and rose.

Mace reached for the bottle of wine. "How about one for the road?"

"I don't think so. It's been a long day, and I'd like to get home."

"So this is really how it's going to be between us?"

I nodded.

His sea-green eyes faded to a murky olive drab. "Will I see you tomorrow night at the concert?"

"I'll be there. I'm looking forward to meeting some of the other officers and board members."

Mace grabbed the wine and glasses and followed me back to my office. I dumped the laptop and files and retrieved my coat. He donned his, placing a glass in each pocket and tucking the bottle into the crook of his arm.

We rode down the elevator in silence. Outside the building he insisted on hailing me a cab. When one pulled up to the corner, he opened the back door for me, then bent down and kissed me gently on the cheek. "I'll see you tomorrow."

I felt a tug in my belly. Part of me wanted to kiss him back, but the emotion sprang from sadness and regret rather than any physical need or attraction, and the last thing I wanted to do was lead him to think I could be swayed in my decision. As far as I was concerned, the spark that had sizzled over dinner several months earlier had been doused for good later that same evening.

I wanted a man in my life, but I was neither foolish enough nor desperate enough to latch onto one with a drinking problem and who-knew-what other serious emotional issues. I'd made enough mistakes where men were concerned. All I had to do was look back at the list of my failed relationships. Maybe after so many, I'd finally learned a valuable lesson—the one about looking before leaping.

As the cab pulled away, I reminded myself how lucky I was to have discovered the darker side of Mason Hightower before I let myself succumb to his sexy Indiana Jones grin.

~*~

Somehow I managed to get through the rest of the week. Mace was tied up in rehearsal all day Thursday and surrounded by crowds of well-wishers and fellow musicians during the reception after the concert. On Friday morning he flew back to Nebraska. Our next face-to-face meeting wouldn't occur until the board met in April.

~*~

I hadn't had much time to think about my date with Neil, and all of a sudden, it was Saturday.

"Why do I feel so nervous?" Mitch and I were in the basement doing laundry. For a change, Joni had taken off for parts unknown.

"I don't know. You tell me." He picked an ivory silk bikini out of his clothes basket and tossed it aside. "I don't know how these got in my hamper, but I am *not* washing my sister's unmentionables."

"Maybe they're not Joni's. How did things go with you and your date last night?" Mitch had asked out one of the women he met during the Seven-Minute Date.

212

"Not *that* far. Besides, I thought we were talking about you."

I finished loading the washer and turned it on. "I suppose it's because of tomorrow. All of a sudden I feel so old, even though I know thirty-two isn't old—at least not to anyone other than my mother. And to her it's only old if you're still single."

Mitch dumped a scoop of detergent into the other machine and set the dials. "Tick-tock. Tick-tock. You're worried about that biological clock, aren't you?"

"I've been brainwashed into worrying about it." I slumped into a chair at the small table in the middle of the room and propped my chin in my hands. "It's kind of hard to shake off at this point. My fifteen-year high school reunion is in a few months, and I'm beginning to dread going. To listen to Mom, I'm the only one not involved in driving carpool to soccer practice."

Mitch joined me at the table. "Do you want to drive carpool to soccer practice?"

"I don't know. I'm tired of being alone, though. What if I never do find someone to share the rest of my life with?"

Mitch reached across the table and cupped my hands in his. "You're pinning a lot of hope on tonight. That's why you're so nervous. Don't set yourself up for a fall, Polly. You don't know anything about this guy."

Was that a hint of warning I heard in his voice? "Why? What do you know about him that you're not telling me?"

"Nothing. I hardly know him. He seems decent enough. I just don't want to see you get hurt again. Take it slowly. Okay?"

I told him about seeing Mason Wednesday night and my thoughts afterwards. "I promise. I don't want to be hurt again, either."

He squeezed my hands. "Good. Let's get some coffee while the washers are running."

"My place or yours?"

"Yours is one flight closer, but I make the coffee. You only know how to make dishwater."

I rose from my chair and punched him playfully in his bicep. "True, but it's the best damn dishwater you'll ever taste."

Mitch laughed. "Polly, mark my words, you will go down in history as the maker of the finest gourmet dishwater the world has ever seen." He wrapped his arm around my shoulders, and side-by-side, we headed upstairs.

Why couldn't I find someone like Mitch?

~*~

I'm a sucker for a guy with a devilish smile. As I think back on all my ex-boyfriends, I realize that's the feature that first drew me to each of them. Smile at me a certain way, and I melt like a scoop of Ben & Jerry's on a hot summer day. It doesn't matter whether the guy's a saint or a cad. As long as he's got the smile, my brain heads south.

Neil Pearson had a killer smile. I couldn't keep my eyes off his sexy mouth throughout dinner. The rest of him wasn't too bad, either. Add to that a wry sense of humor, sparkling conversation, and the ability to listen as well as speak, and it wasn't long before all my good intentions took flight. The temperature started soaring, and I started melting.

Always with past relationships, my hormones first had to attack my heart before they took control of my body. My head-over-heels tumbles take time. Slowly, the smile eats away at my defenses and burrows into every cell in my body until I become a quivering mass of love-struck need. There's no fighting it. The hormones win out every time.

In hindsight, I'm not sure I've ever been in love, but each time I'd fallen, nothing could have convinced me otherwise. Things were different this time, though. I wasn't in love with Neil Pearson. I hardly knew the guy, but damn if I didn't want him. Now.

I could tell he felt the heat. He created quite a bit of his own. His eyes smoldered when he gazed at me—which he did all night. He wanted me as much as I wanted him. Every gesture, every unspoken word, told me so. The chemistry flying across the table was incendiary.

Look before you leap. Look before you leap. I repeated my new mantra silently to myself a dozen times during the entrée alone. Determined to keep my wits, I ignored my wine and drank glass after glass of ice water. All that water led to several trips to the ladies' room, where I patted my cheeks and neck with wet paper towels, took deep calming breaths, and gave my wayward hormones several stern, silent lectures.

During my third trip to relieve my bladder, I gazed at my reflection in the mirror and laughed out loud. I was acting more like Mom during one of her menopause rushes. What in the world had come over me? I had never flipped out so quickly and so completely over a man—especially one who'd never even held my hand, let alone kissed me. Damn that smile of his! If I had an ounce of common sense, I'd wipe it off his face.

I laughed again—this time a bit more hysterically. I had a sneaking suspicion I knew what had triggered my hormonal whirlpool. Good intentions aside, in little more than three hours, I'd turn thirty-two. Thirty-two and still single. Tick-tock. Tick-tock.

Under the circumstances, if I were having dinner with the

world's most obnoxious nerd, I'd probably act just as foolishly. My behavior was irrational, but no matter how much I tried to convince myself otherwise, strong emotion beat out cool reason any day of the week. I still wanted the guy.

But I vowed not to succumb. In my head I listed all the losers who'd passed through my life and told myself I was better off single than with any one of them. I reminded myself of my promise to Mitch. If Neil was the one, it was better to find out slowly. If he wasn't, I'd be rushing headfirst into another painful disaster, and I didn't want to deal with that kind of hurt again.

I returned to the table with a bit more resolve than I had when I left. I tried to hold onto it for the remainder of the evening.

Saturday night spilled over into the early morning hours of Sunday, and still we sat and talked and the chemistry swirled around us. The restaurant thinned out until we were the only diners left. When the waiters began flipping chairs onto stripped tables and wet-mopping the tile floor, we reluctantly left.

~*~

As much as I wanted to, somehow I worked up the fortitude not to invite Neil in when we arrived back at my apartment. As much as I wanted him to take me in his arms and kiss me senseless, I mustered the courage to step back and extend my hand. "Thank you for the lovely evening."

He stared at my palm and frowned. I knew he at least expected a goodnight kiss—hell, after the silent signals flying across the table all night, he probably expected the whole enchilada. But I was in no condition for even a chaste goodnight peck on the lips, let alone anything deeper. If the man kissed as good as he smiled— and I had no doubt he did—I was a total goner. I wasn't ready for that. Not yet. Not this time.

His frown turned to puzzlement. He clasped my hand in both of his. "I'd like to see you again, Polly."

"I'd like that."

Relief flooded his features. "I'll call you."

"I'll look forward to hearing from you."

I slipped my hand out of his and let myself into my empty apartment. Looking before leaping was hard work.

ELEVEN
Lust, Glorious Lust

Imagine my surprise when I arrived at Uncle Cal's church the next morning to find Arlene sitting by herself in a back pew of the small country English-style stone building. I slid in beside her and whispered, "A little bit out of the way for you, isn't it?" After all, Arlene lived on Staten Island, and All Hallows was located in Caldwell, New Jersey—not exactly around the corner from her.

Arlene fumbled with the hymnal and Bible on her lap and blushed.

I glanced down the length of the sunlit sanctuary to where Uncle Cal sat behind the oak carved pulpit, waiting for the processional music to end. As always, he looked quite formidable in his red-trimmed white clerical vestments, but there was something different about him. I studied his face. It was softer, somehow—more peaceful—even though the same craggy wrinkles still crisscrossed his face, traveling from one feature to the next, and the same puffy bags still hung below his navy blue eyes.

I thought back to Valentine's Day, my mind replaying the scene I had observed at the punch bowl, and suddenly I felt as though someone had dumped a loaded punch bowl over my head. Imagine that! I may not have much luck with my own social life, but it appeared I'd inadvertently managed to bring together two lonely birds with one stone. I nudged Arlene with my elbow. "Is something going on between you and my uncle?"

Arlene bit down on her lower lip, fighting to hide a guilty smile.

Bingo! "Arlene?"

At that moment, the organ music ended, and Uncle Cal strode to the pulpit. As he cleared his throat, Arlene settled back against the pew and sighed. Let her think she'd received a reprieve. I fully intended to continue my interrogation as soon as the service ended.

~*~

An hour later, as everyone else filed out of the sanctuary, I kept my seat, blocking Arlene from leaving. "Are you going to come clean, or do I have to get rough?"

She blushed again and laughed nervously. "I didn't expect to see you until later."

"Later?"

"At your birthday dinner."

Now this was a shock that had to qualify as a ten on the Richter scale. "Uncle Cal invited you to have dinner with my family?" My other uncles occasionally brought guests to Sunday dinner, but Uncle Cal *never* invited anyone, even on a normal Sunday, let alone my birthday.

I knew I risked sounding like a mother hen—or worse, a nosey butinsky, but I had to ask, "Exactly how serious have things gotten between the two of you? You've only known each other less than two weeks."

Uncle Cal came up from behind and placed his hand on my shoulder. "Now, Polly, that's really none of your business, is it?"

I rose and hugged him. Laughter bubbled up inside me. "No it's not, and for the record, I couldn't be happier." I turned back to Arlene and reached for her hand. "For both of you. As far as I'm concerned, this is the best birthday present anyone could give me."

Okay, I lied. I could definitely think of at least one present that would make me happier, but Prince Charming wasn't exactly beating down my door. Besides, I was striving for an unselfish response. If I couldn't find the man of my dreams, maybe Arlene could. After the life she'd led for the past forty-plus years, she certainly deserved more than a little happiness.

Uncle Cal cleared his throat, my over-exuberance obviously catching him off guard. "I'd better put in an appearance at coffee hour." He spun on his heels and headed for the nearest exit.

Arlene's blush grew to a bright scarlet. "We only had two dates, Polly. The last two Saturday nights. Just friendly dinners. We talked. About lots of things." She paused for a moment and trapped me with a piercing green gaze. "About everything."

Just friendly dinners? Maybe. But we were talking about two people who, between them, hadn't dated in over four and a half decades. And a woman who had never divulged the secret that kept her trapped in the past to anyone other than me. Whatever force had drawn them together on Valentine's Day had to be pretty powerful. I raised my eyebrows and grinned at her. "So nothing happened?"

Arlene gasped. "No, of course not."

"It will."

Her bright scarlet cheeks deepened to purple.

One question remained, though. "So what about your mother?"

She hesitated.

"You haven't told her anything yet, have you?"

She inhaled sharply, pressing her twisted fingers into a tight knot against her abdomen. "Worse." Her voice faltered as she spoke. "I lied to her. She thinks I went to a bridal shower for a coworker the first Saturday night and the wedding last night. I even took her shopping with me for the gifts. I tossed them into the Salvation Army bin on my way to meet your uncle each night."

I groaned. "And today?"

"Your birthday party. I arranged for her to get a ride to and from church with a neighbor."

"Does Uncle Cal know?" My uncle regarded lying and deceit as near-mortal sins. He'd given a fair share of blistering sermons on the subjects over the years—not to mention the scathing lecture I'd received when I was five years old. He caught me lying about how Aunt June's cookie jar wound up shattered on the kitchen floor. To this day I find it difficult to tell a lie, and when I do, I keep glancing over my shoulder to make sure my uncle isn't within earshot.

Arlene grimaced. "He's not happy about it."

I wouldn't think so. "Maybe you should take him to meet your mother."

I bit back the rest of my thought. I had developed an unhealthy dislike toward a woman I've never met, but, under the circumstances, my feelings were justified. If someone as virtuous as my uncle could see beyond a sin committed by a teenager over forty years ago, certainly the woman's mother should forgive her.

"We've discussed it."

"And?"

She hung her head and sighed. Her fingers continued to twist and knot, her knuckles growing white from the pressure. "Well, I can't keep making up excuses for running off on Saturday nights." She glanced up and offered me a pleading smile. "We don't have that many coworkers I can marry off, do we?"

"No, we don't." Besides, I had no idea how much Arlene had told her mother about the office staff. She could very easily trap herself in a whopper of a lie if she weren't careful. From what I knew of her mother, I doubted the woman would tolerate even the most minor fib. And once she caught Arlene in one, she'd make her life even more miserable.

Arlene thought for a moment. "I suppose we could have a few baby showers coming up and maybe a going-away or retirement party?"

I shook my head. "I don't think so."

"No, I suppose you're right. It's about time I replaced the macaroni in my spine with a backbone."

"Good idea."

She sighed again, unknotted her fingers, and nervously combed them through her hair. "You don't know my mother, Polly."

I locked arms with Arlene and led her towards the church dining room. "True but she doesn't know Uncle Cal."

~*~

Having one of my uncles bring a date to my birthday dinner seemed odd, but because it was Arlene, I didn't mind. For years my birthday celebration had consisted of my parents; my uncles; my aunts and Arthur, when they were alive; Joni; Mitch; and occasionally—very occasionally—my significant other of the moment. Strangely enough, as I looked back over the past ten years, I remembered very few birthdays where I was actually dating someone. No wonder my mother has a cow every time my birthday approaches.

Joni and Mitch, who had taken the train to Summit with Uncle Emerson and Uncle Aaron, both raised eyebrows on seeing Uncle Cal with Arlene. None of my family seemed the least bit surprised, though. Apparently Uncle Cal had informed them ahead of time, leaving me—obviously, still considered the baby of the family in some ways—out of the loop.

Or maybe it was meant to be a birthday surprise. I decided to give him the benefit of the doubt.

As we took our seats around a large circular table at Chez Pierre, one of my favorite New Jersey restaurants, I discovered my uncles had a bigger birthday surprise for me up their collective sleeves. Although they hadn't mentioned a word about Carlos since Christmas, they hadn't forgotten about him. In the ensuing weeks, they'd worked diligently towards seeing that he took responsibility for Tiffany and their children.

"How did you manage it?" Joni, Mitch and I asked in unison. As much as we'd hoped the indomitable foursome could work some major miracle, in the backs of our minds, we had our doubts. From what we'd read and seen on the news from time to time, the three of us suspected the system contained enough inherent flaws to impede their kind of divine earthly intervention. Besides, we expected Carlos to fight them tooth and nail.

"Equal portions of blackmail, threats, and the promise of eternal damnation," said Uncle Francis with a straight face but a twinkle in his eye.

"Not to mention the assistance of one parole officer and one former juvie officer," said Uncle Aaron. His face beamed. "Between them, they exerted enough pressure to convince the boy that it was in his best interest to have Francis handle his finances."

Uncle Francis, who had received his undergraduate degree in accounting before receiving the Lord's call, was appointed Carlos' financial advisor. He established a custodial account, doling out a weekly allowance to the scumbag.

Uncle Francis moved Tiffany into a nicer apartment—one complete with an ongoing supply of hot water and heat and minus any rats and drug dealers loitering on the front steps. He also convinced her to quit her dead-end, fast food job and go back to school. Little Jesse attended daycare at the church while his mother worked toward her high school diploma. With any luck, she'd graduate to a trade school and learn a marketable skill. We didn't delude ourselves into thinking Tiffany was college material.

The balance of Carlos' income was invested in blue chip mutual funds with a trust fund set up for both Tiffany, Jesse, and the baby on the way. No matter what happened to Carlos, Uncle Francis had ensured a nest egg for Tiffany and an education for her and her children.

"And Carlos agreed to all this?" asked Joni.

Uncle Francis puffed out his chest and affected his best Marlon Brando imitation. "Let's just say we made him an offer he couldn't refuse."

Was it legal? Highly unlikely, considering they used coercion, but Carlos *had* gone along with the plan. Maybe in his own slime ball way, he did care for Tiffany and his kids. Or maybe he was smart enough to know when the odds were stacked against him.

"He wasn't too happy," said Uncle Aaron. "He grumbled a good deal."

"But we convinced him it was the right thing to do," added Uncle Emerson.

"And in the end he came to see the light," said Uncle Cal.

Moral of the story? Don't ever mess with my uncles.

I glanced over at Arlene. Uncle Cal could handle her mother, and if by some chance he needed help, all he had to do was call in the clerical posse.

~*~

It didn't take long before the conversation steered over to my date with Neil. As soon as the waiter departed with our beverage orders, my mother began the grilling. "So?" In Mom-speak that means, "Can I book the catering hall?"

All eyes turned to me.

My commando-like hormonal response to Neil the night before had been along the lines of a major histamine reaction—sudden and near lethal. Never before had I experienced anything like it. God only knows how I got through the evening without jumping his bones right there in the middle of the restaurant, let alone once we arrived back at my apartment. The mere thought of him sent heat-seeking missiles caroming through my body.

The last thing in the world I wanted to do was relate my evening with Neil to my family. Except, knowing my family, I wasn't going to get away with *not* talking about last night's date. And I couldn't exactly make a scene or storm out of the room as if we were at my parents' house. Chez Pierre is a very upscale establishment. Monsieur Pierre, the Cordon Bleu trained owner, would shit a French cow.

I willed my voice not to wobble and my cheeks not to blush.

"He's very nice."

"Just nice?" Poor Mom looked crestfallen. She glanced over at Uncle Emerson. He shrugged his shoulders as if to say, he'd tried his best and don't blame him.

"Nice enough to go out with again," I added.

Mom brightened. She opened her mouth, ready to continue the grilling, but Dad interceded on my behalf. "I'm sure when Polly has more to tell us, she will, dear."

"But I—"

"No buts, Mimi. It's Polly's birthday. Let her enjoy herself without an interrogation."

Mom screwed up her nose. She hated when anyone tried to muzzle her—especially Dad. No one ever got away with it— except Dad. She placed her hand on my arm and whispered in my ear, "We'll talk later. Just the two of us."

I smiled weakly. *Not if I can help it.*

~*~

"So dish," said Joni. "What's the scoop with this Neil guy?"

We were back at our apartment building later that night. Joni and Mitch had invited me upstairs for a birthday nightcap. I flopped back against the sofa cushions. "I'm in big trouble. He pushes all the right buttons without moving a finger."

Joni sputtered into her Merlot. "Don't tell me you slept with him on the first date? Our Pollyanna? Stop the presses! Call the networks!"

I whacked her with a pillow, nearly spilling her wine and mine. "Stop calling me that. And no, I didn't sleep with him. I didn't even kiss him."

Joni smirked. "Now that's more like the Polly we all know and love."

"Doesn't mean I didn't want to." I closed my eyes and hugged the pillow to my chest. "God, did I ever want to. Scared the hell out of me. I've never had such an instant, volcanic reaction to a man." I opened my eyes and shifted my gaze between Joni and Mitch. "And we didn't *do* anything. This all happened over dinner at a restaurant. We ate and talked. Nothing more. But you'd think the way my body started reacting that we'd been making out in the backseat of his car!"

"I read somewhere that some women don't reach their sexual peak until their thirties," said Joni. "Maybe your hormones are finally waking up and making up for lost time."

"You think?" I frowned into the dark burgundy pool floating around in my glass. Carlos and his magic fingers immediately sprang to mind. Common sense had deserted me that night, as well. Luckily, I had corralled my AWOL brains before the situation got any further out of control. "If this is the way I'm going to react to men from now on, maybe I'm better off if my hormones don't wake up. I'm not sure I can handle it."

I glanced across the room to where Mitch sat in an overstuffed easy chair, his gaze centered on his own glass of wine. He hadn't said a word since we entered the apartment. For that matter, he hadn't said much the entire evening. "You're awfully quiet tonight."

He lifted his head. "Just thinking."

"About what?"

"You."

"Any words of wisdom?"

He shook his head. "None beyond what I said yesterday, sweetheart. Just take it slowly. I don't want to see you get hurt again."

"No one wants that to happen," said Joni. "But if Polly doesn't start living, she'd going to wake up one day and find life has passed her by."

"Gee, thanks! Am I that much of a lost cause?"

"I didn't mean it like that, Pol. I just think that sometimes you have to take a chance. Not play it so safe."

"I haven't exactly been cloistering myself, Joni. I've got a lengthy list of failed relationships to prove it, in case you haven't noticed."

"All I mean is, maybe your body is telling you something your head hasn't figured out yet—because of all those failures. Intellectually, you're gun shy. Or maybe in this case, it's guy shy. Anyway, you're afraid of listening to your body because you don't want to get hurt again. But your hormones don't know from intellectual reasoning. They react on gut instinct."

"You should know," muttered Mitch.

"I'm not the one with a problem here," she told him.

"Past experience has proven my gut instinct notoriously inaccurate," I reminded her.

"But you yourself said nothing like this has ever hit you before."

She had a point there, but Mitch's advice was equally valid—and probably better for me, considering the two sources. "Hormones or no hormones," I announced to both of them, "I'm not rushing into anything."

"Better rustle up a chastity belt, then," Joni suggested, a smug expression on her face. "Sounds like you're going to need one."

This time I did hit her with the pillow.

~*~

My phone was ringing as I walked in the door from work the

following evening. I'd spent most of the day on a conference call with Mason Hightower and his overly verbose board—for a change. Mace had become a prickly burr up my ass, and the rest of his board wasn't much better. Unfortunately, their connections in the music world had secured several new and lucrative accounts for our firm since the beginning of the year. As a result, Head Lecherous Jerk expected everyone to jump at Mace's every whim. It was my responsibility, as executive director of his organization, to jump the quickest and highest—no questions asked.

I stared at the phone, half-tempted to let voice mail pick it up. With my luck, it was Mace calling—again. Or my mother. I was too tired to deal with either of them. But there was one person I wouldn't mind hearing from, and on that chance, I finally answered.

For the first time that day, luck was with me. Neil was on the other end of the line.

"What do you think about hockey?" he asked.

"I think it's a pretty odd way to start a conversation."

He chuckled. "Probably. Listen, Polly," he continued, "I know this is short notice, but someone gave me a pair of Rangers tickets for tonight's game. I would have called you at work, but I didn't have your number."

"You're inviting me to a hockey game?" I hoped I misunderstood him. On a good day I wasn't keen on spending an evening with fifteen thousand screaming sports jocks in Madison Square Garden. And this had definitely not qualified as a good day. "Wouldn't you rather take one of your buddies?"

"Now, Polly, if you were me, and you had the choice of spending an evening with you or one of the guys, which would you choose?"

I wouldn't choose a hockey game, I thought. Baseball? Definitely. I'd never pass up a chance to see a Mets game. And okay, I know as a New Yorker, never the twain should meet, but I'd even trek up to the Bronx to watch the Yankees if the Mets weren't in town. Dad loved baseball and raised me to love it. When he managed to secure two tickets to each game of the 2000 Subway Series, I jumped at the chance to go with him. Mom didn't mind. She never could understand the heart palpitating allure of sitting on the edge of your seat during a no-hitter.

Even basketball wasn't bad once in a while, but football and hockey left me cold. So how did I decline without sounding like I didn't want to see him? I sighed. "If you had theater or concert tickets, I'd say me, but really, Neil, wouldn't you enjoy yourself more with someone else?"

"No."

I glanced at my watch. If I accepted his offer, I'd have less than half an hour to get ready. As usual, I hadn't eaten all day. My head throbbed, and my stomach growled. All I really wanted to do was nuke some dinner and veg out in front of the television.

I was about to decline his offer when a thought occurred to me. Spending an evening with Neil doing something I hated might not be such a bad idea. Would my body reacted to him in a hockey arena the way it had at the restaurant Saturday night? As tired as I was, I had to find out. "All right," I told him, "but don't expect me to paint my face red and blue. And you'd better not show up in some crazy outfit."

"I promise."

"You also have to promise to feed me. I haven't eaten yet."

"I'll buy you all the beer and cheese nachos your heart desires."

Whoop-de-doo. I suggested we meet at The Garden. Not

wanting to miss the drop of the puck, Neil agreed.

I hung up the phone and went in search of some Motrin. What had I gotten myself into?

~*~

What had I gotten myself into? More than I bargained for. The Motrin didn't relieve the pounding at my temples, even though I took a double dose. Neither did the cold air as I made my way to the subway. As I waited for the train, the blasts of heat from the overhead blowers and the underground stench sent my stomach roiling. By the time I met Neil, I felt like crap, but I pasted a smile on my face and didn't complain—not an easy task under the circumstances.

The Rangers were playing their archrivals, the Philadelphia Flyers. Because only a ninety-mile car ride along the New Jersey turnpike separated the two teams, every seat in the arena was filled with raucous fans, most in Rangers red and blue but many in Flyers orange and black. Within five minutes a fight broke out on the ice, followed by several in the stands.

Ten minutes into the first period, the din of the arena had escalated my headache to near-migraine level. The smells of beer and greasy food wreaked havoc with my stomach. I closed my eyes and took several deep breaths, but instead of fresh air to settle my stomach, my lungs filled with more noxious odors.

A Flyers' penalty gave the Rangers a power play. The stadium erupted in rhythmic foot stomping and chanting. When the captain scored an unassisted goal on the power play, the screaming crowd rose to its feet. Neil joined right in, as excited as the rest of them. "Isn't this a great game?" he yelled.

"Great," I mouthed back. A moment later, beer and popcorn rained down on me from the level above, and I knew beyond a shadow of a doubt, that I was about to lose it. I grabbed my knit cap out of my coat pocket, clapped it over my mouth, and fought my way to the aisle. I prayed I didn't have far to go to find a bathroom.

I never made it. The best I could do was a trash can at the top of the ramp, but it was a hell of a lot better than upchucking on the person sitting in front of me or worse yet, into Neil's lap. I hoped they both appreciated the effort. Closing my eyes, I wretched my guts out over an assortment of debris best left unseen and unidentified.

Sometimes not eating all day can be a godsend. An empty stomach produces very little in rebound, but although my humiliating ordeal ended within seconds of beginning, it seemed more like an hour.

I noticed a growing assemblage—mostly adolescent boys— hanging back across the corridor. My ears picked up an undercurrent of snickering and pubescent humor. Keeping a safe distance, they continued to gawk and joke as I straightened and headed off in search of a restroom. In a few years they'd most likely evolve into the drivers who slow down to gape at a traffic accident, hoping to catch a glimpse of the carnage.

Once in the bathroom, I washed out my mouth and splashed cold water on my face and neck. On the way back, I grabbed a Coke at the concession stand. Despite the embarrassing experience, I felt much better. Even my headache had subsided.

"Long line at the ladies' room?" asked Neil when I sat back down.

I nodded. If he hadn't noticed that I looked like death warmed over earlier, I certainly wasn't going to go into detail about my little excursion. But why hadn't he noticed? I wasn't that good an actress. Surely, my discomfort had shown on my face. I sighed, glad that my stomach and head had kept my hormones duly suppressed. I didn't want to fall for a guy who was so clueless that he didn't notice his date turning a sickly shade of green.

The buzzer sounded, signaling the end of the first period. Neil sprang to his feet. "What can I get you?"

"Nothing, thanks. I'm fine."

"I thought you said you hadn't eaten."

I had my choice of telling him the truth or coming up with a white lie to save both of us an explanation I didn't want to give. I opted for the lie. "I was too hungry to wait. I made myself a sandwich and ate it on the way over."

"Okay. I'm going to get a beer and some nachos. Sure you don't want anything?"

I shook my head and nursed the Coke.

Neil placed his hand on my shoulder and tossed me one of his killer smiles. "Be right back." He turned and inched his way down the row of occupied seats.

When he was out of sight, I fished an ice cube from my cup and rubbed it against the back of my neck. His smile hadn't sent goose bumps racing up and down my spine. His touch hadn't turned my insides to hot, drippy molasses. Was I too wrung out to feel anything, or was Saturday night an aberration brought about by the rapid countdown to my birthday?

Just as I had resolved to take things slowly with Neil, I now decided not to rush into judgment of him. He was caught up in an exciting game. Being a diehard baseball fan, I understood that. Sports fanaticism wasn't necessarily only a guy thing. And my reactions—or lack of them—were definitely clouded by a body that should have remained at home this evening.

~*~

After the game ended, the Rangers pulling out a five-four squeaker in the last seconds of the third period, Neil and I huddled together in the taxi line at Penn Station. "Have you ever seen such an exciting game?" he asked, trying to shield me from the whipping wind.

Truthfully, I hadn't paid much attention to the game. I was too busy concentrating on willing my stomach to remain settled and hoping the din of the arena didn't trigger a resurgence of my finally departed headache. Every nerve ending in my body continued to wobble and jangle precariously, even after heaving up my insides, and it took supreme effort to hide my discomfort.

"How about stopping for a nightcap?" he asked after we'd settled into the backseat of a cab. "I know a little jazz bar in Union Square that whips up some mean spiked coffees."

I knew the place. Jazzed on Java. They served strong coffee and hot jazz, but the only place I wanted to go at the moment was straight to bed. Alone. I smiled sweetly. "How about a rain check? I had a difficult day at work, and I'm anticipating a worse one tomorrow. I really need to get some sleep."

For the first time that night, Neil really looked at me. Realization dawned, his light gray eyes darkening with concern. He reached for my hand and held it firmly between both of his. "You didn't want to come tonight, did you? Why didn't you tell me when I called?"

Why didn't I? Did I think turning down one last-minute date would mean he'd never call again? How very desperate and exceedingly un-twenty-first century of me! And how totally *not* me. Where had I left my backbone earlier that day? I suffered through a miserable few hours with only myself to blame. "I should have. I didn't realize how exhausted I was. I'm sorry."

He raised my hand and placed a kiss on my fingertips. "I feel like an insensitive boor. Forgive me?" His whispered breath raised goose bumps on my flesh. The heat of his lips traveled straight to my belly. I began to melt, and he hadn't even employed one of those killer smiles. "I'll make it up to you, I promise. How about Saturday night? Dinner. Dancing. And absolutely no hockey."

I turned my head to face him. He had twisted in his seat. Only a hair's breadth separated us. "Sounds nice." My words rang breathless in my ears. Sexy. As sexy as Neil made me feel with merely a gentle kiss to my fingers. I shuddered.

An instant later his lips settled gently over mine—thank God for the Tic Tacs I'd popped in my mouth after my date with the trash can—and all thought of my earlier discomfort fled. He wrapped one hand around the back of my neck and drew me closer, intensifying the pressure on my lips. His other hand still held one of my mine, trapped between our bodies, his knuckles brushing my breasts. Even through the thick layers of winter clothing, I responded to his touch. My breasts swelled. My nipples tightened, straining against the lace of my bra.

He took his time, exploring, nibbling, tasting. When I parted my lips, he accepted the invitation, delving farther with his tongue, probing deep inside my mouth. His kisses washed over me like a narcotic, and I reacted like an addict, desperate for more.

Neil pulled back enough to work open the buttons on my coat. He slipped his hand inside and underneath my sweater, moaning into my mouth when he made contact with my bare flesh. He cupped one of my breasts, then found my hardened nipple and rolled the tip between his thumb and forefinger. My stomach clenched, and I moaned back into his mouth.

"I've wanted to do this from the moment I first saw you," he said. His fingers danced circles around one nipple and then the other. "This and so much more."

And I wanted him to. I wanted him to strip me naked and take me right there in the cab. Aroused to a fevered pitch, I arched into him, melding our bodies together. The hell with taking things slowly.

"But not tonight," he murmured. His voice was husky and ripe with need, but he withdrew his hand, pulled back, and slowly buttoned my coat. I shivered at the loss of his warmth, his touch.

A moment later, the taxi drew up to the curb in front of my apartment.

Neil reached for the handle but before opening the door, he turned back to me, cupped my face with his palm, and whispered in my ear, "I want you well-rested and wide awake because I intend to keep you up all night begging for more." He accentuated his words with one of his killer smiles.

My response, a deep, needy moan that rocketed from my womb to my throat, amused Neil and embarrassed the hell out of me. I felt myself turn scarlet—from my toes to my scalp. He chuckled. His fingers skimmed across my cheek, over my lips, and down my neck. My breath caught in my throat. His hooded eyes narrowed into two sensuous slits. "Saturday, my love. I promise I'll make it worth the wait."

I moaned again.

~*~

Neil stood me up Saturday night.

TWELVE
When I Smile, You'll Know I Finally Got Laid

Friday night I came home from work to find a message from Neil on my voice mail.

"Polly, I'm afraid I'm going to have to cancel tomorrow night. One of our major accounts flew in unexpectedly for a brain-picking session, and my head was nominated for weekend duty. I'm sorry, babe. I'll call you Monday."

So much for looking forward to getting laid. Thoughts of Neil had kept me in a constant state of arousal all week. I couldn't eat. I couldn't sleep. Every time I closed my eyes, my mind started conjuring up triple-X rated pictures of the two of us. I was in lust like I'd never been in my life. It was sheer hell. The only thing that kept me going all week was the knowledge that come Saturday, I'd get to live out those highly erotic fantasies. Wrong again. Welcome to my life—someone's idea of a sick joke.

The next night, instead of getting naked with Neil, I donned a pair of ratty thermals, popped *Sleepless in Seattle* into my DVD player, and curled up on the sofa with a bowl of popcorn, a box of tissues, and a full-blown case of the *why me's*. I couldn't even invite Joni and Mitch to a bitching session. They both had dates—which only made me feel even sorrier for myself.

Two hours later, Tom and Meg had found love on top of the Empire State Building. I should be so lucky. This was not the night for happy ending movies. I needed characters who understood my pain. I air-popped another bowl of popcorn, drenched it with melted butter, grabbed a bottle of white Zinfandel, and switched to *Shakespeare in Love*.

As Viola washed onto shore in the New World, tears washed down my cheeks, but I cried for myself, not Viola and the Bard. At least they'd known love for a little while—unlike me and my loveless, sexless, pathetic existence. I might as well become a nun.

My pity party kicked into high gear. I rooted around in the freezer for a package of frozen brownies and popped them into the microwave. Then I popped the tearjerker of all tearjerkers into the DVD player. Sometime around three in the morning, I finally fell asleep. The last thing I remembered was Rick telling Ilsa they'd always have Paris.

~*~

I woke the next morning with a stiff neck, puffy eyes, tear-stained cheeks, and an incessant buzzing in my head that I first attributed to the empty bottle of wine on the coffee table. When the sound shifted from one long buzz to a series of sharp insistent notes, I finally recognized it as the outer doorbell.

Whoever it was, I was in no shape for an unexpected visitor. I crawled off the sofa, my head spinning from last night's feeling-sorry-for-myself binge, and yelled into the intercom, "Whatever you're selling, I either already have it or don't want it. Go away."

"Is that any way to speak to your mother?"

Mom! Just what I didn't need this morning. "What are you doing here?"

"Why? Am I interrupting something?" Her voice sounded hopeful.

I wish. "No, of course not."

"Oh." She sent one of her dramatic sighs of disappointment through the intercom. "Well, are you going to make me stand out in the cold, or are you going to buzz me in, dear?"

I pressed the button to release the outer door lock, then scrambled back to the sofa and hunted under the cushions for the remote control. After clicking off the TV, I grabbed the empty popcorn bowl, the plate of brownie crumbs, and the wine bottle and shoved everything under the sofa. A moment later Mom knocked at the door.

She didn't say a word as she slowly scanned me from head-to-toe. She didn't have to. A shake of her head and the pinched expression on her face said it all. "You're alone?" she asked, craning her neck to spy down the hall towards my open bedroom door, but it was only a formality. She already knew the answer to her question.

I ran my fingers through the tangled rat's nest of my hair and avoided her stern gaze. Only my mother could become disappointed over *not* catching her daughter with a man in her bed. If I were in a better mood, I'd laugh out loud, but I was in a lousy mood, and Mom's prying questions were like salt in an open wound.

She exhaled forcefully as she strode across the room and plopped a grocery bag onto the kitchen counter. "Take a shower, and get dressed," she ordered. "I brought breakfast."

"Yes, ma'am." I resisted the urge to salute. There was no use arguing with her when she stepped into her General Mimi persona. I didn't bother asking again why she'd come or where Dad was. She'd tell me in her own good time. Besides, I wasn't exactly in the best shape to pick a fight or enter into a debate with her. She'd browbeat me into a pulp, and I'd done enough self-flagellation the night before.

That was the trouble with pity parties, I decided, as I shuffled off to the bathroom. You always felt a hell of a lot worse the morning after the night before. I deserved a good swift kick in the rear, and Mom was exactly the person to give it to me—even if she came for some other reason. I'd spent the night wallowing, for God's sake! And for what? A cancelled date? It wasn't like I was in love with the guy or anything. I just wanted him to screw my brains out. How pathetic!

If I was that desperate for a good lay, maybe I needed a vibrator instead of a man. After all, wasn't I the girl who couldn't have sex without emotional commitment? Neil and I had no emotional commitment to each other. The fire burning between us was nothing more than unadulterated animal lust—nature's way of ensuring survival of the species.

Yet, if Neil hadn't cancelled last night, I would have greedily spread my legs for him. How much worse would I now feel, had last night gone as planned? All my latent Jewish-Catholic-Episcopal guilt answered the question for me.

So why did I still want the man in my pants? "Pathetic," I mumbled as I shook my head and stepped into the shower. "Polly Pathetic."

Half an hour later, I still felt like shit—both physically and emotionally—but at least I'd cleaned myself up. A blast of ambrosia hit me full force when I opened the bathroom door. Bless her busybody heart, Mom had left a steaming mug of coffee sitting on my nightstand. I clasped it between both hands and drank greedily.

"Must have been some party last night."

I spun around to find her lounging in the doorway. In one hand she held the empty wine bottle, the popcorn bowl and brownie plate nestled in the crook of her arm. Her other hand waved the DVD cases.

I grimaced. "I always suspected you had mindreading powers, Mom, but when did you develop X-ray vision? Or do you make a habit of snooping under sofas?"

She offered me one of those you-can't-pull-anything-over-on-your-mother smiles. "Next time you want to hide something, dear, you might consider shoving it *all the way* under the furniture."

I smiled back at her through gritted teeth. "I'll remember that."

"Excellent." She turned and headed down the hall. "Now let's have some breakfast, or we'll be late for church."

"Church?" I followed after her. The light began to dawn through my hungover head. Mom rarely came into the city on Sunday mornings. If her soul were in need of organized religion, she usually attended either Uncle Francis' or Uncle Cal's church. She couldn't fool me. She'd come into the city to scope out Neil.

"Yes, dear, Uncle Emerson has a wonderful sermon planned for today. I didn't want to miss it."

If memory served—and granted, after last night's binge, I couldn't necessarily trust any part of my brain—Uncle Emerson wasn't giving today's sermon. A visiting minister from the Unitarian-Universalist Association in Boston was scheduled to preach on the joy of giving. In other words, it was that time of year for the congregation once again to open its collective wallets and pledge support to replenish the shrinking coffers.

I settled into a chair at the table and reached for a toasted bagel. "He won't be there," I said. "You've made the trip for nothing."

She passed me a tub of cream cheese. "I don't know what you're talking about."

"Neil." I studied her out of the corner of my eye as I scooped up a glob of cream cheese and spread it over my bagel. "He won't be at church this morning. He had to work over the weekend."

"Neil who, dear?"

I gave up. If Mom wanted to act the innocent, fine. I was on to her. "Where's Dad? Why didn't he come with you?"

"He promised to help Uncle Cal with something this afternoon and didn't think we'd get back in time."

Translation: Dad didn't approve, so Mom went without him. "I see." I bit into my bagel.

"So how are things going with that nice young man you met a few weeks ago, dear?"

Grrr!

~*~

Much to my surprise, Neil showed up at church. He waved me over from halfway down the aisle as Mom and I entered the sanctuary. When we approached the pew, he rose, clasped his hands around mine, and kissed my cheek. "I was hoping you'd be here this morning."

I settled down next to him with Mom on my other side. "I didn't expect to see you."

He shrugged and grinned. "Time off for good behavior. I'm picking the client up at his hotel at one."

244

Mom elbowed me in the ribs—her subtle way of demanding an introduction. Luckily, the service began as soon as I finished introducing them, thus forcing her to keep her mouth closed—at least for the next hour. Sort of.

"So why weren't you out with him last night?" she whispered in my ear during one of the hymns.

"He had to work," I whispered back.

Mom chewed on the inside of her cheek for a moment before responding. "A workaholic? As much as I want a husband and children for you, dear, I don't want a son-in-law who never has time for his family."

"Don't worry. I have no plans to marry him."

"So why are you wasting your time with him?"

"*Shh!*"

She clamped her mouth shut as the hymn ended and took her seat. I sighed and stared ahead, focusing on the large stained glass window framing the pulpit.

On my right, Neil brushed his corduroy-clad leg up against mine, sending a tingle of hot pleasure surging through me. Accident? Or was he deliberately trying to turn me on? I glanced over at him. He glanced back, a rakish grin on his lips.

Damn him! How dare he come on to me in church with my mother sitting right beside me! I stole a glance to my left. Mom stared straight ahead, but her features had hardened to granite. There I was, stuck between a rock and a hard place—literally. Damned if I do, damned if I don't.

I didn't hear a word of the sermon. For the next hour I operated like one of the ventriloquists' dummies. On cue, I stood, sang, sat, as if I had a hollow wooden head and someone were pulling my strings.

When the service ended, Neil checked his watch, then extended his hand, skimming my breasts as he reached across me to Mom. "It was a pleasure meeting you, Mrs. Harmony. I wish we had time to get to know each other better, but I have to pick up a client."

Mom shook his hand. Coolly.

"Another time?"

She nodded, her lips curving up into an almost indiscernible smile.

"You weren't very pleasant," I said, after Neil left.

"He's only after one thing. Have you slept with him yet?"

"Not that it's any of your business, but no."

"Good. Don't. He'll only wind up hurting you."

"Now how do you know that?"

"A mother can tell these things, dear. I've kept my mouth shut before, but I'm not doing it any longer—not with your track record. Time is too precious." She rolled her eyes and sighed. "And to think Emerson fixed you up with that sex fiend!"

"Mom!" It was one thing to voice her opinions in private. I could even tolerate her butting into my life when other family members were present. As much as it irritated me, I knew she spoke out of love and concern. But I drew the line in a crowded church where anyone could overhear her.

I quickly scanned the nearby crowd inching out of the sanctuary. One elderly woman lingered behind us, her ears perked inches from Mom's back. When I glared at her, she shuffled off in the opposite direction.

Mom continued, her voice growing more strident. "Don't *Mom* me, Polly. I'm not blind, you know. Wait until I get hold of your uncle." She growled deep in her throat. "He's got some heavy explaining to do." With that, she steamrolled her way through the crowd toward the corridor leading into the church dining room.

"I'm *really* looking forward to dinner this evening," I mumbled under my breath to no one specific.

Someone tittered behind me. Not wanting to know who else had heard Mom's tirade, I didn't turn around to confront the culprit.

~*~

Somehow we all made it through dinner that evening without war erupting. Dad attempted to settle Mom down before any of the uncles arrived, and I placated her as best I could, but I'm not sure she believed anything either of us said. She was definitely not a happy camper and made certain everyone knew it. Uncle Emerson received the brunt of her hostility during the meal, with me a close second. We had both let her down.

For a woman who spent her life as an overachiever, she now viewed her only daughter as her one great failure. Of course, she never came right out and said it in so many words, but neither did she hide her disappointment that my life wasn't going as she'd planned it. Mom liked being in control. Of everything.

I tried to shrug the evening off, but Mom had really gotten to me this time, mostly because in my heart I knew she was right about Neil. He *was* seducing me. No doubt about it, but I shared half the blame. I wanted him to seduce me—even though I knew I'd hate myself in the morning.

Why couldn't I be like Joni and enjoy sex for sex's sake? Why did I have to clutter physical pleasure with all sorts of emotional baggage?

~*~

I posed that question later that night in Joni and Mitch's

apartment. The last thing in the world I expected was the answer she gave me.

"Maybe you've got the right idea," she said, twirling a lock of her white-blonde hair around her index finger. "Sex is great fun, but when you love someone, sex is no longer just sex, no matter how good it feels. You're making love, and all of a sudden, feeling good pales in comparison. The sex becomes mind-boggling and earth-shattering."

I stared at Mitch.

He stared back at me. "Did we just hear what I think we heard?"

"I think so."

We both stared at Joni. Mitch leaned over and grabbed her shoulders, forcing her to look directly at him. "This has gone on long enough," he said. "Spill it. Who are you, and what have you done with my sister?"

Joni smiled sweetly, lowered her gaze, and blushed. I don't think I'd ever seen her look so demure, and I *know* I'd never seen her blush. "There is something I've been meaning to tell both of you. I...we've been waiting for the right time."

"We?" Mitch dropped his hands to his sides. A stunned expression settled across his face.

"Someone we know?" I asked.

Joni nodded. She turned to me. "I was hoping you'd find someone before I told you."

"Why?" And then it hit me like a thunderbolt. "You're not dating Former Significant Other, are you? Joni, how could you fall for that louse?"

She laughed. "Relax, Pol. I'm not seeing Former Significant Other. I'm not just *seeing* anyone."

"What's that supposed to mean?" asked Mitch, settling back down in the overstuffed chair across from the coffee table. He folded his arms over his chest and stared at his sister like a stern parent.

Joni took a deep breath and exhaled slowly, biting down on her lower lip. "It means he's asked me to marry him, and I've said yes."

Suddenly, I understood the meaning of a moment frozen in time. Joni's words hung in the air. No one spoke. No one moved. Only the sound of the traffic on the street below proved the world had not stopped spinning on its axis.

Conflicting emotions fought inside me. Joni, my best friend, was getting married. Joni, the ultimate goodtime party girl, was getting married, and I, the quintessential Pollyanna, was still unattached, lonely, and miserable. Although I was happy for her, at the same time, I felt like she'd kicked me in the stomach.

Tears swam behind my eyes. I didn't know whether they were tears of joy for Joni or tears of self-pity—probably a mix of both, but I leaned across the couch and wrapped my arms around her.

Mitch still hadn't moved. Still hadn't said a word. "Who?" I whispered the word over the lump that had risen to my throat.

"Jeff."

I pulled back and stared at her. "*Jeff*? My Jeff?" Joni with her propensity for stud-muffin boy-toys had fallen for soft-spoken, forty-something Jeff with his gray-streaked beard, tweed sports coats, and cordovan loafers? Joni, who loved to dance the night away at Holland Tube, and Jeff, the two left feet Klezmer klutz? We had definitely entered *The Twilight Zone*.

Mitch found his voice. "Polly's boring cantor Jeff? With the roses?"

Joni laughed again. "He's really not boring once you get to

know him."

How was this possible? Putting aside the fact that Joni was the complete opposite of everything Jeff purported to want, there was the irrefutable fact that he couldn't deal with me being only one-quarter Jewish. How could he accept Joni? "But you're Catholic," I reminded her.

"Not any more."

"What!" Mitch shot out of his chair.

"Remember those classes I told you I was taking?"

I nodded. "You said they were for work."

"I lied."

"You converted!" It all began to make sense. Joni's change of wardrobe and attitude from in-your-face sexpot to finishing school chic, her secretiveness over the past few months, her disappearing acts.

"When did all this happen?" asked Mitch. "And why keep it a secret from us?"

"It began the night of Polly's dinner party. I can't explain it, but something happened when I pulled Jeff into the hallway to get rid of those damn roses that were causing Polly's sneezing fit."

"That's why you were gone so long?" I asked.

She drew her knees up to her chest, wrapped her arms around her legs, and nodded. A distant smile played across her lips. "We started talking. Jeff realized the moment he saw me and Mitch that you were sending him a message. At first he was upset. I tried to explain, but somehow before we knew what was happening, we'd both forgotten all about you, Polly. It was like all that crap about love at first sight isn't really crap at all. We simply knew immediately.

"At first I fought it. So did he. I acted especially slutty that night to prove to him it would never work out between us. I didn't want someone like him. We were too different—worlds apart in attitudes and everything else. We argued about it for days, but in the end, none of the differences mattered. Not to him. Not to me." She lowered her chin onto her knees. "Especially after he kissed me."

She closed her eyes and sighed. "By the way, I was all wrong about that age stuff. There's definitely something to be said for a mature lover."

I wouldn't know. As much as I wanted to celebrate Joni's happiness, an ugly jealousy began to roil inside me. The emotion, so foreign, rocked me. Before I said something I'd regret, I had to leave. "It's late." I stood, stretched, and faked a yawn. "Why don't we postpone the rest of our celebrating until Jeff can join us?"

Joni rose from the couch and hugged me. "Thank you. You can't imagine how much I've been dying for all four of us to get together."

Not wanting to rain on Joni's parade, I hugged her back, then forced a smile and headed for the door. Joni and Jeff. I still couldn't believe it, but maybe it's true what they say about opposites attracting. Joni and Jeff were certainly as opposite as they came.

"I'll walk you downstairs," offered Mitch, jumping to his feet.

Once out in the hallway, he began the conversation I was hoping to avoid. "Some shock, huh?"

"Hmm." I nodded as I headed for the staircase but couldn't look at him. Every nerve in my body felt like it was balancing precariously on a thin strand of spider webbing.

At the landing, Mitch grabbed my hand and turned me towards him. "You need to talk this out, Polly. I can see what's going on inside you."

His comment surprised me. I thought I had masked my feelings pretty well upstairs. At least I hoped I had. This was my problem, not Joni's, and I didn't want anything to stand in the way of her happiness or our friendship.

Joni and Mitch had grown up under less-than-ideal conditions, receiving little attention and even less love from their mother. I had often wondered if Mitch's lack of commitment and Joni's freewheeling sexuality were defenses they developed to avoid further pain. After all, people kept at a distance can't hurt you.

Maybe Mitch was echoing his own inner turmoil over Joni's announcement. The two of them had relied on each other and no one else for most of their lives. Lovers had come and gone, but no one had ever come between them until now.

I tried for a bit of humor to ease the tension coiling in my belly. "Taking mindreading lessons from my mother, Mitch?"

"Every Wednesday evening from eight to ten."

I chuckled, despite my morose mood, and protested my innocence. "I'm happy for Joni."

"That's a given, but what else is going on?"

I turned away and continued down the stairs. "Do I really need to spell it out for you?"

"I suppose not."

"In your wildest dreams, did you ever imagine Joni would settle down before either of us?"

Shoving the key into the lock, I swung open the door and swept the room with a wave of my hand. Emotion clogged my throat, and I swallowed hard to force it from creeping into my voice. "Every day I wake to an empty apartment. Every night I come home to the same empty apartment. I'm so lonely that for the last few days I've been contemplating having an affair with a man I don't love just to feel something besides loneliness—even if it's only for a little while. Even though I know I'm going to hate myself for doing it."

I stepped inside. Mitch followed. A deep frown settled over his face. "And you know what the real kicker is?" I asked, slamming the door behind us.

"What?"

"I've rationalized that affair by trying to adopt Joni's laidback philosophy about sex. So what does she go and do? She falls in love, damn her, and repudiates everything she's ever claimed to believe in!"

He gathered me up in his arms, his chin resting on the top of my head. "Yeah, she's got some nerve, huh?"

I tried to wriggle out of his grasp. "Don't make fun of me!"

"Shh." He held firm. "I'm not making fun of you, Polly."

"Could've fooled me." But I relaxed against his chest, anyway. It felt good to be held. Especially by Mitch. His embrace comforted me like a crackling fire on a wintry day. My tumultuous emotions calmed a bit. "Things are going to change," I said. "No more reverse Oreos. Joni's breaking up a longstanding act."

"Life is always changing. I guess we'll have to revamp into a duo."

"The bachelor and the old maid?"

Mitch tipped my chin up with his index finger and pursed his lips. "I think we can do better than that."

"Like what? The stud and the spinster?"

He planted a kiss on my forehead before releasing me. "Go to bed, Polly. It's not the end of the world."

I had a feeling my mother might debate that when she heard about Jeff and Joni, but I didn't verbalize that train of thought to Mitch.

He opened the apartment door and stepped out into the hall. "Just don't do anything stupid," he said.

"What's that supposed to mean?"

"Don't try to be someone you're not."

With that he closed the door behind him, leaving me to puzzle out his parting words and the loss that had swept over me once I was no longer nestled in his arms.

I fell asleep that night wondering why I couldn't find a guy like Mitch.

~*~

Neil called me at work the next day. "How do you feel about black tie dinners?"

"I've never actually eaten one."

"Very funny, Polly. Listen, I'm in a rush, but the firm is throwing a party Friday night to introduce our newly appointed CEO. Be my date?"

I won't deny that butterflies had begun fluttering in my belly the moment I heard Neil's voice. But at the same time my head reverberated with my mother's prediction and Mitch's cryptic warning.

Although I never mentioned Neil by name last night, I was certain Mitch had known I was referring to him. It wasn't the first time he'd cautioned me concerning Neil without coming right out and saying something specific. Maybe he thought he had no right to interfere, but if he knew something I should be aware of, I wish he'd tell me instead of driving me crazy with subtle hints. I never was very good at Charades.

On the other hand, even with Mitch and Mom whispering dire warnings in my ears, I still found Neil sexy as hell. The mere sound of his voice over the phone sent my pulse racing and stirred up an itch that hadn't had a good scratching in way too long.

Although I still felt nothing beyond hot and heavy physical attraction for him, if I checked my libido and took things slowly, my carnal lust might have a chance to develop into something deeper. Then, maybe I could stow some of that emotional baggage that now threatened to douse the flames of any potential affair.

"I'd love to," I told him.

"Great. Wear something sexy."

"Excuse me?"

Neil laughed. In my mind I pictured the suggestive twinkle in his eyes and that killer smile stretching across his face. "Hey, these weenie roasts are long and boring as hell. I need something to help keep a smile plastered across my face."

Was that a compliment? "So I'm nothing more than arm candy to you?"

He answered in a voice thick with desire. "Depends. Do you taste as good as you look?"

Oh, God! My stomach flip-flopped. The images his words conjured up sent a surge of heat rising from my breasts into my cheeks. I swallowed hard. "This conversation is veering into territory not meant to travel during work hours," I told him, cringing at the breathless, desperately needy sound of my own voice.

"Maybe we should plan a long lunch, then. Champagne and chocolate-dipped strawberries at The Benjamin? Say around one o'clock?"

The thought of a midday tryst with Neil both thrilled and

horrified me. I could *possibly* envision myself doing something that scandalous further into a relationship but certainly not as a first encounter. I cleared my throat and offered a different suggestion. "Maybe we should both get back to work."

"Polly, Polly, Polly, where's your sense of adventure, sweetheart?"

Before I could answer, he hung up.

For several minutes I stared at the receiver in my hand before settling it back into its cradle. Where *was* my sense of adventure? Did I even have any? Joni, Mitch, Mom, and my own reservations aside, I wondered if maybe I might not be too cautious for my own good. When a guy turns your insides to mush at the mere sound of his voice, it has to mean something, doesn't it?

On the other hand, perhaps I was merely experiencing a major case of desperation-coated infatuation. All I knew for certain was that I'd lost all sense of perspective where Neil Pearson was concerned.

THIRTEEN
Be Careful What You Wish For

As usual, I was running late Friday afternoon, thanks to an end-of-the-day emergency call from the president of the Cloggers Association. "The board has been receiving irate calls from our membership," she informed me in a very clipped tone.

"About?"

"The hotel you chose to replace the one that went bankrupt in Tulsa. They're extremely unhappy."

"What's wrong with the hotel?" I grabbed my conference folder. After a quick shuffle through a stack of papers, I found the information I'd sent the membership on the Hilton in Daytona Beach, Florida. I'd bent over backwards to find the cloggers a new site after their original hotel went bankrupt. At this late date, they were luck to have any facility.

"It doesn't offer free shuttle service from the airport like the other one did."

I bit down on my tongue to hold back the string of four-letter words threatening to erupt from my throat and willed a tone of diplomacy into my voice. "True, Ms. Fitzgerald; however, the hotel is not far from the airport, and there is taxi service."

"The Tulsa hotel offered us free transportation to and from the hotel. The board feels the Hilton should do likewise. After all, we're doing them a favor."

"How do you figure that?"

"Honestly, Polly, it's obvious that they had a convention cancel on them in order to have so many rooms available for us at such a late date. You and I both know that hotels book conventions and conferences at least a year in advance. If we hadn't booked those rooms, they'd lose quite a bit of revenue, wouldn't they?" She exhaled impatiently. "I'd say, the least they can do to show their appreciation is provide us with free transportation."

"And how do you propose they do that if the hotel doesn't own a fleet of shuttle buses?"

"I'm sure they can rent them from somewhere."

And if not, they could always hire a fleet of flying pigs to transport the cheapskates. I bit down further on my tongue until I tasted blood. "Ms. Fitzgerald, do you have *any* idea how difficult it is to find a hotel willing to host your group?"

"I beg your pardon?"

"Your cloggers have specific requirements. We need large ballrooms with wooden floors and hotels willing to have those floors subjected to a week of abuse. And you want to pay as little as possible for those facilities."

"Your point, Polly?"

"My point is, your members should feel grateful I was able to find them a suitable substitute venue on such short notice and stop bitching about a ten-dollar cab ride!"

Silence greeted my outburst. Finally, Eunice Fitzgerald cleared her throat. "It wouldn't kill you to ask them."

"Yes, Eunice, it would." With that I ended the call. I had no doubt she'd be on the phone to Head Lecherous Jerk within minutes, but thanks to Trophy Wife Number Four, Head Lecherous Jerk had taken off early for a long weekend on some private island in the Bahamas.

I glanced at my watch. Thanks to Eunice Fitzgerald's call, I had less than two hours to get home, shower, and change before Neil picked me up for dinner. Grabbing my coat, I raced out of my cubicle and headed for the elevator. As I stood waiting for the car, I heard Arlene's phone ring. Eunice had wasted no time calling back.

A part of me felt guilty dumping Eunice on an unsuspecting Arlene—but only a small part. Arlene now had Uncle Cal, and I still hadn't had Neil. Or anyone else, for that matter, in quite some time. The way I figured it, she owed me.

The elevator doors opened, and I ducked inside before Arlene came looking for me.

~*~

I arrived home to find a note from Mrs. Dumont, my elderly neighbor, taped to my apartment door. She'd accepted a package delivered for me earlier in the day. Because of the time, I decided to wait until tomorrow to retrieve it. Besides, I could hear Mr. and Mrs. Dumont's television blaring from behind their door. Past experience told me neither of them would hear my knock above the din of the evening news.

~*~

After showering, I wrapped myself in a terry robe and stood in front of my open closet, scanning my wardrobe. As a Harmony, I attended my share of formal events and owned a large collection of evening wear. All qualified as stylish and sophisticated. However, none fell into the "sexy" category, and Neil had specifically requested "sexy."

I thought about running upstairs to borrow something from Joni, but now that she'd divulged her secret love life, I knew she'd already be at Friday night services listening to her cantor's deep baritone.

Besides, Joni towered over me by half a head. Her sexy-looking slip dresses would fall off my shoulders and hang below my knees—assuming she still owned any. With her one-eighty transformation from vamp to neo-virgin, I had a sneaking suspicion all those silky nothings from Versace and Dolce & Gabana had found their way to the Goodwill bin. She certainly hadn't worn any of them in quite a while.

After much scrutiny, I finally selected a burgundy velvet princess cut calf-length dress with long sleeves and a jewel neckline. Neil would have to settle for classic sophistication on the outside and let his imagination supply the rest if he got bored during the speeches.

~*~

I was putting the finishing touches on my makeup when I heard a knock at my door and Mrs. Dumont's high-pitched, sing-song soprano, "Polly, dear? Are you home?"

I didn't have time for her this evening. Mrs. Dumont possessed an extraordinary talent for talking nonstop about everything and anything, and she did it without ever coming up for air. In her youth, she'd performed at the Metropolitan Opera. Sixty-odd years later, although her hearing had failed, her lung capacity hadn't diminished in the slightest.

Even if I hadn't heard her television blasting earlier, I would have left picking up the package until tomorrow when I had more time. If I hadn't, I'd still be standing at her door, listening while she prattled on about everything from what had happened to her favorite soap opera character that day to the latest crisis in the Middle East or the Oval Office.

Due to various ailments, Mr. and Mrs. Dumont rarely left their apartment. Their once active lives now revolved around the television. If it came across the airwaves, Mrs. Dumont had an opinion on it. And chances were, so did Mr. Dumont. A friendly hello to either of them usually lasted a minimum of twenty minutes—on a good day.

At least I'd finished dressing, and Neil would arrive soon, giving me the perfect excuse to cut the visit short. I pasted a smile on my face and swung the door open to find not only Mrs. Dumont but Mr. Dumont standing in the hallway.

"Polly, dear," Mrs. Dumont offered me a broad smile. "Did you get the note I left you about the package?"

"Yes," I raised my voice slightly and enunciated each word carefully, knowing her hearing aids would do the rest. "Thank you for accepting it. I planned to stop by tomorrow when I had more time to visit with you. I'm leaving for a dinner appointment shortly."

Her rheumy eyes scanned my outfit. Then she offered me an approving nod. "You look lovely, dear. Seems to me I remember having a similar gown back in the forties. Or maybe it was in the fifties." She grew thoughtful for a moment, tilting her head and tapping her chin with a bejeweled, arthritic index finger. The large sapphire caught the overhead light and shimmered, as if on cue.

Mrs. Dumont had not stepped foot on a stage in nearly half a century, but she continued to maintain the affected bearing and grace of a diva, every gesture performed with calculated exaggeration. She still dressed for dinner each evening, and thanks to the efforts of a day maid, I'd never seen her with a single hair out of place in her perfectly coifed chignon.

"Yes, I remember now," she continued in a high warble. "It was the mid-fifties, but my gown was more a deep rose than your burgundy. As a matter of fact, I remember wearing it to a party at the Russian Tea Room. We were celebrating something. Now what was it?"

"Ike's second inauguration," bellowed Mr. Dumont, stepping forward and handing me a small, corrugated carton.

"Yes, that's right, dear." She patted his arm. "We couldn't go down to Washington for the inaugural ball because we both had performances that week."

"A group of us decided to throw our own little celebration," continued Mr. Dumont, his voice echoing in the hallway. "It wasn't like it is today where you can watch the festivities from your living room. So we had our own party and toasted Ike well into the night."

"And told him and Mamie about it afterwards," added Mrs. Dumont.

"Next time we spent a weekend at Camp David," said Mr. Dumont, his thick mane of silver hair bobbing up and down as he nodded his head.

Mrs. Dumont brought her hand to the side of her face and stage whispered, "Mamie confided afterwards that the party in Washington was a terrible bore, and she would have much preferred joining us."

"Yes sir, those were good times back then. Before the damn hippies turned our country upside-down and inside-out." Mr. Dumont ended his sentence with a wracking cough.

He'd played bassoon with the Philharmonic until his retirement twenty years ago. Every once in a while, I heard him struggle with the instrument, but although his wife still maintained her lung capacity, emphysema had taken its toll on his. After a few minutes, I'd invariable hear wheezing, coughing, sputtering, and then a string of curses coming from their apartment.

I wanted to end the conversation before he segued into one of his political diatribes. A staunch conservative, he knew of my family background and didn't think much of my parents' politics. Every chance he got, he tried to convert me to supply-side economics and a conservative mindset. To Mr. Dumont, hell was where God sent the liberals, and as he often told me, "You're a good girl, Polly. You can't help who you were born to."

Wanting to keep peace with my neighbors, I did a lot of smiling and nodding around them and kept my mouth shut as much as possible. I also did my best to keep Mom away from them. Mr. and Mrs. Dumont considered my dear opinionated mother a spawn of Satan.

"Well, aren't you going to open your package, dear?" asked Mrs. Dumont, coming back around to the reason for their visit. She stabbed a finger at the box. "Is it your birthday?"

"Two weeks ago."

"Someone must have forgotten." Mr. Dumont chuckled. "Better late than never, right? Go ahead. Open it."

I glanced at the return label. I had no idea who sent the

package, but the last thing in the world I wanted to do was open a box from Victoria's Secret in front of Annabelle and Alphonse Dumont. The contents might send the conservative duo into cardiac arrest. "It's not a present," I lied. "Just some silk scarves I ordered as gifts for the outgoing board members of one of the organizations I oversee."

"Oh." Mrs. Dumont's lower lip pouted outward in disappointment, making me feel as though I'd deprived her and her husband of some titillating thrill. Who would have thought that conservative Republican octogenarians got off on frilly lace undies?

If that was indeed the contents of the package. I certainly hadn't ordered anything from Victoria's Secret, and I couldn't imagine who might have sent me something from the store. Maybe Joni once upon a time but certainly not since she'd discovered religion via Jeff.

Neil's arrival saved me from any further discussion with the Dumonts over the box's contents. I buzzed him through the front door and waited as he bounded up the flight of stairs, the charcoal cashmere overcoat draped over his shoulders, flapping behind him. Beneath the coat he wore a black tuxedo that obviously hadn't been rented for the evening, its pearl gray silk shirt perfectly matching his eyes. A smoke colored silk scarf hung around his neck; a roguish grin covered his face. He looked like a living, breathing advertisement for Hugo Boss—and as always, sexy as hell.

Neil drew me into an embrace, his one hand stroking the back of my neck, the other wrapped around my waist, hugging me close to his body. As he kissed me hello, his tongue quickly flicked between my lips, conjuring up fantasies that immediately swept every one of my good intentions right out the door. How the hell was I supposed to take things slowly with this man when the mere sight of him transformed me into a quivering pile of lust? Not to mention what his kisses did to me.

"Are you wearing them?" he whispered in my ear, the hand around my waist dipping down to surreptitiously stroke my buttocks.

Wearing them? Flustered by his touch, confused by his question, I stepped out of his arms and stared blankly at him. Then it hit me. Neil had sent the package from Victoria's Secret. I raised the small cardboard box I still held in one of my hands.

He frowned but said nothing.

Apparently, I was not the only one taken by Neil's sexy good looks, and before I could explain why I hadn't opened his surprise, Mrs. Dumont started gushing. "If I were fifty years younger, Polly, I'd steal that handsome hunk away from you."

Mr. Dumont glared at his wife and barked, "Behave yourself, Annabelle."

Mrs. Dumont grinned at me. "Alphonse always was the jealous type. Still is."

Mr. Dumont offered a loud hurrumph.

I took that opportunity to introduce Neil to the Dumonts. He shook Mr. Dumont's hand but to my surprise and Mrs. Dumont's delight, he raised the back of her hand to his lips. Mrs. Dumont nearly swooned—or pretended to. "And such wonderful old-world manners! Where in heaven's name have you been hiding this one, Polly?"

Heat rose from my neck to my cheeks. "I'll get my coat," I mumbled to Neil, ignoring Mrs. Dumont's question.

"Take your time," he said, glancing back at the box and then up at me. The glint in his eye left no mistake as to the silent message he was sending. *Open the box, Polly.*

I excused myself and left the three of them in the hall to chat.

As soon as I closed the door behind me, I sat down on the sofa and tore open the small shipping carton. Inside, I found a smaller pink gift box. I lifted the box out of the carton and placed it on the coffee table. I raised the lid and separated the layers of tissue paper.

And then I gasped.

I stared at the contents of the box for several minutes, unsure how to react. How often does a girl receive a black lace garter belt, matching crotchless panties, and silk stockings from a man she barely knows?

I didn't need to search for a gift card. Neil's message was perfectly clear. He intended to consummate what my needy body had begged for in the cab after the hockey game. How could I feel insulted or angered by his gift when I'd thrown myself at him that night? Hell, I was so horny for him that I would have let him screw me in the backseat, had he wanted to.

But I still hadn't figured out what had come over me that night—or for that matter, what came over me whenever I was near Neil. *Near?* Hell, the sound of his voice over the phone sent me creaming! Who was this stranger who had taken over my body? I was turning into Joni, for God's sake—the pre-Jeff, spread-her-legs-for-anyone-for-a-good-time Joni.

Could I do this? Could I strip off my pantyhose, slip on his gifts, and jump blindly into bed with Neil for the pure erotic thrill of it? I fingered the thin wisp of lace that masqueraded as a pair of panties. A shudder coursed upwards, curling my toes and setting my scalp to tingle.

My body urged me on.

My head held me back.

I knew beyond a doubt, I'd hate myself in the morning if I gave into the temptation that clouded my judgment tonight. Mitch's words rang in my ears. *Don't try to be someone you're not.* I stared at the sexy black under things and sighed. I'm just not a crotchless panty type of girl, and I never will be—no matter how much my body burned for Neil. Even if I gave in to my lust and let him scratch the hell out of my itch, my damn conscience wouldn't let me enjoy myself. So why set myself up for a huge guilt trip?

Leaving the box on the coffee table, I grabbed my coat and purse and headed out the door. I needed time. Neil would have to understand.

~*~

He didn't.

I tried my best to make him understand the tug-of-war going on inside me, but the moment he realized he wouldn't be getting any later that night, he went on the attack. "You know what you are, Polly?"

He didn't give me a chance to answer.

"You're a goddamn fucking cock tease!"

He may as well have slapped me across the face. Worst of all, he didn't bother to keep his voice low. The moment he opened his mouth, the cab driver turned off his hip-hop station and perked his ears, keeping one eye peeled to the rearview mirror as he zipped uptown.

Neil didn't let up. "You sway that sexy little ass of yours in my face and then pull back every time I accept your invitation."

"That's not fair, Neil. We hardly know each other. I need some time."

He threw his head back against the seat of the taxi and raked his hands through his hair. "So what the hell was going on in the cab the other night, babe? Exactly what was that little performance of yours all about?"

"I...I don't know. It's not that I don't want to. It's just—"

"Just what? That you've got some weird hang-up about sex? You need a ring on your finger before you'll spread your legs? Is that it?"

"No! I need to know that there's more between us than horny hormones."

"Why? We have the hots for each other. What's wrong with just enjoying that for as long as it lasts?"

"Because I wouldn't enjoy myself if that's all it was."

Neil's voice filled with derision. "How do you know if you don't give it a try?"

"I just do."

"Someone ought to clue you in to the fact that this is the twenty-first century, not the nineteenth. Sex is meant for enjoyment. You don't need commitment, and you won't burn in hell for sleeping with me or anyone else—in case you hadn't heard." He glared at me for a moment, then turned his head to stare out the window for the remainder of the ride.

The cab pulled up to the St. Regis. Neil tossed some bills at the driver and muttered, "Keep the change," before stepping from the cab. I half expected him to walk into the hotel without me, but he waited until I exited and with a hand on my elbow, silently guided me into the lobby and towards the elevators.

Score one for Mom. She'd certainly pegged him. And been right about Uncle Emerson's inability to see Neil for the type of person he really was. But in all fairness, Uncle Emerson was gay, and even though a well-educated minister, how accurate a judge could he really be about the whole hetero thing?

Besides, from personal experience I'd learned that Neil Pearson could charm the ivory off an elephant.

As we road the crowded elevator up to the ballroom, I stole a glance in his direction. He faced straight ahead, his eyes narrowed, his jaw hardened, his mouth set in a grim, tight line.

If he planned to give me the silent treatment all evening, I may as well ride the elevator back down and hail a cab home. I had agreed to attend this function for him. I already spent too much of my life attending boring business dinners, thanks to Harmony cosmetics, as well as the ventriloquists, cloggers, choir directors, and medical illustrators. If Neil wanted to act like an adolescent, he could do it on his own.

I was about to tell him that when I suddenly realized something else. Whatever had ignited that initial incendiary spark between us, his outburst in the cab had completely and permanently doused it. As well as any desire I once had for him.

I shifted my attention to my own body. I felt nothing. No flutter in my stomach. No warm, honey gathering between my legs. Not a single telltale remnant of the lust that had scorched my insides since that initial dinner not quite two weeks ago. The man whose voice and smile had toppled my equilibrium, now left me cold. All because he wasn't getting any pussy tonight.

It struck me that curbing my libido had been one of the smartest things I'd ever done.

The elevator came to a halt. The doors swooshed open, but I remained inside, jabbing a finger on the button to hold the door open. "If you're not going to speak to me all evening, I'm leaving."

He glanced out into the vestibule before answering me and nervously shifted his gaze up and down the corridor. "That's a rather childish attitude," he said, turning back to me.

"Why? Because I refuse to subject myself to your passive-aggressive silent treatment all evening? Or because I refuse to act the whore to your juvenile fantasies?"

"Lower your voice," he hissed between gritted teeth.

"I haven't raised my voice."

The elevator buzzed. I'd held the door open too long. Neil grabbed my arm and pulled me out of the car. The doors swished closed behind us. "Look, can we just get through this dinner and talk about everything else later?"

"I'm not sure there's anything to talk about."

A soft ding heralded the arrival of another elevator to our left. A middle-aged couple in tux and designer gown stepped out. The man nodded to Neil. "Pearson."

Like a chameleon, Neil's demeanor transformed. His body language shifted from irate would-be lover to kiss-ass executive. He offered the man and woman a warm smile. "Sir. Mrs. Maxwell."

The man glanced my way. A puzzled expression crossed his brow. "Polly? Polly Harmony?"

It was then that I recognized the couple—Edgar and Lillian Maxwell. They owned a summer home out in the Hamptons, directly across the street from the house where my parents and I vacationed every summer while I was growing up. "Hello, Mr. and Mrs. Maxwell." I extended my hand. "Nice to see you."

He grasped my hand in both of his and placed a paternal peck on my cheek. Then he glanced back over at Neil. "You've got a winner here, Pearson. Fine young lady. We watched her grow up." Mr. Maxwell turned to his wife. "How long has it been, dear?"

"Why I'm not certain," she answered, kissing my other cheek.

"It must be years."

"Ten years," I offered. "My parents sold the house in the Hamptons and bought one on the coast of Maine."

"Sensible move," said Mr. Maxwell. "Nice and secluded. The Hamptons are getting overrun with Hollywood types. Can't walk anywhere without dodging gossip columnists and getting camcorders shoved in your face."

"And forget about a peaceful evening out," Mrs. Maxwell added. "One might just as well stay in the city for the weekend. It's certainly quieter and less crowded."

Neil wrapped his arm possessively around my waist. "We should go inside," he suggested. "I don't want to be accused of waylaying the guest of honor."

Mr. Maxwell chuckled. "Ladies?" He held an arm crooked for each of us. "You don't mind, do you, Pearson? It's not often an old geezer like me gets the chance to escort two beautiful women."

Neil dropped his arm from my waist and took a step aside. "Not at all, sir."

How typical of my luck. Not only do I run into Neil's new CEO before I get a chance to duck out, but the guy turns out to be an old summer neighbor. With little choice other than completely embarrassing both Neil and myself in front of the Maxwells, I smiled up at the guest of honor and slipped my arm through his.

It was going to be a long night.

~*~

When Neil invited me to the dinner, he'd described the event in terms of an intimate affair for a select number of Wall Street executives and members of the media. I expected a small private dining room. Instead, we were ushered into a large ballroom. A raised dais with a long table ran the length of the front of the room. Round tables, draped in ivory linen and topped with arrangements of delicate white orchids, were scattered around either side of a parquet dance floor, now filled with several hundred mingling guests.

White-gloved waiters, bearing trays of champagne and caviar, silently snaked their way through the silk, satin, and sequined groups of New York's most established elite. In fact, I'd wager half the upper East Side of Manhattan was gathered in that room —at least those who resided in the Seventies and Eighties between Fifth and Park.

I also knew enough about organizing such affairs that they weren't slapped together within a few days. The men and women mingling and munching and exchanging eloquent *bon mots* filled their social calendars months in advance.

Mr. Maxwell was immediately swarmed by well-wishers. Neil, who had obviously decided to take advantage of our chance meeting with the Maxwells by doing a bit of brown-nosing, offered to fetch a waiter with drinks. While he was gone and Mr. Maxwell was accepting congratulations from a group of brokers, I turned to Mrs. Maxwell, intent on satisfying my curiosity. "When was Mr. Maxwell appointed CEO of Traeger, Young, and Ledbetter?"

"Last month," she said, "but he doesn't officially take over until Monday."

Neil returned with a waiter in tow and immediately muscled his way in beside Mr. Maxwell as the waiter offered flutes to first me and Mrs. Maxwell, then to the band of tuxedo-clad, middle-aged suck-ups hovering around their new boss.

Mrs. Maxwell pulled me aside. "Disgusting little worms, aren't they?" Her face puckered as though she'd sipped vinegar instead of very expensive champagne.

I shifted my gaze back to the men. The group hovering around Mr. Maxwell, Neil included, reminded me of pigs fighting for a spot at the feeding trough. I just never expected Mrs. Maxwell to be thinking the same thing, let alone voice such thoughts aloud.

"Your gentleman friend is very handsome and charming, Polly," she said, smoothing out an imaginary crease in her emerald satin sheath.

This was no non sequitur. I remembered Mrs. Maxwell as being a shrewd woman, and I detected a hidden insinuation behind the casual remark. However, I nodded in agreement and let her continue. After all, I'd fallen for those looks and that charm. Thankfully, not too far nor too hard before I realized what lay beneath the surface.

"Let me offer you a bit of advice," she said. "If your boyfriend wants to score points with my husband, he should know that Edgar has little tolerance for lap dogs, yes-men, and bootlickers."

Neil Pearson wasn't my boyfriend. After this evening, I strongly suspected we'd no longer even be friends and not only because we had different outlooks on sex. Something else didn't sit right with me. I couldn't put my finger on it yet, but I would. Eventually. And I suspected that when I finally did figure it out, I'd be very angry. With Neil as well as myself.

I offered her an appreciative smile but said nothing. There were some things a man had to find out for himself. After all, you could lead a pig away from the trough, but you couldn't force him to diet.

Mrs. Maxwell eventually wandered off to greet some friends, leaving me to my musings. For the next half hour I lingered on the fringes, sipping champagne, nibbling on canapés, and making small talk with the various guests I knew who stopped by to chat. At the same time, I kept one eye on Neil as he continued to stick like epoxy to Mr. Maxwell.

When the lights dimmed, the signal to take our seats, Neil finally remembered he'd brought a date. "We're at Table Seventeen," he said, frowning after returning to my side. As he guided me along with the crowd, he whispered, "Some asshole screwed up the table assignments."

"How do you know?"

"As a junior V.P., I should at least be at one of the front tables, if not the head table with Maxwell. I tried to switch us, but the cards for the front tables were already gone."

How tacky! I glanced up to find myself the recipient of one of his rakish grins—as if his would-be manipulation of the seating amused him and therefore, should amuse me. I waited for the hormonal assault his bad-boy smile had produced in the past, but instead of arousal, I experienced annoyance.

Was Neil now trying to get back on my good side due to my connection to the Maxwells? I thought of Mrs. Maxwell's words of advice and nearly suggested he simply crawl up onto Mr. Maxwell's lap. We still had dinner to get through, though, and I had already placed myself firmly on Neil's bad side by refusing to partake in his after-dinner entertainment. I decided to keep my mouth shut and not tempt fate. Getting through the next few hours would be difficult enough.

As we approached Table Seventeen, off to one side of the ballroom, I experienced a momentary surge of relief. Mitch. At least I'd have a buffer if Neil turned surly. As a columnist for *The Wall Street Journal*, I'd expected to find him at the dinner, but with the way my luck had gone so far this evening, I never expected to find him at the same table.

Mitch sat next to a tall, thin blonde. Her body twisted in her seat, she spoke over her shoulder to a couple passing behind the table. As we approached, she turned back to Mitch. One look at her, and my momentary surge of relief transformed into a thick, churning bile.

Could this night get *any* worse?

FOURTEEN
Adolescent Angst—Revisited and Revenged

Regina Koltzner! I'd recognize that bitch anywhere—even if fifteen years had passed since I last saw her at our high school graduation. Even if she'd purchased herself a set of 38 double D's in addition to a fake mole on her upper lip à la Cindy Crawford.

All the silicone and tattooed artificial melanin in the world couldn't mask Regina Koltzner's vicious arrogance—or the minuscule hairline scar at the corner of her left eye, a visible reminder of five-year-old Regina's efforts to bath—or so she claimed—a neighbor's kitten. Frankly, knowing Regina, I suspected she'd tried to drown the poor animal.

Mitch stood to greet us. "I hope you don't mind," he whispered to keep the other two couples at the table from hearing. "I finagled the seat assignments and got us placed at the same table."

Neil forced a smile but his eyes narrowed, his jaw tightened. He scowled at the two other couples, apparently neither pleased with the choice of table mates nor Mitch's interference. "How thoughtful of you."

He pulled a chair out for me, guaranteeing himself the seat next to Regina and nodded a terse, mumbled greeting to the two other couples without offering introductions.

Having already met the other members of our party, Mitch did the honors. The source of Neil's annoyance quickly became apparent. Not only hadn't he gotten to sit with the Maxwells or the other senior members of the firm, but Mitch had placed us at a table with a low-level junior sales associate and a secretary—not exactly where a ladder-climbing vice-president expected to find himself at such an august function.

Mitch continued with the introductions, nodding first to me, then Neil. "Polly Harmony. Neil Pearson." Then he motioned to Regina. "And this is my date, Régine."

Régine, my ass! I knew Regina Koltzner when I saw her. *Régine* lifted one perfectly arched eyebrow at the mention of my name but gave no hint of recognition.

"Just Régine?" asked Neil, gracing her with one of his trademark smiles. "No last name?"

"Just Régine," she answered in a thick accent. "Very simple. Very memorable."

And very phony.

"You're French?" Neil asked.

"*Oui.*" She pointedly ignored looking in my direction.

Like hell. She was no more French than the potatoes that came out of the deep-fat fryer at McDonald's. The fraud grew up in Summit, New Jersey—to a German-American father who owned a chain of quick printing businesses and a Polish-American mother who played flute with the New Jersey Symphony and gave private lessons from their home.

I could never forget the face of the person who made my life a living nightmare for so much of my childhood and teen years. *Régine* was Regina Koltzner. I'd stake my inheritance on it. Even if she now called herself Régine—dropping her last name along with a few years from her age, no doubt. Even if she now employed a fake French accent and lied about her nationality.

No matter how you dress her up, a rat is still a rat and a bitch is still a bitch. If you could even call what Regina wore, a dress. With the top of her gauzy, flesh-colored spaghetti strap gown barely covering her nipples and her purchased cleavage dipping below the table, the outfit looked more like two transparent scarves taped to her upper body. Regina was certainly making the most of her newly acquired assets.

"And what brings you to the States?" asked Neil.

Was he now sucking up to Regina as he had Mr. Maxwell? Or was he coming on to her to get even with Mitch for switching the seating? I couldn't believe it! Actually, I could. I was getting an eye-opening education this evening, thankfully *before* I'd committed myself to a foolhardy tryst.

"I'm the new accessories editor at *Vogue*."

"How fascinating! Have you been here long?"

"A few weeks."

"First trip to the States?"

"*Oui.*"

What a crock of shit. I closed my ears to Neil's sycophantic patter and Regina's lying prattle.

What had I seen in Neil? What was it about him—or me—that had turned me into a quivering mass of need around him? Desperation, I decided. Pure and simple desperation. Given the timing, I probably would have fallen as fast and hard for any of the other Seven-Minute Date bachelors—even the *Star Trek* nut or the one covered in tattoos and piercing—had any of them called. What a self-indictment!

Of course, it hadn't hurt that Neil Pearson was drop-dead gorgeous, and I, obviously, was very shallow, never bothering to scratch beneath the surface of those good looks to see what the man was really like under all that oozing testosterone and phony charm. Polly Pathetic rides again.

I glanced over at Mitch. Although he kept his ear tuned to the flirtatious conversation between Neil and Regina, his eyes focused on me. Not wanting my thoughts conveyed by my face, I forced a smile, but I sensed he saw right through me. He usually did. Mitch's talents were wasted in finance. He should have become a shrink. With his mind-reading abilities, he'd figure out a patient's inner workings without having to hear a word.

After all the guests had taken their seats, the usual requisite speeches, peppered with trite jokes, preceded dinner. Each witticism filled the room with laughter thoroughly disproportionate to its level of amusement. Each speech produced the mandatory standing ovation at both its commencement and conclusion. I sat back and closed my mind to the droning monologues. You've been to one self-congratulatory business dinner, you've been to them all. Only the names and faces change.

Throughout the meal, I toyed with each course, eating little. Anger, annoyance, hurt, and suspicion had formed a pact and lodged itself firmly in my throat. I felt used and manipulated and stupid. To top it off, every one of my childhood insecurities had suddenly roared back to life—thanks to Regina—and she hadn't had to utter a word to trigger their release.

Throughout the meal, the wife of the junior sales associate, seated to my left, drew me into banal conversation. I didn't mind. It took my thoughts off Neil and Regina and my own self-flagellation.

However, between the appetizer and entrée courses, I learned far more than I ever cared to know about Feng Shui. Mrs. Junior Sales Associate had recently finished a three-week course in the Chinese art of what-should-go-where in order to balance the elements of your life. I wondered why Mom hadn't caught the Feng Shui bug yet.

After two glasses of champagne, one glass of wine, and very little food, the creative and destructive orders of wood, fire, earth, metal, and water began to make sense to me. According to Mrs. Junior Sales Associate, a person could straighten out her life simply by making sure her possessions—and thus, her elements—were harmoniously placed. Maybe my initial attraction to Neil had something to do with my elements being out of whack.

Right. And maybe I should hang a crystal around my neck and tape magnets to my pressure points. Talk about desperation! I figured I was really losing all sense of reality if I was beginning to consider such nonsense. I helped myself to a mouthful of baby asparagus, hoping a little food would clear my mind.

With the din of several hundred voices filling the large ballroom, conversation with anyone else at the table became a strain on my vocal chords, not to mention an exercise in futility—especially since the person sitting to my right had glued his attention to the French fraud seated to his right.

I nibbled at more asparagus, drained the remaining wine from my glass, and listened glassy-eyed as Mrs. Junior Sales Associate segued from Feng Shui into last night's episode of some TV show

I'd never heard of. Seemed Mrs. Junior Sales Associate was a huge fan of the star.

"I met him once, you know?" she gushed. "At Bloomingdale's, of all places. Can you imagine? He was buying undershirts, of all things! Just like a normal person. V-neck Jockeys. The same as Jeremy wears."

"Jeremy?"

"My husband." She frowned, then motioned to the man seated to her left.

"Jeremy. Of course." I mumbled an apology. "Sorry. Long day."

"Yes, but isn't this all so elegant? I wouldn't have missed it for the world. I bought a new dress for tonight and even treated myself to a special manicure today. See. The designs match my gown." She held out her hands to show me the intricate, multi-colored swirls of yellow and orange that dotted a base coat of fire engine red, ten miniature wagging replicas of her rayon-polyester blend, paisley patterned designer knockoff.

"Lovely." As I raised my wine glass for a refill from a passing waiter, I mused whether the success of the star whose name I couldn't remember, had anything to do with the juxtaposition of his undershirts to his five elements.

~*~

Towards the end of the main course, a band began setting up at the base of the raised platform. Dance music commenced with the serving of dessert. At the sound of the first note, Neil rose and offered his hand to Regina. I stared after them as they made their way to the center of the room. I wasn't the only one.

Regina's dress, or lack of it, garnered the stares of everyone else within sight of her as she passed among the tables to the dance floor. For the first time, I caught the full effect of the outfit as the gauzy wisps of skin-toned fabric skimmed over her breasts, cinched in around her waspish waist, then fluttered in sectioned angles over her hips and thighs, stopping several inches above her knees. Around me, women gasped and men blocked admiring snorts with fake coughs.

A waiter placed dessert in front of me, a heart-shaped cup of dark chocolate filled with raspberry mousse and sprinkled with shavings of white chocolate. I pushed the confection aside and reached for my coffee. As I sipped, I watched Neil and Regina dance. They guided intimately across the floor, swirling around other couples, like longtime lovers, oblivious to anyone but each other.

"Would you like to dance, Polly?"

I glanced up to find Mitch standing beside my chair. I placed my cup back on its saucer, tossed my napkin alongside my untouched dessert, and rose to join him. "Yes, I would."

He took my hand and led me to the crowded dance floor. "Want to talk about it?" he asked, drawing me into his arms as the band segued from *All I Ask of You* into *The Music of the Night.*

I pondered his question for a moment before answering. "Depends. Are you playing shrink or big brother?" This was hardly the most conducive venue for spilling my guts. Still, I suddenly realized, that as the evening had progressed, something changed inside me. Maybe it was the wine or Mrs. Junior Sales Associate's numbing chatter. Or maybe it was me coming to my senses at last.

Although initially consumed with resentment, anger, and hurt, much of those feelings spawned from the initial shock of seeing Regina after all these years. The reminders of an often unhappy childhood, thanks to her unending cruelty, had flashed before my eyes and sent me reeling.

I'd already begun the process of exorcising Neil from my emotions before we came upon Regina. His attraction and attention to her only helped speed up the process. Once again, I had nearly succumbed to a manipulative man. At least in Neil's case, I never made the mistake of thinking I was in love with him as I had with Former Significant Other. The attraction was purely physical from the onset.

In a way, I owed Regina. Neil had already begun an about-face upon discovering my connection to the Maxwells. Had Regina not come on the scene, I may have weakened and given him another chance. I hardly needed to add masochist to my list of flaws.

Mitch broke into my thoughts to answer my question. "Shrink. Brother. Friend. Does it matter? I can tell you're upset."

More with myself at this point, though. Although I thought his behavior childish and reprehensible, Neil's actions only reflected on him. I didn't care enough about him any more. "And you're not?" I asked, eyeing Mitch suspiciously. "After all, my date seems to have usurped yours."

"Easy come. Easy go."

"Have you slept with her?"

Mitch stopped dancing and stared down at me. "That's not like you, Polly."

He was right. Joni enjoyed supplying graphic details of her sexual encounters, but Mitch, although he dated many beautiful women, kept his bedroom exploits to himself. I tried to ignore Joni's bragging and never pried into Mitch's private affairs. "I know, but I haven't been myself lately. In more ways than one."

"Are you regretting something?"

My sexual attraction to Neil was hardly a secret. Mitch and Joni had acted as a sounding board throughout the past two weeks as I ruminated over my wildly, out-of-control hormones and whether or not to act on them. "No."

In the background the band moved on from Andrew Lloyd Webber to Lerner and Lowe's *I Could Have Danced All Night*. Mitch raised an eyebrow, his features clouded with concern. "Nothing?"

"Not about Neil. I came to my senses earlier this evening. I had already decided we were on our last date."

Mitch exhaled—or was it more a sigh of relief? "What made you wise up?" he asked, gathering me back into his arms to resume our slow sway around the crowded dance floor.

"A pair of crotchless bikinis."

"You're kidding."

"No."

His arms tensed around me. "Are you okay?"

"I'm fine. I just came to realize I'm not the crotchless bikini type. If I were, I wouldn't have hemmed and hawed over whether or not to have an affair with him in the first place. I don't know what came over me the last few weeks. Maybe it was a reaction to my birthday, but I'm over it now. And I'm definitely over Neil. I can't deal with a relationship based solely on sex."

I hesitated. I didn't want to come across sounding didactic. "I'm not passing judgment on anyone else. It's just not me, and it never will be. You were right, Mitch. I can't be someone I'm not. I need more out of a relationship."

He relaxed his grip. "Good."

"You knew all along, didn't you?"

"About what?"

"Neil."

"Let's say I've heard rumors."

"What kind of rumors?"

"That he's a hunter. Bag 'em and bang 'em. Then move on."

I shuddered at his crude choice of words, but after this evening I couldn't defend Neil against the indictment. Somehow, it made sense. "And he chose me for his next conquest. With a push from Uncle Emerson."

"Apparently so, but I doubt Emerson has a clue about that side of Neil's personality."

Neither had I. "Neil can be quite charming."

"True, and remember, everything I heard came third and fourth hand. You women don't have a lock on catty, backstabbing behavior."

That explained why Mitch kept cautioning me but never came right out and said anything. His comment also brought me back to Regina. "About your date...."

I followed Mitch's gaze as it swept across the dance floor to Neil and Regina. Not a whisper of air separated their bodies. With her arms hooked around his neck and his wrapped around her waist, his hands settling over her well-toned buns, their dance had turned to foreplay. "What about her?"

"Known her long?"

"This is our first date." He paused for a moment before adding, "And our last."

"Good."

"Do I detect a hint of jealousy?"

"No." I knew Mitch well enough to know he'd eventually see through Regina's false façade. Mitch could take care of himself. He'd been doing it all his life. Besides, unlike me, he had a way of keeping his heart out of relationships, protecting himself from getting hurt—the legacy of growing up the son of Rainbow Hues.

"Why do I get the feeling you know more than you're telling me?"

I glanced over at Regina and Neil, then offered Mitch a teasing smile. "Let's just say some people aren't what they at first seem." Let Regina carry the mantle of backstabbing cat. I decided not to stoop to her level.

Mitch steered us in Neil and Regina's direction until we were dancing alongside them. They remained in a world of their own, totally oblivious to us or anyone else. Finally, Mitch cleared his throat and tapped Neil on the shoulder to get his attention.

Neil did nothing to hide the annoyance that sprang to his face, but Mitch jumped in before he could say anything. "Since you two seem to be enjoying each other's company so fully, why don't I take Polly home?"

Neil brightened. "Sure you don't mind, Hughes?"

"Not in the least."

Neil went back to nuzzling Regina's neck. He never even bothered to say so much as a goodnight to me. I stepped out of Mitch's arms and sidled up to Neil. "By the way," I whispered in his ear, loud enough for Regina to hear but not Mitch, "they're implants, and she grew up in Summit, New Jersey."

Neil froze. Regina turned as red as Mrs. Junior Sales Associate's rayon-polyester gown. I offered them both a way too innocent smile and twirled on my heels. As I headed off the dance floor, hand-in-hand with Mitch, I glanced back over my shoulder. Neil and Regina stood motionless, glaring back at me. I decided to toss them both one parting shot. "The beauty mark's a fake, too."

"What was that all about?" asked Mitch as we exited the ballroom.

"Merely a little bit of closure."

So maybe I briefly unleashed my evil twin. Call me a bitch. But to quote Joni, "And you say that like it's a bad thing?"

Besides, turnabout is fair play, isn't it? Regina Koltzner had made my school years a living hell. Exposing her chicanery felt damn good and a suitable ending to both a rotten day and my quasi-relationship with Neil.

~*~

Never one to mince words or hide her emotions, Mom was thrilled to hear I had decided not to see Neil again.

"There was just something about him," she mumbled.

There certainly was, but I kept that to myself, since I now wondered if perhaps my recent hormonal meltdown had nothing to do with Neil and everything to do with me. Maybe I merely suffered an allergic reaction to turning thirty-two. Maybe I was in heat, a state subconsciously induced out of a desperate need to fulfill at least one of Mom's wishes—and yes, one of mine, as well.

I won't deny I'd like to have a child. Mom was right. My biological time clock had inched its way towards the eleventh hour of my reproductive life. Although, I doubt she'd be too happy to find her only daughter pregnant *sans* husband—considering there was never the slightest possibility of exchanging *I do's* with Neil. I might have been tempted to invite a guy I didn't love into my bed, but I certainly wasn't stupid enough to marry him.

After hearing the unexpected but welcome news that I'd severed ties with Neil, Mom even made peace with Uncle Emerson. The poor man had suffered the brunt of her wrath over the past week, and believe me, that's a fate worse than death.

Then she began plotting.

FIFTEEN
Mom Takes Control

For some time now, I've had the sneaking suspicion that my relatives sit around in the evenings debating various schemes to marry me off. Some people belong to book groups. Others join support groups. I decided Mom had established the Help Find Polly a Husband Society, a secret fraternity with restricted membership—her and my uncles. Dad, of course, would have no part of it.

Weekly meetings probably consisted of Mom, the dictatorial leader of the group, sending my uncles out to comb their flocks in search of eligible male suitors between the ages of thirty and forty-five. Each week they gathered names, presented reports on the suitability of each, then took a vote as to the best candidate to unleash on me. The lucky winner was handed my phone number.

Mom most likely coerced my uncles into cooperating through some diabolical form of blackmail or threatened torture. I can imagine the lengths she goes to: Find Polly a husband or risk having Mimi show up on the golf course every Monday, a fate worse than death—for my uncles as well as every other golfer at the club. So naturally, they complied. And every few weeks I found myself stuck with yet another loser in an ever-growing list of losers.

To give my uncles some credit, the men they thrust upon me usually started out nice enough. However, they never get to know these men the way I do. I attributed that to a drawback of their profession—people always act their Sunday best around the clergy, whether it's Sunday or not. Which is probably why Uncle Emerson thought so highly of Neil.

~*~

The first of the latest crop of phone calls came less than twenty-four hours after Sunday dinner. The caller introduced himself as Barry Endicott, a divorced nephrologist. He'd been introduced to Uncle Francis by a mutual acquaintance during intermission at a recent Placido Domingo concert.

"Given the Pope's recently diagnosed kidney disorder," I said, "I can understand how a nephrologist and a priest might strike up a conversation, but how exactly did I enter into the discussion?"

Barry chuckled. "Your uncle came right out and asked me if I was seeing anyone. When I said no, he pulled out a picture of you."

"Subtle, isn't he?"

I agreed to meet him for a drink in SoHo after work the next day.

"I'll be the one wearing a red carnation."

Forty-five minutes later, I received another phone call. Mom had apparently opted for a full frontal assault this time, rather than spreading the prospects out over time.

His name was Donald Ghermann, a software engineer who

recently upgraded Harmony Cosmetics' computer system. He spent fifteen minutes singing Mom's praises—literally. I closed my eyes and envisioned myself back in *Mr. Rogers' Neighborhood*. Donald had that same monotonous, singsong, talking-to-toddlers inflection to his voice. Fred Rogers had bored me into a daze as a child, and Donald Ghermann was running the risk of doing so as an adult. I tried to imagine him with a personality, but when I closed my eyes, I saw a wimpy old man in a red cardigan V-neck sweater.

Besides, it sounded like he'd rather have a date with Mom. Other than his profession and how he got my number, he hadn't mentioned a thing about himself, nor had he asked anything about me.

"Are you free Saturday night?" he finally asked.

I felt my evil twin surfacing and bit back a few of the caustic remarks springing to my mind. *Be nice, Polly.*

Don't be a wuss. Tell him to get off your planet, evil twin retorted.

I opted for a copout lie. "I'm afraid not."

"Next Saturday, then?"

"Already booked."

"You don't want to go out with me, do you?"

Bright guy. He catches on fast. However, he sounded so disappointed, that I relented. Maybe he was shy around strangers. Maybe it had taken a lot of courage for him to pick up the phone to call me. And maybe I was being too much of a bitch—for a change. "How about lunch Saturday?" I asked, although a niggling feeling in the pit of my stomach warned me I'd regret my sudden streak of compassion the moment I hung up the phone.

"Saturday?" He hesitated for a moment. "Um, sure. I guess I

could swing that."

We made plans for him to pick me up at noon.

I prayed he'd improve in person. Surely there had to be *something* interesting about Donald Ghermann. After all, my own mother gave him my number. She couldn't be *that* desperate to marry me off—or could she? I thought about calling Dad to get the scoop on the guy, then changed my mind. If he turned out to be as dull and boring as his voice, I'd rather not ruminate over my misplaced compassion all week. Better to put Donald Ghermann out of my mind until Saturday.

~*~

Caller Number Three struck at work the next day. I had Arlene to thank for that. He's her second cousin once removed on her father's side. Arlene considered me the Cupid that brought her and Uncle Cal together. Since she felt she owed me, I imagine she was easy prey for Mom to lure into the cause.

Buzz Flynn owned an auto parts store on Staten Island. "But not just *any* auto parts store," he bragged. "The biggest and best on the rock. I pull in the big bucks, baby."

As if that was supposed to impress me. I was tempted to mention that Staten Island was actually an enormous mound of colonial landfill, rather than a rock, but tamped down my sarcastic side once again. People tend to get a little testy when you remind them they live on a huge chunk of petrified garbage.

Buzz was coming into Manhattan for an auto parts show at the Javitz Center Wednesday. He asked if I'd have dinner with him afterwards. Once again, against my better judgment, I agreed to a date. Call me a sucker or a glutton for punishment, but I didn't want to hurt Arlene's feelings without first giving Buzz a chance.

After hanging up from Buzz, I approached Arlene. "Your

cousin called me."

"Oh." She stared down at her shoes. "And?"

"You've gone over to the other side, haven't you?"

Her brows knit together as she hazarded a glance upwards to meet my gaze. "What do you mean?"

"Did my mother coerce you?"

Arlene sighed. "Buzz isn't so bad, Polly."

"*Isn't so bad?* As compared to what?"

"Other auto parts salesmen?"

"Arlene, after all I've done for you! How could you?"

"Your mother wouldn't let up." She waved her arms in frustration. Her eyes pleaded with me. "You know how she is."

Did I ever. Arlene didn't stand a chance against Steamroller Mimi when she set her mind to something. I patted her arm. "Yeah, she can be a bit overbearing. Even the strongest among us can't stand up to her at times." And Arlene, downtrodden most of her life by her own mother, was certainly no match for Mimi, the Mom on a Mission.

"She kept pestering me for the names of anyone I knew. "Buzz is my only unattached relative. I told her I didn't think the two of you had anything in common, but she said something about nature and destiny and how it's not for us to interfere."

"No, only her." Funny how Mom's feelings about people not interfering in other people's lives never extend to her. She's convinced she has some divine right of intervention because she knows better than the rest of us. Just ask her.

"How bad is this cousin of yours?"

Once again, Arlene refused to meet my gaze. "It's not a matter of good or bad, Polly. He's just...different. Not your type."

"Who's type is he?"

She didn't answer. I couldn't tell whether Arlene suddenly came down with an attack of family loyalty or if she was trying to cushion an impending blow. Either way, I figured I was screwed.

And Mom had some heavy explaining to do.

~*~

At five o'clock I grabbed my coat and headed off for my date with Caller Number One.

Barry Endicott had suggested Dash of the Past, a newly opened retro-bistro at the northern edge of SoHo. The entire restaurant was fitted out to resemble a Levittown, Long Island living room from the early sixties, complete with walnut Danish modern tables and chairs, Mondrian posters on the walls, and waitresses dressed like Jackie Kennedy in pastel Chanel suits with matching pillbox hats. Since most of the twenty-something clientele jamming the place weren't old enough to remember the Reagan administration, much less Kennedy's presidency, I wondered about the appeal. I also wondered why Barry chose such a chaotic place for a first meeting. How do you get to know someone when you have to shout to make yourself heard?

I fought my way inside. Forget about *get to know*. How do you *find* someone you've never met in a standing-room-only crowd? Especially when most of that crowd stands at least half a head taller than your own five-feet-and-not-much-more petite frame? Shouldering my way around one group after another, I searched for an unattached male who looked like he was waiting for someone.

I laughed when I found him. True to his word, Barry Endicott wore a red carnation pinned to his lapel. He was seated at a small table for two at the back of the restaurant, shielded from the noise and confusion of the front bar area.

"A red carnation. You must be Barry."

He rose to greet me. "Polly?"

I nodded. "I thought you were joking about the carnation," I told him, settling into the seat opposite him.

"Nephrologists aren't known for their sense of humor."

"And here I expected an evening of nonstop scatological jokes."

He offered me a blank stare. "Pardon?"

Surely, a nephrologist knew the definition of *scatological*.

That could only mean one thing. I shrugged and offered him an apologetic smile. "Guess you're right. No sense of humor."

Uncle Francis had a great sense of humor—one I'd inherited, much to my mother's chagrin. Caustic, biting, and usually sarcastic, Uncle Francis curbed his acerbic wit around many of his parishioners and most of the church hierarchy, but he rarely held back around family. Had he fallen behind on his quota and gotten desperate to produce an eligible bachelor for Mom's approval? What else could possibly explain sic'ing me with a humor-deficient doctor?

A waitress approached our table. "Ready to order?"

Dash of the Past specialized in martinis. As I quickly scanned their cocktail menu, I discovered twenty different varieties, including some rather questionable ones like a brandy Alexander martini and a grasshopper martini. Chocolate and peppermint flavored martinis aside, the drink reminded me too much of Mason Hightower. I passed. "Margarita on the rocks with salt, please."

She jotted down my order, then turned to Barry. "And for you, sir?"

"Perrier straight up with a twist of lime." He eyed me over his menu, the corners of his mouth dipped into a slight frown. "I'm on call this evening. My partner's got the flu. Would you like to share an appetizer sampler?"

"Yes, thank you." As usual, I hadn't taken a lunch break. Aside from my morning bagel, I'd existed on too many cups of coffee and nothing else all day. The thought of Buffalo wings, fried mozzarella sticks, and stuffed mushrooms sent my saliva glands into overdrive.

I wish I could say the same for Barry and the rest of my glands. Although a bit on the pudgy side, he was a good-looking man with a thick head of wavy dark chestnut hair that barely missed skimming his shirt collar. He wore a conservatively cut navy suit with a white shirt and a solid cobalt tie, but I chalked his lack of style up to his profession. Nephrologists deal for the most part with elderly patients, and old people expect their doctors to dress a certain way.

No, the extra fifteen or twenty pounds aside, the problem with Dr. Barry Endicott wasn't his looks. The problem was his dolorous attitude. The man barely cracked a smile. His shoulders sagged, and his dark brown eyes had an emptiness about them. He looked downtrodden and miserable and a million miles away.

"Has your partner been sick long?"

My question seemed to startle him back into the present. "No, why?"

"You look tired. If you'd rather do this another evening, I'll understand."

He closed his eyes and massaged the bridge of his nose. "I'm sorry. I'm not making the best impression, am I? I guess I have something on my mind."

"A case?"

"All of them, actually."

The waitress arrived with our drinks and appetizer order, placing the sampler platter in the center of the table and a small plate in front of each of us. "You folks ordering dinner?"

"I don't think so," said Barry. When she walked away, he apologized. "I shouldn't have asked you out. There's too much going on in my life right now to pay proper attention to a relationship."

"That's all right."

"No it's not. The medical profession killed my marriage. I have no business getting involved with someone else until I make some major decisions."

He picked up his appetizer plate and stared at it. "My grandmother had a set of dishes exactly like this." He glanced around the room. "And similar furniture. Know why I like this place?"

"Because it reminds you of her?"

"Because it reminds me of a time when I was happy. Back before all the pressure to succeed. To be a doctor. To make everyone proud of me. I never wanted to be a doctor. I wanted to be a painter like my grandmother, but my father wouldn't let me. He threw away my art supplies."

Thank you, Uncle Francis! Dear Lord, I couldn't believe this was happening to me again. Weren't there *any* normal guys left in the dating pool? Any guys not going through midlife crisis or holding a torch for a dead spouse or involved in a Twelve Step program or in need of a Twelve Step program? Why did I always manage to get stuck with the neurotics, the manipulators, the weirdoes, and the jerks?

Barry needed a shrink, not a date. And Uncle Francis needed

to spend more than a ten-minute concert intermission with someone before handing out my phone number to total strangers. I pushed aside my untouched margarita and reached for my handbag. "I'm sorry, Barry, but you're right. You definitely need to get a few things straightened out in your life before you start dating again."

I opened my purse and fished out a pencil and scrap of paper. "You can reach my Uncle Francis here," I said, jotting down the phone number of the rectory. "Maybe he can help you. Or suggest someone else." I passed the paper across the table and rose.

Grabbing my coat from the back of the chair, I hurried to the exit.

~*~

When I arrived home, I found a message on my machine from yet another of Mom's hopefuls. I erased it.

Then I dialed the Grand Instigator. "Stop doing this to me," I yelled into the phone when she picked up. "You're driving me crazy!"

"Polly, darling, what is it?" I heard her call to my father, "Howard, grab the extension. It's Polly. There's something terribly wrong. She's hysterical."

My father picked up. "Polly? What's the matter? Are you hurt?"

"No. Just sick and tired of everyone trying to run my life."

"Since when do we run your life?" asked Mom, her voice rising with indignation. "You've been living and working on your own for years."

"Look," I said. "You're going to have to accept the fact that I may not ever get married and give you that grandchild you so desperately want. I missed the boat, Mom. I'm not settling for the dregs that are left."

"Calm down, dear. You're not making any sense."

"I'm making perfect sense. I just arrived home from an aborted date with one of Uncle Francis' picks. You're driving everyone so crazy, they're passing my phone number out to strangers, Mom! Strangers with problems."

"I think you're exaggerating, Polly. Your uncles love you. We all love you. No one would ever give your name to someone unsuitable."

"No? Wednesday, thanks to your meddling, I'm stuck having dinner with Arlene's cousin. The guy's a loser, Mom."

"Did she say that to you?"

"She didn't have to. She couldn't think of anything nice to say about him other than *he's not that bad*. Is that what you want for me?"

"No, of course not, dear."

"Then stop meddling."

"I don't meddle. I never meddle."

"Right. What about Saturday?"

"I don't know anything about Saturday. What's Saturday?"

"Lunch with the computer repairman who has a crush on you!"

"What!" Dad practically roared into the phone.

"He doesn't have a crush on me. He's a nice young man, Polly. You'll see."

"No, you'll see, Mom. This is it. I agreed to these two dates but no more. Don't you dare try to fix me up with anyone else." I slammed the phone down before she could respond.

A moment later the phone rang. I yanked the cord out of the wall. Five minutes later Mitch was pounding on my door.

"So, I see she called the cavalry in," I said.

"What the hell's going on? Mimi just called and insisted I come check up on you."

"Nothing's wrong." I stomped across the room and yanked open the refrigerator. "I threw a tantrum and refused to eat my vegetables. That's all."

"She said you were hysterical and not making any sense. Want to run that one by me again?"

"God! Why don't I ever have any food in my apartment?" I slammed the refrigerator shut and reached for a bag of stale potato chips.

"Is that a rhetorical question?" Mitch came up from behind and yanked the bag out of my hands. "Dinner?"

I shrugged. "Looks like it. Want some?"

He tossed the bag on the counter. "Hell, no. No wonder you're not making any sense." He grabbed my hand and pulled me to the door. "Come on. I'll feed you. Then you can tell me all about it. Whatever *it* is."

Mitch cooked me an omelet loaded with sweet peppers and shitake mushrooms. While we ate, I told him about Barry and my pending dates with Donald and Buzz.

"Cancel them."

"No. I promised I'd go out with them. It's only one dinner and one lunch. Then I'm through. No more fix-ups from anyone."

"Good. How about some dessert?"

"Is it sickeningly sweet and decadent and loaded with fat and calories?"

"Absolutely." He rose and carried our plates to the sink. "But I do have some chocolate sauce we can add, just in case." He returned to the table with two pints of double chocolate chip gelato and two spoons. "One for you and one for me." He handed me a pint and a spoon.

We moved over to the sofa, but before either of us could enjoy the first spoonful, the front door swung open, and Joni and Jeff walked in. "Oh great," I mumbled. "Now we'll have to share our dessert."

Mitch laughed.

"What's going on?" asked Joni.

"Poor Polly's having a rough day."

"Poor Polly's having a rough life," I muttered. "Hi, Jeff. You don't want any gelato, do you?"

Joni shifted her gaze between me and Mitch, then grabbed Jeff's arm before he could answer and spun him around towards the door. "I just remembered I forgot to pick up a few things at the pharmacy. Let's go, Jeff. I need a lugger. See you two later." With that they were gone.

"Ah, true love. She leads him around like a puppy dog, and he laps it up." I smiled down at my pint of double chocolate chip gelato. "You're all mine." I scooped up a spoonful and lifted it to my mouth. Mitch stared at me. "What?"

"Nothing."

"No, not nothing. Why are you looking at me like that?"

He flashed me a wicked grin. "Will you grow fat with me, Polly?"

I sighed. "Best offer I've had in ages, Mitch. Let's dig in and get started." He dipped his spoon into his gelato, and we fed each other the first mouthfuls. As the rich chocolate melted in my mouth, the stress seeped from my muscles. I leaned back against the sofa cushions, closed my eyes, and ran my tongue over my lips. "Heaven."

"Not quite," whispered Mitch, "but we're getting there." He slipped another spoonful of gelato into my mouth.

~*~

On Wednesday my worst nightmare of dating hell came to life. When Arlene referred to her cousin as *different*, she'd uttered the understatement of all time.

Buzz Flynn was a sitcom stereotype come to life, all macho attitude and no taste. He wore too much gel in his slicked back red hair and too little clothing over his bulging pecs. Beneath his open, full-length black leather coat, a forest of thick chest hair poked through a half-buttoned lime green silk shirt. Around his neck dangled a chunky gold chain. A fake Rolex encircled his left wrist, and a cubic zirconia pinkie ring glittered from his right hand. A pair of black leather pants completed the bad taste ensemble, showcasing certain anatomical features I'd rather not consider.

No wonder Arlene ducked out of work early. I was willing to wager she really didn't have a dentist appointment. No, Arlene the Chicken had flown the coop. She didn't want to be around when her cousin came to pick me up after work. She knew I'd kill her. And then I'd kill Mom for pressuring Arlene into subjecting me to her cousin.

As I stood in the lobby and stared at Buzz, I came to two immediate conclusions. First, I now understood why he remained single. What woman would want him? And second, the office definitely needed a back exit for speedy escapes.

I quickly introduced myself and hastened him back into the elevator. The last thing I needed was to have Jay the Jerk get a look at Buzz the Bozo. I'd never hear the end of it. Actually, I wasn't too keen on *anyone* seeing me with Buzz.

Just when I thought things couldn't get any worse in my

pathetic excuse for a life....

They did.

My eyes and nose began to itch as soon as I got within three feet of Buzz. Once we stepped into the elevator's confining quarters, I nearly gagged. He smelled like a rose petal-draped runner after a marathon through a field of overripe pumpkins. "That's interesting cologne," I said on a gasp.

"You like it?"

My sinuses swelled. My voice grew hoarse and breathless. The tabloid headline flashed before my watering eyes: *Man Marinates in Cologne For Two Days. Date Drops Dead After One Whiff.* "It's rather....potent."

"Yeah? Good." He looked pleased with himself. "Truth in advertising. Don't you love it? In my business I come across so many products that claim to put out and don't come across." He clapped his hands together. "I can see from your reaction that this baby's a winner. Definitely worth the hundred bucks a bottle."

He *paid* for that stench?

The elevator came to a halt and the doors swooshed open. I rushed for the exit and filled my lungs with fresh air. It didn't help. My head pounded. My sinuses throbbed. My knees grew weak. I leaned against the building to steady myself. In a breathless whisper I managed to ask, "Exactly what is that stuff you're wearing?"

Buzz pumped out his chest. "High Octane. Guaranteed to push all the right babe buttons. Guess it's pushing yours, huh Polly?" He wiggled his eyebrows.

I groaned. The idiot had misinterpreted an allergic reaction for a pheromone swoon. I turned my head to avoid breathing in any more High Octane and took several deep breaths. "Well, actually,

Buzz, the truth is, I think I'm allergic to you. I mean your scent. Your High Octane." I waved my hand to fan the air. "Whatever. This isn't going to work out."

"Allergic? How can you be allergic to something women go crazy over?"

I shrugged my shoulders and sneezed. "Life's a mystery, Buzz." I backed further away from him, stepping out into the street to hail a cab.

"Hey, wait!" he called as a taxi pulled up and I reached for the door. "I was going to take you to dinner at AWE. What if I wash it off?"

A date at the American Wrestling Enterprise theme restaurant? Be still my beating heart! "Frankly, Buzz, I think you might have to soak in a tub of tomato juice for a few weeks before you get rid of that stench. In the meantime, watch out for skunks in heat." I climbed into the cab and shut the door behind me.

The welcoming aroma of hot, spicy food filled the taxi. I leaned forward and saw the remnants of the driver's Mexican dinner on the seat beside him. At least *something* in my life was going right. I muttered my address, leaned back in the seat, and inhaled deep eye-watering, sinus-cleansing breaths of roasted jalapeños and habaneras.

~*~

Two down. One to go. I shuddered to think what I might face Saturday afternoon. Several times I reached for the phone to cancel my lunch date with Donald Ghermann, but each time I hung up before I finished dialing.

"I don't want to go out with a Mr. Rogers clone," I whined to Joni Thursday night. "Why does my mother do these things to me?" We sat on my couch, pigging out on Flames of Calcutta, a specialty of Curry in a Hurry, the Indian takeout place down the street. For the past twenty-four hours, I'd craved nothing but hot and spicy foods, my body's way of helping rid itself of the histamines produced by Buzz Flynn and his High Octane stench.

"Then don't go out with him."

"I already said I would."

"So now you've turned into Horton the Elephant? *I meant what I said, and I said what I meant*? Isn't Pollyanna bad enough? Come on. You've had a rough week. Why subject yourself to someone you've already decided you're going to hate?"

She had a point. Still...."No, it's better if I suffer through the date. That way I have plenty of ammunition to use against Mom the next time she tries to pull a Yenta the Matchmaker on me."

"True." Joni washed down a mouthful of Flaming Calcutta with a swig of Corona. "Damn, this stuff is hot!"

"Enjoy it while you can. It's not kosher."

"No problem," she said, scooping another forkful into her mouth. "Jeff and I have an understanding. As long as I keep a kosher house, I can eat anything I want elsewhere."

Joni and Jeff were in the process of planning their wedding—the only reason the two of them weren't together this evening. Jeff had taken Mitch out to dinner to ask him to serve as best man. Masochist that I am, I agreed to Old Maid of Honor duty. Come the second Saturday evening in April, Uncle Aaron would marry Party-girl Joni to Cantor Jeff.

A week later, Arlene and Uncle Cal planned to tie the knot, and once again I'd secured the role of Old Maid of Honor—only two of the many little ironies that comprised my so-called life. At least I got to choose my own dress for both events and didn't have to stand at either alter decked out in lavender organdy.

~*~

In less than a week, I'd added three more reasons to my Top Ten List for calling it quits after the first date. Mason, Jeff, and Jeremy had supplied Reasons Number Eleven, Twelve, and Thirteen. Some of my Seven-Minute Dates had fallen into one or more of the original ten reasons. The rest had given me Reasons Number Fourteen through Twenty-one.

I had Neil to thank for Reason Number Twenty-two. Then there was Dr. Barry, Reason Number Twenty-three. Reason Number Twenty-four came courtesy of Buzz. Which brings me to Donald Ghermann and Reason Number Twenty-five.

~*~

Donald arrived at my apartment forty minutes late. I'd almost given up on him and gone out. In hindsight, I wish I had. "I'm sorry," he said through the outside intercom when he finally showed up. "I ran into a few problems."

I thought about asking if he knew Alexander Graham Bell had invented a handy little gadget for just such emergencies, but instead, I merely said, "Second floor on the left," and pressed the buzzer to release the front lock.

A moment later I heard a raucous commotion out in the hallway. I swung open my door to find two small children in full tantrum mode and a very harried looking man trying to quiet them down. He was failing miserably.

"Daddy! Gabe hit me!" cried a little girl around three years of age.

"Did not!" said a boy of about five. "Lindsay's lying, Daddy!"

"Did, too! Did, too!"

"Polly?"

I nodded—reluctantly.

"Donald Ghermann. I'm sorry about this." He turned to the little girl and shoved a pacifier in her mouth. "Here Lindsey. Suck on your binky. Daddy will buy you a Happy Meal in a few minutes."

"I want pizza!" yelled Gabe, jumping up and down. "Happy Meals are for babies." He reached over and pinched his sister's arm.

"Ow!"

"Gabe, stop that!" Donald shoved a second pacifier in the boy's mouth. "Apologize to your sister."

Gabe mumbled something around the rubber nipple that sounded more like a curse than an apology, but his father ignored him.

Donald combed his fingers through his receding hairline. "My ex-wife was supposed to have the kids this weekend, but she needed to go out of town on business at the last moment."

"Mommy went skiing with Jason," said Gabe.

Donald flushed a deep scarlet. "Yes, well...."

"She said we couldn't come," added Lindsey, spitting out her pacifier with a sniffle and a pout. It dropped to the floor. She yanked on her father's pant leg. "I want to go skiing with Mommy!"

"You don't know how to ski," taunted Gabe.

"Do, too!"

"Do not!"

Donald bent to scoop up the pacifier, but before he could grab it, Gabe kicked it through the railing. It bounced all the way down to the first floor.

"My binky!" Lindsay's shriek echoed throughout the hall.

Donald glared at Gabe, then went scampering after the

pacifier, leaving me alone with two children who looked like they were about to kill each other.

"Don't even think it," I warned them.

A moment later Mitch stuck his head over the third-floor railing. "Everything okay down there, Polly?"

I raised my chin and mouthed, "Help!"

Two minutes later, convinced of his folly, Donald hoisted both brats into his arms and left in search of a fast food restaurant that sold both Happy Meals and pizza.

"Got any more gelato up there?" I asked Mitch. He laced his fingers between mine and led me upstairs. "Why can't I find someone like you?" I asked.

Mitch stopped and turned to me. "Maybe you're too blind to see what's been right under your nose all along, Polly."

"Mitch?"

He lowered his head and captured my lips with his.

IN THE END
...and They Lived Happily Ever After

"Finally," said my mother and father in unison when we broke the news to them a few weeks later.

"I knew the two of you would come to your senses eventually," said Uncle Aaron.

"Just needed to get everything else out of their systems," said Uncle Francis.

"Atta girl!" said Uncle Emerson, wrapping me in a hug.

"About time," said Uncle Cal, patting Mitch across the back.

I stared at my relatives. Six not-so-innocent Sylvesters grinned back at me. Yellow Tweety-Bird feathers peaked from the corners of their mouths.

"We were set up," I told Mitch. All along there had been a deliberate method to their meddlesome matchmaking mania.

"I'm not complaining."

Neither was I.

Like my mother and father before me, Mitch and I were married by my four uncles in a combination Catholic-Episcopal-Jewish-Unitarian ceremony. Jeff was best man and sang at the reception. Joni and Arlene served as dual matrons of honor. Neither wore lavender organdy.

But that night I surprised my new husband when I stepped out of my wedding gown and revealed a pair of crotchless black lace panties.

POLLY'S TOP TWENTY-FIVE REASONS
TO CALL IT QUITS
AFTER THE FIRST DATE

25. He has joint custody of the kids from hell and brings them on the first date.

24. He's a throwback to a lesser life form.

23. He's going through a midlife crisis.

22. He believes crotchless panties are a suitable first gift for a burgeoning relationship.

21. He's not bright enough to qualify for a career in fast food.

20. He's an obsessive jockaholic on a road trip mission.

19. He thinks *soap* is a four-letter word.

18. He buys his clothes at the Hell's Angels thrift shop.

17. He's in love with himself.

16. He's still in love with his dead wife.

15. He's a New Age crystals and magnets freak.

14. He's a *Star Trek* junkie.

13. He can't carry on a conversation past the third sentence.

12. You invite him in for coffee, and he strips down to his birthday suit while you're making a pit stop.

11. He brings his dog on the first date.

10. He's thirty-five and still living with his mother.

9. He shows up for a formal gala at the Met wearing black jeans and a tuxedo print T-shirt.

8. He shows up for a picnic in Central Park wearing a three-piece Brooks Brothers suit, white shirt with French cuffs, and a conservative blue and red striped tie.

7. He kisses with his eyes open and puckers his lips like a fish

sucking up plankton.

6. He has a list of his former girlfriends tattooed on his left bicep.

5. He spends the entire date talking about his ex-girlfriend.

4. He spends the entire date psychoanalyzing you.

3. He brings his own silverware to the restaurant and disinfects all surfaces with antibacterial wipes before touching anything.

2. He conveniently forgets to mention he's married.

And the number one reason to call it quits after the first date—

1. Your parents or one of your great-uncles fixes you up with him (which means he most likely falls into one of the above categories.)

ABOUT THE AUTHOR

USA Today and Amazon bestselling and award-winning author Lois Winston writes mystery, romance, romantic suspense, chick lit, women's fiction, children's chapter books, and nonfiction under her own name and her Emma Carlyle pen name. *Kirkus Reviews* dubbed her critically acclaimed Anastasia Pollack Crafting Mystery series, "North Jersey's more mature answer to Stephanie Plum." In addition, Lois is an award-winning craft and needlework designer who often draws much of her source material for both her characters and plots from her experiences in the crafts industry.

Connect with Lois at her website, www.loiswinston.com, where you can learn more about her and her books, sign up for her newsletter, and find links to follow her on social media.

Made in the USA
Columbia, SC
29 November 2020

25812524R00195